BLACKBIRD

BLACKBIRD

Tony Cartano

Translated by Sheila Fischman

MACMILLAN PUBLISHING COMPANY

New York

Macmillan Publishing Company
866 Third Avenue, New York, N.Y. 10022
Collier Macmillan Canada, Inc.

Library of Congress Cataloging-in-Publication Data
Cartano, Tony, 1944-
Blackbird.
I. Title.
PQ2663.A785B5513 1987   843'.914   86-23600
ISBN 0-02-529270-6

10   9   8   7   6   5   4   3   2   1

Printed in the United States of America

for Françoise

"A cage in search of a bird."

—KAFKA

I.

Blackie's Notebooks (I)

❧❧❧ I hesitated for a long while before taking pen in hand, probably for the last time. At the age of eighty-five (eighty-six?), when the body quakes to the pressing calls of death that waits, snickering, on the fringe, why must I open the big yellow spiral-bound notebook, as if that act would turn back the course of existence and wipe out everything so I could start from scratch? Would that stop the clock, make it give way to the real life which, even today, they insist they're saving me from? They say that I'm crazy. So they've locked me up. All of them—the Roths, Friedmans, Golds, Rossmans, Bernsteins, from the Bronx and Broadway, joined now by Dr. Clockwork and his patients—Garry the psychopath, Snuffie the junkie, Jack the schizo, Jerry the ape-man, Pat the tigress, Andy the short-order cook who thinks he's Rockefeller, Hans the Nazi, Linda the fat stripper and nutty Lola, her daughter . . . there's no end to the list of diabolical but all too solid creatures who have haunted the corridors of my life like monsters for more than thirty years. I don't remember them all because it's easier to forget than to confront the demons of an existence that's too present, too weighty, to permit any literary subterfuge. . . . I have both loved them and hated them. And their names, their twitching, their clowning, their cries, and their tears will no doubt return, frequently, uncontrollably, to disturb the peaceful course of my solitary nights when I've determined to tell what happened, to restore the truth.

And if people no longer believe me, if they dismiss my words as unimportant infant's prattle, or an old degenerate's

1

rambling, even if they gag me again, nothing will stop me from the final weighing up of memory traps, of the successive exiles that couldn't destroy me completely, from extracting the lesson from a fate that, even if it wasn't exemplary, still gives me grounds to take up the pen I'd laid aside for so many years and aspire to something new once more. Just for myself, if need be. I've nothing left to prove. Despite misfortune. Despite bad luck. Despite all the corpses that come between me and the men and women of today. If Dr. Clockwork allows it, though (because, knowing him, he'll find where I've stashed the three yellow notebooks), perhaps the present generation—I don't know much about them, only the little I can guess behind the tormented features and bodies of the young madmen who live here in the hospital—will be able to recognize the voice of a writer who, against my will, this generation considers a master.

Today, though, I am called Blackbird, the only name I'm known by. In fact I wonder if I really want my identity revealed. In any case, as far as Roth, Friedman, Gold, Rossman, and Bernstein from the Bronx and Broadway are concerned—as well as Dr. Clockwork and his menagerie—I've never been anything but Blackbird or, more familiarly, Blackie.

They claim it's all written on my American passport, but what they don't know is that Blackbird is the name I chose one May morning in 1939 when I came ashore on the Promised Land in the Port of New York City. They're convinced it's a nickname they gave me, but I know it's not true, I know all the secret echoes of a patronymic planted deep in my guts like a not so benign tumor. I've realized for a long time now that their fine talk is only a dreadful lie concocted to deny my very existence, obliterate my history, consign it to nameless oblivion. But on my frozen features, contorted by illness, fatigue, and electroshock, on my hands, gnarled because I dreamed too much of the signs they might have traced to conjure up a fate quite different from my own, in my scarlet lungs, on my breath, my withered heart and penis, one name is deeply carved. And that secret, the final one, I shall not reveal. Not before I'm sure the claws of death have sunk into my neck and won't let go. I escaped it *in extremis*, during an earlier existence that I hold in reserve. By reliving that life now, I can launch a final challenge at the void, although I know that illusion is often misleading.

On the threshold of the void, at the final moment, there is always some question that will make you rise from your bed, spit out the venom sealed in your body, and come back to life after everyone has condemned you, after parents, wife, lover, and friends have consigned you to the utmost suffering of an everlasting hell.

I won't reveal my true bird's name. I lost it one hot summer's day at the Klosterneuburg sanatorium near Vienna, in the heart of old Europe. I've been stripped of it forever, because the whole world declared at the time that I'd given up the ghost. My soul, perhaps, had gone, but not the body that would walk down more roads, even harder and more arid than those in the dawn of a life devoted to lost happiness. And when lost happiness is truly gone, when even the dream of finding it is out of the question, aside from an eternally hopeful quest, all that is left to do is stop crying out "I'm not dead," to value life enough to deny it. At such a time silence, withdrawal, and solitude may seem a safe enough refuge from pursuit, suspicion, and memory. In vain. . . . But it's too early to conjure up the details of that first death. For the moment, it's enough to know that the man Vienna called, let's say, Franz, Karl, Alban, Hugo, or Stefan—it doesn't matter—he ceased to exist more than fifty years ago. In my mind, in my dreams, in reality, perhaps only the Anton of the passport has ever existed. Very well, for all eternity, long live Anton Blackbird!

If I revealed my name, it would give Clockwork and his acolytes another reason to think me lost, and make it too easy for the others to consider me stark raving mad. They'd also say, I'm sure, that it's impossible, unthinkable, they'd say there's ample evidence of the death of the writer I claim to be, and in any case I don't write nearly as well. . . . Of course, all those years without the verbal scales, the exercises, the rudiments! That would make it easy for them to sanction the idea of schizophrenia, turn me into a perfect thesis topic for psychiatrists and sophisticated art critics. I cannot suggest, even vaguely, the style of the Other. And yet, if I dare to write as I do and declare that I *am* the Other, then that's who I must be. Otherwise it would be worse than suicide. And suicide means little to me now, for I have wished for it and lived it too often to think it still conceals some absolute virtue.

That was why, at the time, I tore up a number of my manuscripts, and ignored my opus to escape the death that was closing in on me, even emanating from my wife, Dora, whose zealous affection was wasted on a living corpse. I knew that to escape with my life, I would have to sell it to the Fates. And I have known ever since that suffering is not creative, and that there's no haggling with destiny.

I survived. While humanity was being splattered with shaming blood, I was giving piano lessons to the children of the rich in New York. Until I got news of Milena's death, which hit me harder than any bullet or bomb. The details were all in a letter from her husband. The bastard was finally taking his revenge. Milena had never loved him. She'd loved many other men, some women too, and finally me; she taught me the sweetness and sadness of love, the storm of the senses that, before we met, had only grazed my cold skin. Milena made me a man. She was mother, sister, mistress—all women in one joined together, in an overarching will to survive. When she was taken from me by her husband, by the twists and turns of her existence and the torments of my own, my health was destroyed. That is what posterity calls my disease. But when Ravensbrück took her from me for good, I could no longer resist the weight that oppressed my entire being, and I said that I wasn't who people thought. I revealed the identity which linked me inseparably with Milena, as if I wanted that extravagant act to take me with her into the catacombs of horror which I'd long shut my eyes to. What was the good of living, even a little, when Milena was dead? So bravely, with such dignity, and so absurdly, poor woman. . . . That was when the people on Hester Street started saying I was mad. As if, under the circumstances, such words still had any meaning! That was when I chose to be put away. For on that score too, there must be no ambiguity. "They" think they're responsible for my confinement. How naive— and how ironic! In a way, it's what I've called my second death. Perhaps the only one that's genuine. The one I lived with for so many years, in the pit of my stomach which breeds only sterile fantasies. But there's always a third time, and this third one, though not genuine, will be the right one. Oh yes, today I can allow myself a joke that, at another time, I would have considered in poor taste and liable to make my words seem trivial. It's time for the comedy to end. The choice is simple, then: either everything must be preserved, or everything destroyed. If I retain the slightest fragment of those moments that compose the texture of my life, if I consider it of any interest and hence worthy of falling into Clockwork's hands (I've got my eye on him!), then nothing must be scorned, rejected, or forgotten.

With the same rigor, the same desperate energy that made me order Maximilien to destroy the sheets of paper stained with my blood, soiled with my sweat, soaked in the pain that had given some meaning to my first forty years, I can now take back my wager, free myself from the pact, and make a bid, at last, on what is essential. Not content with being merely crazy, I am christening my death pangs with a second life.

2.
Bestiary of the Yellow Notebook (I)

ᴠᴠᴠ *Blindly, the bird pecked at the shell. The cool air of evening draped itself about him. His frail body trembled and his beak pierced the gummy fibers that joined him to the source. As if the earth's belly were opening up a thousand cracks to the setting sun, allowing its vitals to be cut to pieces. . . .*

Feebly, the bird cried out. Once, twice. Life. Suddenly, the fierce odors, the myriad sounds, the chattering force him to open his eyes; the light gleams like a scalpel; all of nature turns out to greet him. And the bird has no time to wonder what is happening: he must, immediately, perform the routines dictated from within, that come from the broken shell now resting on its bed of straw. The beak, like a surgical probe, preens the knotted feathers, tears apart the liquid night still covering the flesh, the trembling skin. With a sharp, precise twitch the neck is set free. The feet stir. And the eyes sparkle, look up to the stars that have just appeared in the sky. The lamb and the dog bend over him. The lamb bleats, the dog barks—tenderly. And the jaws and feet of all the sudden throng of insects rustle upon the luminescent leaves.

Hidden behind a tree trunk, the cat is smiling. And the tiger that has just burst into the clearing roars, showing all its teeth.

The night falls silent again, and the clouds stretch lazily, like herds of wild cattle grazing. Licked by moonbeams, the bird cheeps with all its might. Life is worth living.

3.

Clockwork's Notes (I)

❧❧❧ I've seen some pretty amazing cases in the course of my career, but there's no question which one was most intriguing—the case of Antoine Choucas, alias Anton Blackbird. I had just been made chief of the clinic when he was brought to me here at Bellevue. I remember it very clearly. It was August 7, 1945, the day after our atom bomb wiped Hiroshima off the map.

When the head nurse brought him into my office, she slipped over to me and whispered, "Careful—they just took him out of the straitjacket a couple of hours ago." Though we never had to restrain him again after that day, more than thirty years of internment don't seem to have made the slightest improvement.

At the time, he was a small man of fifty-two. Stocky, with short legs and broad shoulders, you could picture him as a boxer except for his delicate features—aquiline nose, black hair and eyes, well-shaped eyebrows, an adolescent's mouth and lips. Only his forehead, bulging and slightly bald, provided a contrast with his noble expression, revealing the stubborn, recalcitrant, even feisty side of his personality. But if you went by the overall effect—as I did at once—you sensed you were in the presence of a first-class mind. A poet, a painter, perhaps a musician.

He stood there calmly, chin up. I couldn't help asking the head nurse, "What on earth is he doing here?" She shrugged and left my office, slamming the door.

I told Blackbird to take a seat and immersed myself in his file, as if I were trying to put on a bold front, make an impression, prove I was serious.

7

Blackbird had tried to jump from a twelfth-story window. Alerted by his howling and the racket he'd made ransacking his little apartment, the neighbors had stopped him in time, but it wasn't easy, and blows were exchanged. They said it wasn't the first time: he'd tried gas ("Could have blown up the building," according to the testimony), the bathtub, a rope— the works. And increasingly over the past few months, the piano teacher had been terrorizing the neighborhood, claiming to be one of the greatest writers of the century. I admit it took me a long time to penetrate the mystery, to discover the identity of the alter ego whose fame had not yet reached America. (Did I ever succeed? That's the question. With Blackbird, you must always be wary of appearances.) First, I had to retrace the early background of the man whose actual name was Antoine Choucas and who, contrary to his own declarations, was neither Jewish nor Austrian, but a Frenchman who'd killed his own father.

His life as inmate and lunatic became so entangled with mine that I must be extremely patient and careful now, so I can tell our story with the exact rigor that is fitting in such cases.

4.
Blackie's Notebooks (II)

❧❧❧ When I came to Vienna I was sixteen, maybe seventeen years old. Adapting to life in the capital was hard at first, especially the customs of the school where my father enrolled me. We were immigrants and didn't speak German as perfectly as our background might have led people to assume. In Prague, I'd forgotten the subtleties of our mother tongue, so I suffered greatly from the teasing of my new classmates, who laughed at my accent and my blunders. Still, I was grateful to my father for letting me attend the same school as the privileged offspring of the Viennese bourgeoisie. I have to admit he had an appetite for life, a sense of ambition he kept trying to instill in me. He would grip my shoulders, look me straight in the eye, and say, "We'll win, you know, we'll win and don't you forget it!" With a pang—my mind was ablaze with images of shattered windows, of the fire in the shop on Wenzelsplatz, the hasty departure to escape the pogroms perpetrated by rabid Czech ultranationalists—I listened as he began his litany of revenge and hope. And I acquiesced, not sure if I was trying to talk myself into something, or falling under the spell of my father's authority and conviction.

I was a delicate child, slightly built and very highly strung. The slightest opposition, particularly in class and even more if I thought I was suffering some affront in the presence of a girl my own age, would throw me into crying fits that neither my mother's affection nor my father's anger could appease. They had to put me in a dark room where I could breathe in the rhythm with my waking dreams and regain possession of my thoughts and my body. That infuriated my father. Mama

9

would tell him to leave me alone, saying these outbreaks would disappear in time, that what mattered most was for me to continue being the brilliant student that, in fact, I was. "He'll bring honor to the family name in any case." Then, swaggering and muttering under his breath, my father would put on his butcher's apron and go back to his shop. It didn't stop him, though, whenever he felt like it, from making me play sports that went against my nature. He got it into his head to teach me to box, unable to tolerate my having come home bloody-nosed from school one day, after a fight with a fellow who'd called my mother a kike, a fight that had naturally turned to my disadvantage. Father faced me in a boxer's stance, barking, "Put up your fists, keep your guard up, now raise your left, left, one, two, left, I said the left!" I hit out timidly, then harder, flinging my little fist at the huge mustache that spread from his lips to his ears. "Now your right, uppercut!" Then he would inevitably wait for the moment to deliver what he called his "counter" to my face. My ears would buzz, my teeth would chatter, my blood would seem to boil, and I'd slump, abject, to my knees. My father would roar with laughter, followed by a flood of remarks about my weakness and everything I still had to learn. "You mustn't drop your guard like that, and your one-two should be a lot faster or he'll get you right on the chin, or the liver." Of course, he always arranged it so we had these bouts when Mama wasn't around. And he knew I wouldn't complain when she returned. When she was there, he was content to "toughen me up," teaching me, for instance, to punch a wall. "It's good for the knuckles." Mama was quick to intervene: "Hermann, look at what you've done to his pretty hands!"

One day, though, these little sessions he loved nearly turned to disaster. Not content with fists, he wanted to teach me how to handle a saber, "in case of a duel, later." He had devoutly kept a pair of sabers that belonged to his great-uncle, I think, who himself had inherited them from his father, who had fought against the armies of the French Revolution. I no longer recall just how this horrible scene came about, but I'm sure my butcher father would have skewered me, run me through like a vulgar side of veal, if I hadn't, with a quickness he acknowledged, dodged his blow at the last moment. The trouble was that as I was moving, I slipped, and as I fell, the flat of the saber struck my left eye. I didn't have time to wonder—any more than my father did—what would have happened if I'd fallen on the point. Blood gushed out. Terrified, I screamed. My father too. Furiously at first, at my clumsiness. And then with fear, as he picked me up in his arms, pressing me tightly against him and crying, "Anton, Anton, I didn't mean . . . Anton, forgive me!"

At the hospital they were able to save my eye. I wore an eyepatch for almost a year, and it took another year for the resulting scar to go away. But I didn't lose the eye. And even though I never totally regained the use of it, after a few years only people in the know might have guessed, from a slight squint, what had happened. In any event, from that day on my mother made my father swear he'd put a stop to his violent games. He kept his word.

I had always been gripped by a physical fear that seized my guts, actually made me vomit, whenever I witnessed a scene of brutality. The mere sight of a schoolyard brawl would freeze me so rigid that if I got caught up in the action I'd let myself be beaten black-and-blue without even reacting. At least this was true until the saber fight. After that, my father never touched me again, not even to lay a finger on me; but he demonstrated his vigor and his will to power through other means which I shall speak of later, ways less brutal perhaps, but ultimately more destructive.

Concluding that I must train myself to stay one jump ahead of my obsessive fears, I took up the challenge. In the utmost secrecy (I'd rather have died than let him know what I was doing) I trained myself, stepping up my physical exercises, increasing the level of difficulty every day, going over the advice he'd lavished on me point by point. My knuckles got bigger and tougher from contact with the cold walls. On the floor, I worked my abdominal muscles. Whenever I could, I'd get hold of two-kilo weights from the shop and force myself to lift them above my head till I was exhausted. Finally, at school and on the way home, I'd always find a reason to run, as long as possible, until I couldn't feel the air in my lungs, couldn't see through the thick haze, couldn't even tell if my legs still existed.

So, when I came to Vienna, I was no longer a sickly, fearful child, but rather a young man with broad shoulders and solid muscles. One thing, however, had not changed; my fear, anguish, and timidity—three heads of a monster that would long resist decapitation.

5.
Bestiary of the Yellow Notebook (II)

🜸🜸🜸 Night has fallen upon the savannah. A russet moon reddens the water in the river, which seems to have ceased its roar, as if the rapids were coming up to lick the beach, like a lioness lavishing love on her young. The great carnivores lie on the warm grass. Eyes half shut, they dream perhaps of disembowled bodies still bleeding on the plain, choked with morbid smells. The carnage will not occur tonight, and the breath of the spirits can embrace the sleeping couples. Sated, the wild beasts blend their moans of sensual and filial love as they sprawl in the dust.

On the skeletal tree, the black bird shakes itself. He knows he has nothing more to fear. The sharp-edged teeth are now but hollow dreams. He tugs at his wings, aware of his superiority, of the strength the darkness restores to him. With a thrust he spreads his wings and hurls himself into space. A troop of mocking macaques, ever alert, begin to snicker and applaud. Is this an absurd plunge into a vacuum, or freedom? That is what their hysterical laughter asks.

The black bird straightens up, sloughs off the fear that clings to his whole body, and gradually climbs upward. The concert is over. Nothing is moving now. Everything sleeps.

He charges at the moon, but loses his way among celestial paths.

6.

Blackie's Notebooks (III)

❦❦❦ Vienna fascinated me from the outset. I devoured it. The Ring, the Opera, the Burgtheater, the Kunsthistorisches Museum where I spent all my free afternoons, the old city where we lived on the Bäckerstrasse, in a Renaissance house where the courtyard we shared with a piano merchant echoed with the cadences of his wares, the university I was to enter the following year, where I would bury myself in the vast library and study avidly with the glorious intellectuals of the time. All this irritated my father and thrilled my mother. For him, only the fading splendors of the Empire kept claim to any virtue in a world that, it is true, was on the verge of an unimaginable abyss. Nor was I indifferent to the panache, the luxury, the hubbub of a city that presented such a spectacle of fragile, deadly beauty.

My father and I had something else in common: our immoderate passion for that typically Viennese institution, the café. For him, it was a way to escape the family circle, Mama's recriminations, the meetings of uncles and aunts, the household tasks he would reject with a causal flip of the hand that seemed to say, "Why waste time on such trifles?" What mattered to him was his friends, who counted more than anything, who came before everything—before work (and God knows my father had a high opinion of the butcher's trade!), before his blood ties, before love, even before his fatherland. Only God was above the debate—and even that was uncertain. The café meant noisy discussions, frequent, useless arguments, bitter comments on politics, speeches condemning the new morality . . . relentless chess matches,

14

too. For me, it meant exchanges with friends from the gymnasium or the university, endless fiery discussions, bold remarks on liberal ideas, tirades against the values of a decadent society and regime . . . and a great deal of poring over newspapers as well.

(Insomnia. The nurse has given me a double dose of sleeping pills.)

Prague had been just the opposite of Vienna: a banal, almost provincial city, old-fashioned and dirty, with its collection of bourgeois Germans, including my father, who were surrounded by the masses of Czech workers. Being a German Jew in turn-of-the-century Prague suggested a certain affluence, an intellectual and financial ascendancy, even though its obverse was emerging in the form of the anti-Semitic hydra. But nothing frightened Hermann, who was always prepared to do battle, to get involved in things that didn't concern him, ready to counter the slightest provocation with all his six feet of height and his two hundred and twenty pounds. I frequently witnessed the sight, at once dumbfounded, terrified, and fascinated by my father's strength and determination. He was sure of his rights, unhesitatingly describing all Czechs as "riffraff," "a bad lot of workers," and "revolutionaries." As for Mama, she paid far more attention to the possible significance of events in the street. She would explain to me, with all the implications, the whys and wherefores of the social and political imbroglio in which we lived and struggled. Moreover, I had always suspected her, even though she never betrayed it, of being somewhat indifferent to the rigors of Father's scrupulously observed Orthodox Judaism. What I am sure of is that Mama knew that I distanced myself, quite early, from the religion that should have been mine. . . . For me, the synagogue, rabbis, the Talmud, all had become as empty and arduous as Father's physical exercises. Something inconceivable for him—something I never told anyone before I gained my full independence—was to me so obvious it was not worth elaborating on: God was absent. Only punishment existed, punishment that, for an emotional child like myself, was embodied by the sign outside the kosher butcher shop: a disemboweled ox being pecked at, and devoured, by a huge black bird.

Instead of growing interested in the arcana of the Mishnah, I threw myself into a furious reading of the romantic poets and tales of chivalry. Around the same time—I must have been twelve or thirteen—I took up my pen for the first time with the intention of giving voice to more than a rhetorical commentary—to the conflicts and tears that seethed inside me. I wrote some lyric dramas that were produced at the gymnasium, verses published in magazines hand-copied by my friends and me, epic narratives that mimicked those of the Middle Ages. But this fever was short-lived, and, not content with giving up prayers, I decided that writing was, above all, sacrilegious. One day Father happened on a notebook in which I had copied out some poems: without a word, without a blow, without a single threat, he simply tore it up and threw it in the fire. The flames took hold of my body like an inferno. I myself destroyed everything else I had written and decided to stop writing forever. For the first time. . . .

In the schoolyard next day, big Hans was off guard when he jostled me in his usual way, spewing an endless volley of insults that usually left me unnerved and paralyzed, an easy target for his kicks and prods. That day, however, at the first punch I spun without a word and delivered a solid right hook to the jaw which made my assailant scream in pain. He cried louder when he realized that blood was pouring from the corners of his mouth, and a group of students had formed a circle around us. Bringing his hand to his mouth, he gave me a glare he thought was lethal, but I was no longer afraid. I watched him draw himself up and start to get his heavy frame moving. He was a good head taller than I and he charged like a mad bull. I had my guard up, good and tight, elbows close to my body. I led with my right, left fist in reserve (I'd maintained a false guard ever since the accident to my eye), my weight on the balls of my feet, shuffling lightly. I had no trouble dodging big Hans's assault, and as he lunged I aimed a left that landed right on his nose. He nearly lost his balance, and spun around, ready to grab me, bringing all his weight to bear. I stepped aside smartly but not fast enough, for with his left hand he managed to clutch the hem of my jacket. He pulled me in, locked his arms around my head, and squeezed very hard. The blood began to rush, to pound in my skull, to blur my vision. I tried to free myself with a series of fast and furious blows to his stomach, but my fists just sank into the fat with a muffled, hollow sound. He squeezed harder, puffing like an ox. My neck was about to break and my arms dangled uselessly. I had fallen to my knees. My throat ached, my lungs were ready to burst, the dust on the ground was choking me, Hans was going to stick my face in it, and I didn't want to get dirty, or have to swallow anything, and be forced to spit out the earth which was bound to get into my mouth . . . more than the pain, the lacerations, and the indignity, what mattered was not getting dirty. So I clenched my fist once more and carefully struck Hans in the groin. Three times. At the first blow, he loosened his grip, at the second he let go of me altogether, at the third he collapsed, screaming and clutching himself. Despite Father's admonition—"Only women fight like that"—I had won.

At home, they wanted explanations for my disheveled appearance and my dazed look. Mama lavished attention on me, washed me, and changed my clothes, quickly transforming me into the well-behaved and studious child I should have been, while I gave Father a slightly modified account of what had happened, omitting precise details about the outcome. I simply told him I'd been in a fight. He congratulated me, showing his approval by ruffling my hair.

The storm that shook the city that night was so violent the sign on the butcher shop crashed into the gutter, where we found it the next morning, glistening wet. Father immediately replaced it with another, smaller but just as gaudy, which depicted only the jackdaw, black symbol of the Choucas house. In the beginning, deep in the medieval night, there had been a family of Choucas. Time and phonetic drift had transformed the ancestral name to Huka. I was called Huka. It was my name. Under the circumstances, it was unimportant, Father said, whether people knew that he sold meat, as long as the family name occupied a place of honor on the facade, with the emblem serving as a reminder of our lineage for all to see, a response to the questioning glances of passersby who always wanted to know too much, ill-intentioned people who would be warned by it and would move on.

The twofold and unexpected reversal had the advantage of gaining me a certain autonomy that Father had previously refused. At last I was able to spend time with Oscar, my Czech friend who was neither Jewish nor petty bourgeois, without incurring endless sermons or severe reprimands.

Oscar was the eldest son in a family of seven children. His father worked at the imperial arms factory. Accordingly Oscar, who was an excellent student—in fact, we shared the laurels more or less equally, he in mathematics, physics, and chemistry, I in literature, rhetoric, and history—had won a full scholarship to study at the gymnasium. Physically, he was my opposite: very tall and fair, he seemed to have grown too fast and his small head made him look like a fragile giant, whom you expected to see bend in two like a puppet controlled by an invisible spring. His apparent weakness—narrow shoulders, short trunk, long arms—was offset by the balance and assurance of his legs, which seemed endless, but had the precocious muscularity of a long-distance runner. Oscar was a very good racer, the best in the gymnasium. Thanks to him I acquired a certain competence as well. Together, we were unbeatable.

When the ban was lifted we were able to take long runs through the outlying countryside. It was on one of those afternoons that sensuality first struck me like a whip, clutching me in the pit of my stomach and rising like some warm sap

I couldn't identify, flooding my lungs, my heart, my mind with a novel light-headedness. Until then my rare bouts of sexuality had occurred during childhood—a kiss stolen from a blond cousin whose name was quickly forgotten, the perfume of a distant aunt, the half-naked breasts of my mother, surprised at her toilette.

I was equally ignorant about women's bodies and the goals and effects of promiscuity. I was almost as ignorant about my own body, having barely wondered at the strange faculties that seemed at times to stir and awaken certain intimate parts of my anatomy.

Oscar and I had run through meadows to the forest, and now we were almost out of breath. Dizzy with scalding oxygen, we collapsed onto the grass at a bend in the path. Trying vainly to catch our breath, we managed, though with difficulty, to explode in joyful laughter that welled inside us like fireworks. Several minutes must have passed before, calmer now, we were able to rest in silence, looking up beyond the treetops at the sky. I had forgotten my father, the rabbi, the butcher shop, the gymnasium, all of them cast into the miasma of the city. Shedding my grief and cares, I succumbed to a giddy pleasure that was composed of physical exhaustion, springtime odors, and the serene, clear song of invisible birds that lived in the surrounding woods. Oscar caught me out in the midst of my ecstasy, turning toward me abruptly and asking in a voice that seemed louder than thunder: "Have you ever had a hard-on?"

I'd heard the expression many times, needless to say, and knew more or less what it meant; I'd given it a halo of mystery that lent it a kind of superhuman dignity, as if it were some Olympian feat. But I'd never been asked the question in such a straightforward, provocative manner. As I didn't reply, Oscar added, "Look." Then he slowly undid the buttons of his fly and tugged until he withdrew a hunk of red flesh that seemed enormous. His hands circled the base of his glistening tool so that it stood straight up. Still lying on his back, he raised his head as if to admire this phenomenon. I looked away at first, but then, fascinated by the queer transformation that I'd never observed in myself, I began looking at it closely, scrupulously, inspecting the slightest swelling, the least little vein, the subtlest nuance in color. A triumphant rainbow!

Motionless, Oscar said not a word, merely let me admire his tumescent organ. Then, suddenly, as if he'd had enough of my observations, he replaced it in his trousers, not without difficulty, and, sighing, rebuttoned his fly. Then he stretched out again, laid his head back on his hands, and began to gaze at the stretches of blue sky above us.

And then it happened. Gently, like a wave that is born slowly, obscurely, deep in the water, and growing with the eddies and currents that cross it until it becomes a magnificent crown of foam, that boldly flings itself against the ridge of rocks on the shore . . . stiff, firm, tangible, something I too could grasp with both hands if I desired. The object was supreme as it sought to imbue all of nature with its throbbing, as it pointed beyond the summits of the trees, toward a vertical eternity.

Motionless, I did not utter a word, mindful of the roaring that filled my body. Eyes shut, I abandoned myself to contemplating the sky.

Neither Oscar nor I, from that day on, pursued the mutual exploration of our virility any further. Nor did the slightest ambiguity, or embarrassment, ever compromise our friendship. But the young man who came to Vienna was no longer altogether ignorant of his secret desires, of what drove him to look at the young girls whose charms, he knew now, he would certainly appreciate when the opportunity arose.

The young girls in Vienna had a sort of natural grace that, regardless of social standing or beauty, made them bewitching beings who fed my dreams of tenderness and folly and fueled my thirst for life and love.

Imagine my happiness when I entered the university, where I could at last hear and touch, talk to and have literary arguments with all the girls I saw in the distance at the Prater or on the double-decker coaches that went up and down the Ring.

That was how I met Cosette, a French girl who had come to Vienna to study with Freud. She was much older than I (at least according to the rules of the time and of the circles I was part of); she must have been twenty-three or twenty-four. And the age difference was not the least of the concerns that cast a shadow over our friendship, then our brief liaison. But I was still able to discover what is generally known as love. A love that, though imperfect, had the notable advantage of not being mercenary.

But I realize that memory's retroactive excitement gives the past a light more blinding than the flickers from confused reality, and I am proceeding too hastily. In truth, I admit that at the university I met mostly men. During my first year I took courses in philosophy and in German and English language and literature. In an unexpected burst of generosity, my father had consented; he agreed that I needed time to adapt to the new life, the new space that the Austrian capital offered. I was only seventeen, after all . . . but he hastened to add that when the time came, I would have to turn my thoughts to serious matters. And for him, who saw only grounds for damnation in the subjects I chose, the dire forewarnings of a decadent civilization, unthinkable attacks on the truth and on the necessity of Judaism, only one activity was honest and worthy of our name: business. Because he recognized my abilities and was proud, when you come right down to it, that his son and heir could outwit sons of the finest Viennese bourgeoisie, he was willing for me to complete my education—on condition that it be "profitable." I admit that he differed in that respect from most of the Jewish community of Prague and Vienna, which produced—and would continue to produce—the flower of the country's intelligentsia. He was opposed to my mixing with this subversive riffraff, but my mother, despite her fears, gladly helped me conceal a number of my activities. When she knew I was at the Museum Café, where I spent a good part of the afternoons in heated discussion with Franz, Stefan, Hugo, Robert, and Maximilien on the relative flaws and merits of romanticism and symbolism, she would say I'd been working with her on the shop accounts. Meyrink or Hofmannsthal divided my friends and me into two camps, while on Nietzsche we were unanimous. And when our noisy, joyful troop took an outing to the vineyards of Grinzing to taste the new spring wine, theosophy—in those days the rage of the salons—could wreak its havoc among us as well. We would come home exhausted, drunk on wine, emotions, and theories, our souls replete and slightly reeling, briefly considering a visit to a brothel.

I was nineteen when the dream finally became reality. We were all wild about theater and cabaret, but I'm not sure now if, on that occasion, we were coming out of a play by Kleist (perhaps *Penthesilea*, about the demonic Amazon, in which the verb "to love" was made to rhyme with "bite"), a performance by the Ballets Russes, or a cabaret where we all nursed wild and secret hopes of enjoying liberties with an actress or a singer. I do know the evening ended with copious glasses of Bürsteiner, an exhilarating white wine whose suave, rich aromas make the head swirl. I'd paid no attention to the crowd on the Kärntnerstrasse and had ended up in a bedroom without even thinking about it. I was too drunk to be intimidated, or to take the initiative, so I let the girl have her way, even though the next day I couldn't describe her face. She had straddled me. I do remember that. "It's your first time, isn't it, darling? Never mind, just let yourself go." I don't know what I did or didn't do, but she probably didn't have to feign pleasure to unleash a flood of deliverance in me. In days to come I sought in vain, but I could only reconstitute fragments of images—fierce but at the same time distant and blurred— that seemed light-years away, at the end of a dark corridor stretching out before me, while my testicles felt dizzyingly clenched in a vise, ruling out all play, all glances, all freedom. To say that the experience was entirely negative, or traumatic, sounds like a tendentious interpretation. (I'll leave that to Clockwork!) I kept nothing, possessed nothing of the flesh, but at least I knew that contact with it was no more dangerous than strong alcohol. The result, if there was one, was that I wanted—this time consciously and ardently—to visit a brothel again. But I didn't let myself immediately give in to this urge to try again. Some months passed before the opportunity arose, a period when I studied with Spartan vigor, and began to note the changes occurring in my father's business. Despite his constant flow of explanations and advice for the future, I paid little attention to what was going on, and hadn't realized that his fortune had been growing since we came to Vienna. It had been ages since he'd turned in his butcher's apron for a frock coat, giving his place in the shop to three or four clerks. He had bought first one, then two, then three more butcher shops, assigning managers to them and visiting them regularly to check the books and see that things were running smoothly. Finally, around the time of the Kärntnerstrasse episode, he summoned my mother and me to an extraordinary family council to announce that he'd earned enough on the stock market to "upgrade the family business." Those were his very words. And that was when the black bird became the emblem of Huka and Son. Some fifty employees, vast warehouses, a combined slaughterhouse and canning factory. Father always took me on the inevitable boss's visit, and he never thought for a moment I might dislike it. So it soon became a fearful obsession. Mama and I would both try—and usually fail—to find some good excuse to get out of it. Huka and Son: I had protested feebly this corporate name that linked me so firmly to the blood and money that sustained us. I was on the receiving end. I was pointed out to all as heir apparent. When the emblem somehow came to the attention of Franz or Maximilien (not to mention Cosette!), I was filled with an inexplicable sense of shame, one that left me in a sad physical and mental state from which even the joint efforts of friendship, love, and literature had trouble drawing me. I hated it when Father threw me to the lions—

his account books—or introduced me to the workers as his sole and worthy successor. I didn't understand a thing he said about the firm. And the swirl of account books numbed my mind until I became so nauseated I couldn't eat; they were even more unbearable than the sight of bleeding quarters of beef hanging from their torture hooks. Father was no longer satisfied with merely forcing my head into hemoglobin, he wanted my body to reek of money too. Despite my constant cautious avoidance of the butcher shop, I was attracted to the strange world of knives and saws that glittered in the chiaroscuro of the shop; and I knew that it was sincere friendship that kept me from systematically rejecting the company of the youngest clerks. But not the accountants and bankers, that was impossible! I was well aware that my privileged position allowed me to live the life I describe. I was a member of the Vienna bourgeoisie in the period when the sun was setting on the Empire, just before the Great War. All that I owed to my father, and I was grateful to him. But how the hell could he think that I was able to decide, with the same clairvoyance and tenacity, what should be done to ensure the perpetuation of this golden life unto the future generations that he assumed I would engender? I myself had an ominous feeling that we were living the final moments of a so-called innocence, which the world was experiencing as a reprieve before the storm that would push it to the edge of an abyss whose disastrous, unfathomable depths I could see forming all around me—and within me. Franz Joseph was over seventy. What did he represent to our gratified but desiring young generation? What did all the outmoded pomp, the ramshackle celebrations, the falsely jingoistic military parade, mean to us who thrilled to our reading of new ideologies, who followed passionately anything from one end of Europe to the other that resembled the hope of socialism? Hegel and Rousseau were our masters. Stefan and Franz were enthusiastic about the philosophers of the Enlightenment, Robert read Proudhon, Maximilien had placed his life under the sign of Zionism and dreamed of the state we might help to found on the sands of Palestine. From Prague, Oscar sent me letters in which, in veiled terms, he communicated his passion for the theses of Marx. And I, though closer to the fiercely mystical nihilism of a Dostoyevsky, devoted myself entirely to Russian radicalism and the model of revolutionary purity and asceticism Chernyshevsky's heroes offered me.

Franz, who became a celebrated writer, moved between wars into the comfort of a position officially recognized by the ruling Social Democrats, and toward the end of his life began to sing the praises of Christianity. Shortly before I came to Bellevue Hospital I read in the *Chronicle* that he had died at the height of his apostolic fame, on the West Coast of the New Continent, and far west of the spiritual hopes that then rocked and still stir America. I've always been convinced, for no apparent reason, that he drowned himself in a Beverly Hills swimming pool.

Stefan, like Oedipus banished from Thebes and fleeing with his daughter Antigone to go to Colonus and die, exiled himself to Brazil. He hoped to find there the same reasons for living that made him the most amusing of friends, but somehow in 1941 he found instead good enough reasons to commit suicide.

Robert left us in 1918 to take part in the Spartacist revolution in Munich, where he was sentenced to death.

A few years later, Hugo the engineer suffered a heart attack at the tragic funeral of his four-year-old son.

As for Maximilien, following my orders he destroyed my manuscripts—at least I think he did—then in 1933 he went to Palestine. He must be there still, serene patriarch of one of the first kibbutzim. I cannot, I will not believe, although Pattie the Tigress has been telling me so for three years now, that he was killed by bombs dropped by his own airplanes during the Yom Kippur War. She was in the Middle East at the time and knows what she's talking about: How can I not believe her when, six months later, she was left for dead at an airport after trying to hijack a Boeing 747? Anyway, I've no idea what she's talking about. During all the years I've been cloistered within these hospital walls, I haven't stopped reading the newspapers from around the world that Dr. Clockwork agreed, after a memorable discussion, to have brought to me every morning. And yet, everything Pattie utters in the course of a day strikes me as excessive, and as muddled as the Hebrew that my father tried to ram down my throat, which I tried in vain to forget as soon as independence and solitude made it possible. I belong to no race. That's what my father could never understand. It's what divided us at the time of the great confrontation. "Background," "religion," "origin" were senseless words to me, words that gradually disappeared from my memory. I didn't remember them. My differing desires and necessities had taught me the virtues and the rituals of exile.

As for Oscar, he died in 1944, in the camp at Theresien-stadt.

For a long time I have been possessed by nightmares. Last night again, like almost every other night. A dream blindingly clear, totally obvious.

The hospital is all white. Absolute cleanliness. The walls and wooden floors are gleaming. I have gone down through a trapdoor, guided by bloody hands that held me firmly by the wrists. Underground rooms glow with neon. While stumbling, bound hand and foot, through a maze of corridors and passageways, I soon realized that any hope of flight in this doomed labyrinth was merely the fruit of illusion. I put on, in a process infinitely repeated, divided image of the same motions, over and over again, the white smock. They dragged me through empty rooms where immaculate silence reigned. My footsteps glided across waxed mirrors. I was surrounded by my own image, producing a deafening echo in my mind, revealing an unknown presence that watched me, trapped in its grasp. In all four corners, cameras, flood-lights.

The audiovisual circuit controlled, filtered, and selected all entrances and exits. Only a mysterious airlock, opened by an invisible mechanism inside the walls, gave way to the next room. And when the view opened into a cloudless horizon, where I think I caught a brief glimpse of the street's gaudy spectacle, there loomed directly above me, from a hidden corner, a guardian archangel. His wings enfolded my body and brought me back from any thoughts of freedom. Doors slammed. Why, since they led nowhere? And I backed through corridors that were exactly like those I had just crossed, but with an even more sickening atmosphere, toward the exit.

Then a voice boomed through the loudspeaker. It was Clockwork asking, "Well, Anton, where do you think you're going?"

As the walls came crashing down around me, he added, still invisible, "You must know, my friend, we've seen to everything here. You yourself admitted not long ago that there are advantages to our self-sufficient system that only allows you to think of the reality of the hospital. Have you by chance changed your mind?"

I wanted to answer, to scream as I was still capable of doing during the first months. I opened my mouth, ready to spit out the nightmare that crouched in my chest, yet no sound would escape my lips.

Another time, another night, I know I will find the exit, determine some way to elude the electronic eye. Then Clockwork can shout himself hoarse into his microphone and send his henchmen after me, but there will be nothing between me and the starry sky and the night as bright as northern lights.

I had never doubted that my madness was genuine. Who can permit self-doubt? Nor have I ever let on to anyone, especially not Clockwork, that it might be otherwise. For one good reason: because it was my choice. Ever since 1929 when I nearly died, since the start of my secret and hidden life, since anonymity, since my flight in 1939, since entering the hospital six years later . . . no, in fact my fate was irretrievably sealed in the year of Sarajevo.

A decisive year in many respects. The sense of shared joy and suffering seemed final. Four episodes—amid many others—strike me as sufficient to describe the various twists and turns.

My first experience with prostitutes had left an unbearable mixture of bitterness and appetite in my heart. I had been led there almost against my will, unable in any case to control the desire that was secretly at work inside me. Betrayed by circumstances I wanted my revenge. I knew how to apply myself completely to an event that demanded to be seized bodily, in all its truth. I refused to think that it might be futile. For the ephemeral, all paradox aside, is the necessary, perhaps even the sole condition for approaching the absolute.

I returned, then, to the Kärntnerstrasse. Alone this time. And sober. I took my time choosing the girl: brown hair, big black eyes, she must have been my age, despite thick makeup that accentuated her features and made her look older. I said not a word, nor did she (she could tell from my appearance that I was a young bourgeois and there'd be no haggling over the price). Slowly we headed for the hotel. And silence accompanied us into the room. There she asked me to unfasten her dress. And as she was about to say something to put me at ease, I gently covered her mouth with my hand, signifying that she should say no more. Turning her head toward me, she looked at me and smiled. She understood. I obviously was not accustomed to this sort of behavior and was unprepared for any bold initiatives. But she realized that I intended to be master of the situation. I was not unaware that her profession enabled her to adapt to her client's psychology, no matter how bizarre, and that her only task would be to do everything she could to give me pleasure. I was no cynic, far from it. But I had imagined this meeting with serenity; I had been reflecting on it for months; I had prepared for it as one is slowly initiated into a ritual that imposes trial after trial. So there was no question of overcoming my shyness; something else was at stake.

Whether she liked me or just pretended to enjoy my company is, in the end, unimportant. The main thing was that on that day I thought I was experiencing all the gestures, the perfumes, the headiness of love. From then on, I knew. I knew the warmth of a mouth, the virtuosity of hands, the elasticity of skin, the arching of a back, the shudder of a caress, the violence of a gaze, dampness, shock of skin on skin, the soul opening, the gush from within, the turmoil of the senses, the swaying, explosion, refusal, waiting, irritation, the music of bodies . . .

Nothing would ever be the same again. I didn't realize how true this was. Several hours later, when the desire in our tired, satiated bodies was appeased, I finally found the strength to separate myself from the woman who had taught me pleasure. And yet, when I asked her name as I was dressing, I felt as if I'd been trapped: Julia sounded false, as unreal as the works of literature with which I had screened off my life. Was it a dream? I thought I had absorbed my act, but now, only a short time after consummation, that act was taking on grotesque dimensions. I paid, gave her all the money I was carrying. Julia thanked me coldly and invited me back. I kissed the corner of her mouth and left, lighthearted, but with an uncontrollable pain in the pit of my stomach. My penis was still burning, but a chilly wound opened deep inside me. I was guilty. So soon.

That same evening, as if on purpose I had already thrown myself to the wolves, I was less conciliatory than usual with my father. I was seeking some kind of confrontation, as though I wanted to punish myself, to pay homage to the rebellion that goaded me. Although I usually made subtle compromises, in order to pass off my odd behavior as wayward adolescent moods, receptive to improvement, that night I resisted.

So when Father attacked, I did not take cover. The argument immediately escalated, filled with threats, with storms about to burst.

Father said:

"Study is necessary, of course, but life comes first."

"Life? Blood, piss, shit . . . and the will to power that blinds men."

"How dare you? The problem with you young people is, you don't understand the meaning of words—you throw them in our faces like curses. Language is a gift from God, for the glorification of His name."

"And of the golden calf."

My mother interrupted, trying to change the subject and put an end to the quarrel that, this time, was assuming dangerous proportions.

"You look so tired, Anton—why not eat your soup and go to bed."

"He must work. No, he must 'study,' as he says. And tonight I am giving the lesson."

And once again the subject was our generation's profligate manners, our lack of courage. Father didn't understand why I had stopped defending my friends. I told him I was seeing less and less of them. In fact, I'd gotten tired of the drunken arguments and the aesthetic spats that, not long ago, had seemed as necessary to my life as my heartbeat. Dialogue had given way to solitary questioning. Certainties did not content me; what fascinated me was doubt. And at the time, my generation had not learned to doubt. We would discover it shortly, at great cost. Father, though, had changed. He was less sure of himself; I even had the impression that some secret fault had appeared in his religious convictions, as if History were beginning to catch up with him, to submerge him . . . as if he had a premonition of disaster. I had been surprised to see his resignation in the face of increasingly virulent attacks on the Jews. The business of the *Protocols of the Elders of Zion*—a total fabrication by the czarist police in support of who knows what international conspiracy to justify anti-Jewish oppression—had become enormous. And when there were anti-Semitic outbursts in Vienna, I was astonished when Father hung his head and gave in. As a bourgeois and a wealthy businessman, he thought he was safe from such dangers. But when insulting slogans were scrawled on his own shops, he was forced to acknowledge the evidence. The fortress he thought he'd erected around himself was useless. He too was fragile. He too had surrendered.

So there it was. Just as he was flagging and as I began to

resist (though I wasn't consciously trying to take advantage of his relative weakness), confrontation became inevitable. And he threw himself into it with as much determination as I. He knew there was no other way to escape, no other way out of the crisis we were both undergoing. One of us must give in— or give the other a reason to think that he'd won. Fight and flight.

"You don't go to the café anymore to find out what's going on and you think I'll swallow your tall tales," he said.

"What's important isn't at the café."

"Ah yes, your great principles . . ."

"They're better than cynicism and pride."

"And God, Anton. And faith."

"I believe in truth and love."

"I'd like to know where you found them. At the university? The whorehouse? May the fires of hell . . ."

". . . flood us, quench us, and kill us, for there lie the sources of pleasure."

"Blasphemy!"

"I'm a man without roots."

Then Father hurled himself at me, sneering, "A man!" He gripped my collar, raised his arm. I pushed him away roughly, and my voice shot out "I advise you not to touch me!" with electric force.

Frozen with warring strength and frustration, he stared at me. I lowered my eyes, turned, and went to lock myself in my room. I threw myself on my bed and buried my head in the pillow to stifle the clamor and shouting from the other end of the corridor. Father and Mama must have been discussing me, each one trying to drown out the other, and to obliterate my rebellion. I didn't have the strength to cry. Or to undress. For ages, sharp, painful thoughts buried me under successive waves of rancor, anguish, fatigue—and enthusiasm too. I had reached a turning point. I knew it. But I was afraid to negotiate the curve, fearing I lacked the necessary courage and speed for the direct route to the sanctuary of ideas that stirred me. I planned my future, deciding, notably, to stay at the university rather than transfer to the Institute of Commercial Studies as Father had suggested. I resolved to drop my group of friends from the Museum Café and, finally, to speak to the young woman I had noticed in my literature class. I determined to forget Julia, and to start writing again.

In the silence of the night I masturbated while thinking of Julia one last time. And then I slept.

All these decisions would have had some meaning if, a few days later, the first red patches hadn't appeared. My glans had started to swell and a sharp pain ran through my body when I urinated. Then small white pustules, the size of a pinhead, appeared, and the pain seemed to subside. But it was replaced by an aggressive, tenacious odor that wafted up to my face whenever I undressed or took out my penis to pee. I would hold it delicately in my fingers and cautiously examine it, unable to do anything but observe the extent of the disaster and inhale the terrible smell that seemed to come from the meatus. Shame gave way to fear—fear of discovery, of course, but far more profoundly, the fear of dying, of rotting from this extremity before I'd had time to discover all its possibilities. Already, it was escaping me to dissolve in horror. I did not, would not believe in punishment. Father's power, his desire for revenge, his authority didn't go that far. No, what terrified me was the specter of syphilis. I devoured all the books in the university library that dealt with the disease. Spirochetes, roseola, Venus's necklace held no secrets from me, and I frequently locked myself in the bathroom to compare my symptoms with the descriptions in medical treatises. This development was all the more painful and tragic because I'd decided to take the plunge with Cosette. I had seated myself beside her on a bench in the amphitheater, and our shared passion for Novalis soon led to a conversation that continued after the lecture, in a café near the Rathaus. We saw each other every day. And when we didn't have class, I would wait for her outside Freud's lecture, which was the main reason for her being in Vienna. She had started studying medicine at the Salpêtrière in Paris, and her father, one of

the most brilliant scientists in France, had not only consented, but encouraged her coming. She described him as an
enlightened man who believed in progress and, faithful to the
philosophers of the Enlightenment, fought the good fight simultaneously on the medical and political fronts. He admired
Freud, whose renown had finally crossed national borders,
and was also a supporter of Jaurès. Cosette, too, was a pacifist
during this prelude to war, and was enthusiastic about psychoanalysis. I was aware, of course, of the works and lessons
of our Viennese master, and had read his *Die Traumdeutung*,
but this key to dreams had only partially convinced me. The
process was new, and combined many aspects of our generation's revolt against the conformity and ancient history that
had us smothered in intellectual laziness, an alienation of the
senses which dated from another time. And yet, I saw this
breakthrough into dreams not as a sacrilege—I'd leave that to
Father—but as one more illusion that, under the persuasive
mask of truth, would convince us a little more of the folly of
our passions. Later, Freud's article on Dostoyevsky and patri-
cide would only further confirm my reluctance to accept that
death (or art—same thing) could be reduced to a neurosis or
a destructive urge that was determined by illness, acceptance
of punishment, and obsession with sin. Of course, I recognized that these factors were partially valid, though they
seemed very limited in comparison with the shadowy wasteland where they had been discovered. But I think now that
my refusal sprang from the excessive fear I would experience
if I found that the core of my own life was locked in these
mysteries. In any case, Cosette's twofold admiration for
Freud and Jaurès led us to see one another daily. One evening I took her to dinner at a tavern near the Opera. She
sampled some Viennese dishes for the first time and I introduced her to the delightful beef dish, *Tafelspitz*. We didn't
talk much about literature or psychoanalysis. Had we exhausted the subject? Were we already in love? I don't know,
but I loved hearing her describe Paris, a city that attracted
me, fascinated me, that I dreamed of visiting one day. We

made a pact to go there together. I could already picture myself on the grand boulevards, the Champs-Elysées, strolling arm in arm with Cosette, who would love me as much as I loved her. We would have a tiny room filled with books, close to the Sorbonne. Obviously, my head was filled with all the clichés I'd read in novels of the Belle Epoque. But I was happy. I would have been utterly happy if, as I said, the thing hadn't come to intrude in my most secret self, if this obsession hadn't lodged between my legs, devouring my ambitions, dissipating my hopes, destroying any possibility of a joyous and carefree embrace.

After dinner, I walked her back to her little boardinghouse on the Judenplatz. On the doorstep, as she was shaking my hand, I felt certain that if I made the first move she would welcome a kiss, or even allow me into her room. I looked away from her gleaming eyes, picturing my reddened penis. Then I briskly freed my hand, as if I were afraid of contaminating her, and strode toward the next street without a word of farewell. I heard her cry out behind me—"Anton . . ."— but I did not turn around. Fearing she might try to catch up with me, I started running and didn't stop until I was part of the crowd still strolling on the Graben. . . .

I swore I wouldn't see her again. That way, Father couldn't reproach me for loving a foreigner or tell me for the hundredth time that I could never marry a goy. I loved Cosette. But it was Julia there between my legs, stigmata of gratified desire, of a supreme pleasure that fate had stolen, taken back from me, for having believed in evil spells! And so I decided not to see Cosette again. The next day, I stopped attending the literature class. I found a café far from the center of town where I was sure I wouldn't run into anyone I knew. And finally, after long hesitations and reflections on how to get out of the horrible situation I'd gotten into, I decided to consult Dr. Schnitzler.

The disease had progressed, and I realized I was exposing myself to serious danger. But aside from my tormented conscience, I didn't see how I could easily remedy the situation. I couldn't consult Dr. Rosenbaum, our family physician, because he would rush right off and tell the story to his friend Hermann Huka. I could picture him, his eyes twinkling, having a good laugh over it. He would poke fun, and condemn me.

Besides, I was reluctant to expose my dilemma and my body to the impersonal gaze of someone I didn't know. But inspiration struck as I passed a bookstore: Schnitzler. He was a famous writer. I'd read most of his work, seen some of his plays. More than any writer, he had explored the unfathomable depths of sexuality. Physician and writer—yes, that was what I needed now, with chaos threatening both my body and my mind. I knew at once that I could talk to him, explain, display both my outer and my inner wounds.

Dr. Schnitzler was a celebrity in Vienna. Everyone knew the large suburban house where he lived. I decided to go there at once. After traveling all that distance, of course, I could only make an appointment to return the following day. That night was sheer torture, but the mere notion that I would soon know the degree of my sentence relieved me.

"Take these pills three times a day, and it is vital that you come to my office every day for treatment."

The verdict was concise, almost terse. And Schnitzler did not lecture me, though the whole time that his gloved hands were examining the tip of my penis—moments that seemed like hours—I kept expecting him to denounce my indiscretion and childish ignorance. He said nothing until he went to his office to write out the prescription, when he looked at me and said:

"You said your name was Anton Huka, is that right?"

"Yes." (I waited for him to add, "Oh yes, the son of . . .")

"Aren't you the Huka whose poems I read a while ago in *Poetica*?"

I was dumbfounded. Schnitzler had read me!

"You're still writing, I assume."

I dared not deny it.

"Yes, I'm . . . working on something." (It was only a half-lie. I had already decided to resume my writing.)

"Let's talk about all that tomorrow, shall we?"

The consultation, which could have been a Calvary, ended in resurrection. I almost blessed the disease that had led me to Schnitzler. During our café and salon indictments we young diehards, steeped in romanticism, had criticized his writing, we had derided the light comedies that relied on facile effects and pandered to the basest instincts. But here was the writer, the physician, welcoming me, putting me at ease, restoring my self-confidence, inviting me to take part in rituals I had considered despicable, although they stemmed from profoundly human concerns.

That evening I had another fight with Father, less violent than the last, but ending with his threatening to disinherit me. My "Who gives a damn!" made him breathless, sent him into a violent coughing fit from which he emerged only to shut himself away with his account books. Everything had been said. He knew, I'm quite sure, that now it was only a matter of time, but he clung to the secret hope that the hand of God would come and stop me at the edge of the precipice.

The following day Schnitzler painted my glans with dilute peroxide. I was nervous, but able to tolerate the pain, as I would in the days to come, for he never alluded to any sort of punishment, to any indirect way of "paying."

When he spoke of the decadent era we lived in, he did not intend to stigmatize my personal behavior; he had his sights on collective responsibility. It was not I, Anton Huka, son of Hermann Huka, who had sinned, but an entire society with no outlet for its anguish except the one pleasure left among the ruins: debauchery.

As Schnitzler was placing a gauze bandage on the circumcised part of my penis, I asked him about theories of morality.

"It's obvious, my friend, that the comedy of sexuality is the one thing shared by all social classes, all individuals."

"You . . . you believe that," I stammered, grimacing with pain.

"I believe nothing. Have you read my novel *The Road to the Open?*"

"Yes."

And then I realized that, quite unintentionally, I had chosen to consult a doctor who was a Jew. An amazing coincidence. I gasped.

As if he knew the reason for my distress, Schnitzler alluded once more to his story of a Jewish doctor-poet, a genuine pariah who lived in isolation, in a society corroded by bigotry, by all sorts of prejudices, guided by fanatical patriotism. The fable seemed—need I say—exaggerated. I was reluctant to give the doctor any more personal details. So I was not unhappy when our conversation ended shortly after with practical advice on curing the insomnia that had been tormenting me quite a while.

The penis, Cosette, and Julia populated my nights, and phantoms danced an endless saraband about my frantic dreams.

Throughout the following week of my "shock treatment," I had an extended conversation with Schnitzler that should have filled me with the same enthusiasm I possessed at first. Oddly, my passion was dwindling with each consultation as the conviction I'd had from the outset, about dealing with an exceptional man, became ratified. I grew wary. To the author of *La Ronde* I must be simply another experimental subject, to be gradually transformed, through successive confessions, into a guinea pig for his theories of eroticism.

Alone in my bedroom I had started to write, to note down the strange and contradictory feelings that had enveloped me. My meeting with the writer was an ideal subject for a short story. After several pages, I realized I had been vouchsafed material for a novel with possibilities I hadn't dreamed of. So I began to exploit it, though I lingered over how to proceed. Who should be the protagonist? The doctor or the patient? Should I make their meeting the symbolic motif of some strange reflection? Were the fragments of dialogue I'd put down liable to build to a dramatic crescendo, to crystallize an extreme position? Who would be the winner—for in the end there was a confrontation—patient or therapist?

The matter was settled at our last session, when Schnitzler said peremptorily:

"Ah, dear friend, there's nothing poetic about life. You have to live with your faults."

Masks off! How could I have fallen into the trap of illusion? Strange how I allowed myself to be periodically fascinated by the effects of mirrors. Dazzled by my own gaze, by the blinding light of my anxieties.

At home, I reread what I'd written and decided to abandon the extravagant project then and there. It was the first in a long series of aborted manuscripts which posterity has seen fit to turn into the cornerstones of a "budding opus." What a farce! The novels, the real ones, touched the public only indirectly. They were written before my "first death," and taken with me into my tomb of silence, as long as they were destroyed by Maximilien, who kept his promise.

Oh yes, my illness—Schnitzler had told me, incidentally, while giving me the routine check with a stethoscope, that he could hear a disturbing and raucous murmur in my chest.

"Do you smoke?"

"No." (True, for tobacco. Schnitzler needn't know about the opium fantasias with Stefan and Maximilien.)

He had recommended that when "this problem" was "in working order" again, I come and see him about the murmur. It should not be taken lightly, he added. Had my penis, then, become something trivial? Was he an imbecile or a sadist? Didn't he know that what caused me to swell at one extremity was entwined with what was already gnawing at me inside? Not the same symptoms, nor the same disease, but one single appetite for death was burrowing, coiling within me like a gluttonous snake ready to spring on an easy prey—my complacent body, offering itself to the stings of destruction.

As for the disease, let me finish up and quickly outline the role it played in my life. It caused unhappiness and happiness, it spared me the horrors of imperial and international butchery, it caused me to lose Cosette and kept me under paternal sway for some time, and it finally led me to write some of my finest pages but also left me unsatisfied, clinging to my phantasmagoria, unable to make any constant or sustained effort, unable to finish what I had started, though it was, quite obviously, a last-ditch effort to feel hope.

The truth is that I was probably living through the final moments of adolescence and, like the old world, that period of my life corresponded with the twilight of the age of the masters. Soon the continent would be sacked and burned, and the railings that sheltered Europe, that, in turn, protected us, would be shattered. Bruised flesh, shredded bones, pulverized bodies. Souls and statues thrown from their pedestals. Who could still believe in masters? And yet, my alienation clashed more and more violently with the incredible perseverance with which everyone—Father, Stefan, Robert, Oscar, Maximilien, and the rest—clung to life-saving ideologies. Man has never been able to live for himself; so true, it has become an intolerable commonplace. We always need to lean on tottering crutches that we use at the first opportunity as bludgeons, clubs, death-dealing cannons.

Still, I too had to pay my final tribute to the masters. It was probably a good thing. . . . In order to forget Schnitzler, Cosette, and my violent confrontations with Father, I became unreasonably infatuated with that very fashionable personality Rudolf Steiner. I had met the bard of theosophy two or three times. The lectures, which I attended with my café friends, imprinted on my questioning mind, though they didn't completely transport me. But that didn't stop me from wanting to meet him.

His black frock coat, his luminous gaze, his determined manner. On his desk, the *Annals of Natural Philosophy*. We spoke of reconciling science and metaphysics. I came to consult him. About my condition. About the illness that was

splitting my mind and body. And I let Steiner think me a
follower. Despite my confusion, he suspected nothing. I listened to him, fascinated by his power, but deep down, something told me that my aspirations lay elsewhere. I, too, spoke
of the end of the world. Without qualms I boarded the foundering ship of the apocalypse. A splendid opportunity. Impas-
sioned, I launched into the secrets of creativity, what impelled me to write. Captivated by the spiritualist, I swore to
become a vegetarian. It seemed a good way to infuriate Father. And in fact, from then on, meat disgusted me. I ate less
and less, using dietetic theories as protective armor. I thought
it would conquer the disease that oppressed my carcass more
each week. Over the next few months I lost a good twenty-five
pounds. The solid frame I had doggedly constructed developed cracks. My muscles weakened. My resistance ran out. I
grew short of breath. And Mama became concerned about
my health. She talked to Dr. Rosenbaum, whom I refused to
consult at first. One day, however—probably to avoid hurting
her and also because I knew the effects of the disease were
irreversible and it was no use pretending—I decided to go
through with it. It's true that wartime privations exacerbated
my declining vitality and new dietary whims. Despite his privileged position, Father was not totally immune from the disasters overcoming our country. The high cost of living, the
black market, abetted the naturalist position I confronted him
with and caused my everyday fare to deteriorate until my
rations were quite inadequate for a man my age. "If he won't
eat meat, the hell with him! It's still cheaper than vegetables!
Who does he think he is, anyway? I'm not the Prince of Bos-
nia-Herzogovina!"

But I hadn't finished with Steiner. My interminable
speeches had swamped him, and I sensed that he'd nodded
off in his chair, or just shut his eyes to escape me and engage
in some meditation that was beyond my reach. Once in a
while he emerged from his reverie (or his sleep) and noisily
blew his nose. He had a head cold, a runny nose. He would
stick his finger in his nostrils, snorting like a metal forge. . . .

7.
Clockwork's Notes (II)

❧❧❧ I was sick at heart when I succeeded in deciphering this part of Blackie's notebooks. It couldn't be—but yes, I'd read those lines somewhere. The very words, turn of phrase. "A runny nose," "a head cold," "his finger," "his nose." I'd seen them somewhere before. I didn't know if the phrases were identical, but that day I was sure that Anton had read Kafka's *Diary*. It was a sizable clue, a discovery whose potential repercussions terrified me. And if . . . but no, clues are always just a clever way to disguise the truth. And I knew that once again, Antoine Choucas was starring in a comedy of forgery, introducing the artful strategies of plagiarism. He was deliberately steering me down the wrong track, but I didn't hold it against him. By doing so he'd revealed a shred of his secret, a tiny scrap of his solitary past. One question remained: Where could he have gotten hold of the book? Very mysterious. Besides, in the work of that "Other"—who was perhaps not the right one—there was no phrase "snorting like a metal forge."

8.
Blackie's Notebooks (IV)

ꕥꕥꕥ Well, it happened. Father decided my vocation was to attend the Institute of Commercial Studies. The next day would be June 28, 1914. Franz Ferdinand would die. And blood would flow from Europe's right flank, reddening the Serbian lands, splashing the Balkans, Prussia, Belgium, France, Russia . . . And nothing would matter anymore. Anyway, Dr. Rosenbaum diagnosed pulmonary catarrh. I started to spit blood. He recommended the sanatorium. Perfect timing. . . . It was early summer and very hot in Vienna. I felt I was suffocating. The mountains would probably be good for me. But I didn't want to leave, because the memory of Cosette continued to torment me. I hadn't seen her in six months—didn't know whether she'd left Austria and returned to Paris, where the vengeful "Marseillaise" replaced the sentimental melodies of the *caf concert*. My desire was unavoidable, I had not decided to yield to it; but I wanted to go back to her, take her in my arms, hold her close, cover her with kisses, tell her I loved her. As in the song. . . .

My unconscious prodded me. The pacifists were campaigning against the war, and that night they held a meeting at the university. I went.

Father ranted and raved, but his speeches ran off me like water. I would never go to the institute. I would go to the mountains. I would be a writer. Whatever the cost. . . .

For one evening, the question of peace brought together Vienna's anarchists, revolutionary socialists, progressives, and democratic humanists. The amphitheater was packed and tense. Everyone was talking about the ultimatum. A speaker took the stage. Recognizing one of their own, the anarchists clapped wildly. The ovation stole through the entire audience, as if it were an entity looking for comfort, for reassurance of the desire for life welling up in all the hearts chanting in unison. We feared provocations from the extreme right. The police were rumored to have orders to stop the meeting. I too applauded. The speaker spoke of our brothers—French, Russian, German—who like us at that very moment, with the same words, were refusing a holy war, a capitalistic war. The Americans were with us too: On the other side of the Atlantic, in the land of liberty, Red Emma, the courageous Emma Goldman, stood up to the police wanting to lock her up for calling for desertion. "Workers of the world, don't turn your bayonets on yourselves. Don't let them drive you to fratricidal suicide and . . ." He didn't have time to finish his sentence. From the back of the hall came a loud cry. "Police!" And it seemed as though the rats were crawling out of the ground from all sides. Infiltrators appeared in the four corners of the amphitheater, wielding truncheons, while uniformed men smashed those in the back rows with their rifle butts. In accordance with their beliefs, the organizers had made no arrangements for crowd control. Havoc and mayhem. People escaped as best they could. The ship was leaking at every seam. The crowd jumped out windows, spraining ankles, breaking legs, and were picked up by police, who had circled the university buildings as if it were a genuine siege. Blows and insults rained down. The offended Fatherland cried out for revenge.

After the initial shock had worn off, a few anarchists and revolutionary socialists banded together to face the truncheon-bearers. Some were armed with chair rungs, but most were empty-handed; nonetheless they closed ranks, ready for a confrontation, allowing the crowd to escape through a side entrance. Rendered briefly powerless by their courage, I let the tide carry me to the edge of the scuffle. I could hear my father screaming, "Get your guard up, left, left!" But the roaring crowd soon covered the voice that urged me there. I was overcome by my paralyzing fear of crowds. And I'm not ashamed to admit that I had only one thought at that moment—to join the people rushing down the corridors of the university. I threw all my strength into the battle to escape the human lava blocking the side door. I managed to get through, and as I started running down the dark tunnel before me, I crashed into a woman and knocked her down. I almost stepped over her—then I recognized the grimacing face. "Cosette!" I knelt, took her in my arms. "Cosette!" She looked at me, stupefied. Blood was trickling through her blond hair. Without thinking, I got her to her feet, put her arm around my shoulder, and dragged her along as best I could. She quickly regained consciousness, her pace speeded up, and soon I no longer had to support her. She had recognized me. "Anton!" And then nothing mattered but our bodies joined by a shared desire to live, launched toward a shared hunger for light.

I knew the labyrinth well and had no trouble escaping the police net. We took refuge in a café near the Rathaus, where a few months earlier I had tried to forget Cosette, and we waited for calm to return to the neighborhood so we could leave. I told her everything. Everything that had happened since the Judenplatz, and why I had deliberately avoided her. She took my hands in hers and with tears in her eyes said simply, "Come."

We crossed the Lueger Ring in front of Beethoven's house. We walked side by side, without a word. As we passed the Scottish church, Cosette took my arm. My mind was blank. I didn't realize what was happening, but let myself be led like a blind man toward a horizon darkened by banks of clouds about to burst in floods of iron, fire, thunder. As we came to the Judenplatz, the storm opened like a river lock. Heavy drops lashed our faces. Cosette looked at me and began to laugh. Pulling my arm, she drew me along as she ran. The square is small, and we were only about one hundred and fifty feet from her pension. Still, we got soaked. When we got to her room, breathless from our flight and from scaling the stairs, we looked at each other again, hair dripping wet, faces cool and pink. Cosette stroked my cheek. I came closer, to touch her. I took her in my arms. Our lips joined, an endless swirl of pleasure to which I yielded with a shudder of my entire being. We swayed in a single movement toward the bed. . . .

How can I find the words, so distant now, to describe the crumpled cloth, her shirt plastered to the skin by rain, the delicate gestures, the hand that stroked, caressed, lacerated? How dare I, a dying man, be party to a description of an ageless ritual: two stripped bodies?

How long it was, how delicious (how trivial!), the moment when we clung together, clutching the edge of the parapet over the void. . . . And when we were dragged down, when we gave in to our vertigo, when I had to respond to death as it clasped me in its tantalizing arms, I discovered I was impotent.

I crumpled into the void. My body was nothing. Scalding tears scored my face. Forever. Nothing would ever be the same. Desire, youth, life—all lost. Even years later with Milena, when passion would take me to heights I had only guessed at with Cosette, that break, that fault, the leap into the unknown, would return to haunt and torment me when I least expected it. It was all the more uncontrollable because, under different circumstances, full, complete virility could make me temporarily believe that I'd conquered my demon.

Cosette demonstrated a tenderness that crowned my feeling of helplessness. Wanting to reassure me, she acted like the adult, emancipated woman she was, who for that very reason had attracted the inexperienced young man that I was. Smiling, she kissed me, ruffled my mop of hair, lavished encouragement and advice. To no avail.

She stroked my cheek one last time, then got up and put on

her clothes. "It doesn't matter," she said with a smile. But I knew it wasn't true. Deep in her eyes I could see dark glimmers of bitterness. With feigned indifference she added:

"Anyway, I'm leaving for France tomorrow."

I lacked the strength to tell her that I too was leaving Vienna, to seek refuge on the heights of Semmering.

9.
Bestiary of the Yellow Notebook (III)

🪶🪶🪶 He started and stepped aside. Among the eyes that had flocked together to witness the trial were some, rimmed in black, that blinked intermittently, and the flash of brewing storms streaked their fleeting gazes. Downcast at being heard, he yielded to the muffled rumbling of distant drums. The horde was approaching. In the lead, a big male who directed the frenzied procession led the way in triumph. As he passed, heads bowed and shouts of approval greeted them.

He had stepped aside. As if that slight movement could make him invisible, as if his incongruous presence in this remote place weren't enough to draw all eyes to him.

The circle closed. The cacophony ended. A silent menace swelled the tree branches and all of space strained to uproot the sleeplessness that had endured too long.

The horde dragged behind it the remains of a fantastical bird. He had been sacrificed by the community, for an irreparable crime. He had been discovered caressing a woman's neck with his feathers. Then his spur had suddenly penetrated her tender flesh. The embrace was so brutal, the tail had shed some feathers. And the beak had bitten hungrily into the breast swollen with desire and blood, that wept tears as round and strong as the criminal's cries of love.

The male in charge of the animals in the clearing pointed to the corpse. It must be gutted, cut to pieces, and consumed. That was the price of purification. The hateful murderer was condemned to consume the remains of the Other.

The flesh opened to reveal chasms of blood. He thought he would faint. His nose was thrust into an intricate network of

47

blood vessels and muscles. The air was so thick inside the carcass that he could hardly open his mouth. His feet clutched at the grass on the sinking ground. He wished for strong vines under him to launch him on the flight toward death. But jungle, savannah, forest had been destroyed as the charnel house spread across the land, and though his wings beat in a vain search for longer, bolder adventures, the desolate spectacle never changed. Every time he touched down, the feeling of still-warm bodies under his claws forced him to take flight again. Without respite. The eddying glances around him didn't let go, didn't give him a moment's peace. He consumed unhappiness at its source.

Deep down he sensed stupor gaining ground. The vital organs embedded in a solid vein of terror no longer responded to him. As his beating grew weaker, he felt his heart on the edge of his lips and a volley of insults rose from the crowd. Thief, sham, swindler, murderer! Then the big male's bodyguards came forward to roll him in the dead beast's belly and sprinkle him with its blood. They pulled on his wings until his beak could no longer refuse the sacred food. He wept and swallowed the bitterness of his tears, as if that might get rid of the foul taste, reawaken his appetite, wash his entrails, allay his fears.

As he ate, the din grew more infernal. Outside a profusion of cries rose, a torrent of bizarre screams, as if the dead bird's skin had been stretched and turned into an echo chamber. And the circle vibrated to the tom-tom, bodies shifting slowly from foot to foot, faster and faster, in place.

Suddenly, the big male approached the one under sentence of death, pressed with all his weight on his chest, and expertly gripped the crown of feathers that adorned his lower belly. He tugged at it, then stood, brandishing the trophy above his head. The cries of rage grew louder then, until inside the victim's head there was only emptiness. Yellowish snot filled his nostrils and ears. He was choking. Life was beyond his reach.

And then, as he was about to breathe his last, his belly jerking spasmodically, the young queen broke away from the purifying group. She quieted the crowd with a gesture. Her eyes like glowing embers begged her father to grant life to the sentenced one.

. . . I saw her approach. Her hair covered her face and fell in splendid sheaves on either side of her body, hiding all but her bosom, which pulsed like the perfectly drawn lobes of a heart in the open air, exposed to all eyes. She leaned over me, knelt, and touched my shoulder. I heard the rustle of her wings as her heart beat faster. Her blood was bright red, clean, full of light. She was beautiful. She offered me her throbbing breast, and my swollen lips closed gently around it. I stayed there for a long time, until my body filled with warmth. Then I rediscovered the use of my feathers and, bracing myself against a multicolored wheel, I slid into her. Her long hair mingled with mine and my serpent's head easily found the passage that led to her heart, to the place where my bite would be fatal.

10.

Clockwork's Notes (III)

❧❧❧ Our relationship was difficult to establish. At the first interview, Blackbird didn't want to say anything. He wouldn't answer my probing questions, and would respond to banalities with a mere yes or no. I quickly realized my efforts were useless. I'd have to start all over again, begin by observing him, let him have his way, give him time to adapt to his new environment, his new companions, and the new personality he'd discovered he possessed. Perhaps, too, I'd have to wait for an auspicious time, even provoke him to a point where he'd shed his carapace, abandon himself—and if I was lucky perhaps that moment would come soon.

But then he just stared into space, behind my head, as if I weren't there.

Some weeks later, the first rift appeared. I'd noticed that Blackie refused to participate in recommended activities. He always stayed apart from the others, avoided their quarrels, their cries of distress or rebellion, as if he were deep in meditation. Until the day one of my assistants asked me to follow him to the drawing workshop and showed me the works Blackie had carefully stored in a large portfolio. I say "works" deliberately, for I was struck at once by the power and originality of his vision. The drawings were savage, indicating a liberating inspiration, but at the same time the line was confident. Their overall mastery of expression was rare inside our walls. Many patients created remarkable pieces that would have been at home in an exhibition, and I know some that have found their way into the collections of connoisseurs of naive art. One of our inmates is an old Viennese painter who had his moment of glory in the period between the wars but, after escaping the Holocaust, sank into the infernal cycle of manic-depression. He's the one Blackbird calls Garry in his notebooks. He died in 1973. Most of his drawings were portraits of women with aggressive features, protruding breasts, and bellies open above a dense mass of pubic hair. And usually these women were armless. The overall impression was one of violent, dominating sensuality. But they were nothing compared with Blackie's sumptuous, gaudy frescoes. Orgies of color, riotous forms, a blend of harmony and disorder produced an absolutely unique effect. It took me some time to get used to his bestiary, to make a stab at interpreting it; even then I was never sure if it came from my own imagination or his. That day I was convinced that, in the past which he'd consigned to oblivion, Antoine Choucas had been an artist, a great artist. At the time, though, I had only my conviction, since nothing in my files or my investigation provided any evidence. Although several months, perhaps even a year, went by before a decisive clue appeared, a chink slowly opened in Blackie's wall of silence. I was determined not to make him talk about his pictures (which I find traces of today in his yellow notebook), but to lead him, with questions and answers, into revealing something that would help me figure him out. One day, he replied scathingly to one of my questions. It filled me with such hope that I had to clamp down on my enthusiasm—and my perplexity.

"Do you know," he lashed at me in a cutting tone I hadn't heard before, "do you know that Freud has just died in London, that Werfel drowned in a swimming pool, that Toller, whom I met in Spain in 1937, has just committed suicide in his hotel room here in New York?"

All these events were at least ten years old, so I tried to understand why Blackbird should be talking about them now, as he stood before one of his drawings. Taken aback, I waited for his next pronouncement, telling myself that here was indeed a highly cultivated individual and that I had been given an important clue. I didn't know then just how important.

"Freud is dead," he added. "I was there when it happened. So stop bothering me with your stupid questions."

I caught the ball on the rebound.

"You couldn't have known Freud—you know very well you weren't in London in 1939." (In fact it was I who knew nothing, practically nothing.)

"How do you know that?"

"From the police report."

"What's a police report but a superficial assembly of truths we can't grasp?"

There we were. The threshold had been crossed, the dam had crumbled. I pressed my luck.

"At the time, weren't you trying to escape from a concentration camp?"

I'd gone too far, too fast. Blackie snapped shut, like a fan. His gaze dulled, his eyes closed, the muscles in his face contracted violently, then he sank into utter apathy. I made one last attempt. Useless. It was over for today. And for weeks and weeks Blackie remained lost in thought, refusing even to go to the art room. We had to start all over again.

I addressed the case anew, mentally reexamining all the elements I'd gathered so far. Something important escaped me. I sensed it vaguely but couldn't tell what it was. I was going around in circles. Rereading the file for the hundredth time, I painstakingly organized the links in the Blackbird case. Until, finally, one point stood out so clearly I couldn't see how it had slipped by me until now. The piano! Why hadn't I thought of it earlier?

I decided the patients would give a concert. The sooner the better, I explained to the director. I insisted that we have talented musicians, and was given the necessary funds. Thanks to Blackbird, I was particularly convincing!

I myself oversaw all the preparations, and on the appointed day I arranged for Blackie to be there when the grand piano was brought in. He was part of the team responsible for arranging the chairs. When four beefy men from the moving company came into the room with their precious cargo, I kept my eye on Blackie. No reaction. Not a muscle moved on his face; he didn't turn his head or even glance at the splendid instrument we'd rented for the occasion. Slowly, with no haste whatsoever, and with his usual precision, he arranged the chairs in neat rows. I had failed. Perhaps I'd been fooling myself. But it was too late to retrack, to postpone the project which my colleagues considered off-the-wall. I still had one hope: the music itself.

The program included Mozart, Beethoven, and Bartók. I'd given the musicians free rein, insisting only that the concert include works from the past as well as more contemporary pieces.

The first part of the program was uneventful. I mean as far as Blackbird was concerned, of course, for the sonatas and quartets provoked hilarity to stupor in the other patients. It was hard to know what was most unbearable to the musicians and to us. Blackie simply sat motionless on his chair. Impenetrable.

But the unpredictable impulse I had so desired occurred during the third movement of Bartók's Fourth Quartet. Suddenly, as the patients' cacophony reached fever pitch, Blackie sprang to his feet and started to scream above the din, "*Non troppo lento!*" And jostling his seatmates, surprised, into silence, he made his way to the string section. I had given orders that he be allowed to have his way, even warned the musicians, who now went on playing as if nothing had happened. When he reached the platform Blackie called out, "Not like that, not like that." And in his powerful voice he began to sing the melody. This time the musicians, not believing their ears, stopped as if petrified, casting questioning glances my way. I nodded to indicate that they should follow him. Blackie ordered, "Repeat the last bar." Which the musicians did, this time under a maestro's direction.

At the end of the *allegro molto*, on the final note, Blackbird stood motionless, facing the musicians. From the corner where I was standing I could see the smile that lit up his sweat-soaked face. In the hall, a weighty silence seemed to have obliterated the other patients. And a few seconds later Blackbird emerged from his trance to shake the violinist's hand. Then he leaned over and whispered something I didn't hear. He headed for the piano, seated himself on the stool, and admired the keyboard, stroking it with infinite tenderness, then played a piece I didn't know, with a virtuosity and sensitivity on a par with the greatest performers'.

And there, at last, was the truth I had been seeking. Anton Blackbird, whoever he was, had once been a great pianist, probably one of the greatest of his day. A path had appeared, and now I must follow it. When the piece was over, I approached the platform, and as he played the final chord, I saw that he was gazing fixedly at the inscription on the piano: "Pleyel, Paris." And his lips stirred gently, several times, mouthing the word: "Paris, Paris, Paris." He rose. I took him in my arms.

(One month later.)

Since the concert, Blackie has not emerged from the silence into which he has settled once again, but he is drawing feverishly. He still refuses to talk to me. As soon as he sees me, he turns his head and moves away. He suspects I've uncovered part of his secret. That part is in the word "Paris." I've made scant progress, though. Of course I questioned Blackbird's former neighbors. The Roths claim that Anton is from Central Europe, the Friedmans that he's from Russia, while others say he arrived with a contingent of Spanish Republican refugees. With all this there's no trace of Paris. During our brief conversations I've noticed that Anton has a slight accent, though his English is good enough to conceal his origins. If the concert hadn't provided evidence that, before the war, the man had been a virtuoso, I would still be completely in the dark. But what I still don't understand is how he could have disappeared from circulation without creating a stir that would have spread even to America. Surely his reputation had crossed the Atlantic. Then what happened? I still haven't the faintest idea, nor can I tell where the revelation might come from. I've arranged to keep the rented piano at the hospital. And I have Blackie taken to it every day. But he remains indifferent. He walks around it, then leaves the room without a word, without a trace of emotion.

I'm going to Paris in a few days, to attend an international psychiatric conference. Deep down, what's important about this trip is the task I've set myself, which I intend to carry out. I'm convinced that the key to this puzzle will be found over there.

II.
Blackie's Notebooks (V)

🐦🐦🐦 I have given in to my recollections. Locked myself inside my memories. And what law, what ban, what authority could force me from it? What have I left to live for, but death by the word?

The process of writing is a superb trick, especially while the body keeps letting you down and your very existence is heading for the dead end of the unspoken. I like that lie. I can hurt myself, tear myself apart, claw at the scrap of perception that remains. I only regret that I can't finish myself off this way. The final illusion (which perhaps spurs me on in this venture) is to believe that my blood is evaporating at the same rate as the ink in the inkwell. Terrifying and blessed blankness . . . words inverted, existence turned upside down, overthrown, knocked awry, to support life's breath for one final moment before it slipped, nails torn out, down a damp chute toward the poisoned fumes that would choke it. Gurgling, bubbling, and opaque. . . . Luckily the night is still clear, transparent. And the signs I trace on paper dance like dim starlight. The night belongs to me. Even though Garry, hallucinating, comes to tug at my feet, he is powerless against my insomnia. Across the hall, Snuffie howls in his sleep, calling Jack, Andy, and Pat to come and help him. Their shadows creep into darkened rooms and stretch over me, lie down on me, beleaguering my body, seeping into the smallest crack, taking advantage of the briefest and slightest weakness that I surrender to their brutal gestures. It is insufferable, unbearable. And I feel pain in my clenched fist, in my wrist. Jerry the apeman howls in his cage. A desire to murder grips my throat. I am suffocating. Another few syllables escape from the pen my trembling fingers grasp in vain. The bastards won't get me. I'll give them the day. In fact, during the day I quite like them, I give in to their charms. Whenever our guards turn their attention elsewhere, Linda doesn't miss a chance to try to arouse me. She tears off her shirt and pushes her heavy red breasts under my nose, rolling and kneading them in her hands, as if to gauge their weight and value. I clutch my pencils. I create, I anticipate the next night's dreams. But none of them touch me, for daytime madness could never mark an old man like me. . . .

In a corner Lola, Linda's daughter, is masturbating. Her right hand under the white smock. Long brown hair masking her face. Her head and shoulders shake convulsively. She has always been able to excite me. The girl gives me strength. She knows instinctively how to reach my impotence. At the sight of her, words start to stir me like blows pounding hard on the barrier of my fears. The world of the hospital does not sadden me; it lets me escape the perils of life. Pat, Garry, Snuffie, and the others are only images from the outside, trying to drag me down into the cave. I've unmasked them. Their games don't bother me, they show me that Clockwork has been forced to the limit to convince himself that I'm mad. But Lola is an oasis for me. She is Cosette, Milena, all women, all my youth: She confirms that slender portion of truth that still pulses inside me.

They would all like to keep me from writing. I know them so well. . . . But their traps amuse me. Clockwork thinks he possesses me with his drawings, his piano, and his speeches, so much so that my time will be counted—to the second— before I return to the notebooks, from which the menagerie, in turn, would like to unearth me. But I am excited by their games and nasty tricks. Even at night my nightmares can't make me forget my essential task. I admit that my power of speech flees during their constant interruptions, their petti- ness, their attempts at seduction or repression. But I've al- ways been able to adjust to such situations. First with Father, later at Semmering, then through the vicissitudes of exile, always living with death. Barriers and restraints have always made me react against what was expected. All I needed to bring me back to this present, to the urgency and necessity of my task, was crazy Lola.

The hardest thing, of course, is to start up when the flow has been interrupted. Words quickly escape desire. But you're always swimming in the same river, although it seems, at times, during these moments of hesitation, of vacillation, that the body is a hollow shell, filmed over and impervious to water. The feeling is all the more unpleasant and destructive, because you still know that nothing is impermeable, neither clothing nor flesh. Soaked, swollen, streaming wet . . .

I am flooded by night. Clockwork can do nothing to me now.

On July 27, 1914 (my birthday), Austria declared war on Serbia. The wick was lit, the European powder barrel was about to explode. I was in the sanatorium.

During the first year of conflict I wrote my first real novel. No need to recall the title; it was, of course, among those destroyed. I had read *Death in Venice*, and Mann's masterpiece left me in such a state of exaltation and vicarious suffering that my own book was bogged down in metaphors created by disease. It had no other reason for being. Then, during the years of carnage, I worked on a second novel, doomed to disappear as well. It was certainly more fully blown than the first; even now I remember it as a singular work; but it was condemned from the start. How could it live when my peers were tearing each other's guts out, while Mama, in despair at my condition and my absence, tormented by the outrageous behavior of Father, whose financial reverses had made him even more bitter and threatening, was gradually being engulfed by a mental cloud that made us fear the worst? And I was there, walled inside whiteness, exulting in my purity, intoxicated by the surrounding heights, but still daring to believe that jousting with absolutes was an act of innocence! How could I be mad enough to believe that writing was hermetic, ascetic? Writing is always a matter of excess. The privilege of the overfed. In a way, the drama of my life springs from a lack of basic nourishment. Perhaps I should have been greedy, so greedy it took my breath away, so greedy I would cough up words, vomit living matter.

At the same time I started keeping a diary. With unpardonable gravity. As if it would allow me, clear-headedly, to put down lies instead of and in place of truth. The torrid summer had given way to an icy winter. Shut in my room, smothered in a heavy dressing gown that Mother had slipped into my suitcase before I left, I let shadows and make-believe overcome me. Now and then the photograph of Cosette (which she'd given me before showing me to her door for the last time) drew me from my phantasmagoria and led me back to the reality scrawled on the wall across from my desk. Her hair, her skin, her eyes, her breasts. The flash of inspiration no longer came from within, it was there, quite visible, stretched over the flowered wallpaper. The consumption that hugged my chest gave way to another pain, far sharper and more precise, with no doubt of its origin. Exasperated by sexual desire, I covered blank sheets of paper with writing until I was exhausted, to erase the image imprinted on my eye, to cover the portrait with a thick layer of scribbling, to dilute forms, odors, and warmth with an unbroken line of anonymous letters to myself.

I judged and condemned myself, once again. What I could not bring myself to do, however, was carry out the sentence. Some pages of the diary escaped the *auto-da-fé*, and they have left their marks on me like stigmata.

Ancient Jewish mysticism contains ecstasies and speculations that disturb me even here in the deep silence of the mountains. But I cannot accept the Law. Not only am I a heretic, but utterly unclean (and I use the word in its strictest sense), despite appearances of ascetic constraint which alone, according to tradition, can open the way to supreme knowledge. The world is evil, certainly, but not doomed. Surely we can attempt to capture the beam of light that persists, beyond shadows and malediction, without becoming mired in a sense of sin. I must admit how fascinated I still am—even as I reject the religion that gnawed at my childhood—by the sumptuous powers, the terrible fits and starts of absolute messianism. To descend to the depths of evil and destroy sin while practicing it—that is what's required now more than ever, during these times of upheaval and butchery. That gives me my most secret hope, the leading line of my life, pulled taut now as a razor's edge, and I am prepared to slit my throat at the slightest urging, at the slightest hint of resistance or retreat.

These were also the terms (or very nearly) of a letter I sent to my father soon after. I waited several months for his answer. It was unyielding, impenetrable, cruel. He called the situation in Vienna "dramatic," he detailed every "privation" he was forced to exact "for my own good," underlined more than once the "special privilege" he claimed I enjoyed, regretted my absence and the help I could have given him if I'd been at his side during this trying time for his own business, the national economy, and the Jewish people. (I'm quite certain that was the order.) In conclusion, he announced brutally and without comment that he'd been forced to "have Mama put away."

Spending time with sick people, being made to face a world where death defines the smallest detail of everyday life, confers a special status on you, and that status is offensive because of its deep but obvious inhumanity. You forget (or think you do) that beyond, in the valleys and plains, in the towns and cities, there is a world buzzing with savage rumors. You act as if death belongs to you, has become familiar, a neighbor. But it is really only a backdrop. Others have depicted it before you; you should recognize its nostalgic charms and its trompe l'oeil.

During those years when my body was the site of a raging battle that nature alone could appease, the outside world was barely recognizable. Perspective was distorted, time disrupted by an arbitrary gear. This "first" illness taught me very little. I was too busy with my private fantasies, too prone to invent stories that resembled reality but were only a pale imitation of it, as though a little substance might make people pay attention to them. I was nothing but "book." When I approached the seemingly tranquil shores of recovery, I was finally able to draw a full breath without panting, and examine the truths I had buried under an avalanche of weak opinions. Mama was crazy; Vienna was crying famine; the war had obliterated my generation. That's what I should have seen.

When I learned my diagnosis, I condemned myself with no appeal. I knew my literature too well not to indulge in the hectic enthusiasm that spurred my precious romantics to excess. Besides, I wasn't afraid of death. I wonder if anyone in the sanatorium was, or if we all imagined it white, immaculate—a precious stone. Because what horrified and fascinated me—I admit it!—was suffering. Suffering to death has ample room for all of human misery. The Calvary that must be climbed to reach the sanctuary. Blows, privations, obstacles. Laceration, bitterness. I knew then (and now more than ever) that there's no coming to terms with death, but that the various stages, the physical pain, are reversible; they can be dealt with more or less successfully, their course, duration, even their nature can be treated. My entire being was nothing but rivers of blood, my thoughts were congestions, tumors. I was invaded not by the disease, but by my obsession with it. I didn't cough much, I spat blood only once or twice over the course of four years, but I knew the indelible mark was there, behind my ribs. As soon as I came to the sanatorium an astonishing languor gripped me and threw me into a panic all the more uncontrollable because it was so unlike my normal disposition. I no longer recognized myself and I spent months in an aura of fever that both exacerbated and interfered with the progress of my writing. My day was filled with events and activities whose ups and downs resembled a temperature chart. It took all the doctors' authority (or rather their honesty and friendship) to make me abandon what I was beginning to take for a predisposition. As soon as I let myself be convinced that a walk would do me good, the fire that was raging in me seemed to die down.

All I really brought back from the sanatorium was landscapes . . . and today they are all I have left.

My outings restored my taste for reading and for letterwriting. I always looked forward to the mail (especially when Mama sent me the latest books from Vienna or Berlin—at least whenever the state of her mind made it possible) and hastened to answer letters from those friends who hadn't disappeared into the war.

I also had the good fortune to make friends with a young English doctor who arrived in 1916. He was well educated and very interested in my work, and we had long conversations about our favorite authors. Thanks to him I rediscovered something of the atmosphere of prewar Vienna which had captivated me and made such an impact on me. His personal library opened new horizons: Katherine Mansfield (she died in 1923 of the tuberculosis she'd contracted six years earlier) and above all James Joyce, who he told me had just left Trieste for Zurich (his *Dubliners* and, even more, the *Portrait of the Artist as a Young Man*, which I'd read in serial form in an English little magazine, were not unlike what I was embarking upon myself at the time). Through him, too, I discovered the American writer Thoreau. I liked Thoreau immediately. He gave me a glimpse of this continent where I had no way of knowing that one day . . . Thoreau, with his sense of freedom, his defense of the natural life, Thoreau who had written that death and disease are often beautiful. Oh, how that remark tormented me, stayed with me. I annexed it, made it the chant of my daily meditations, the emblem of my dream army, and the shield for my nights. Despite everything . . .

. . . after the initial feelings of opacity and laziness came a period of transparency and fury! I changed again. I was far more nervous than usual, so I'd resumed my old athletic activities. I would take long (much too long) walks on the wooded hills until I was out of breath, until I'd reached the greatest heights, and my hand could caress the warm, soft snow with extreme, almost perverse pleasure.

Gradually I rediscovered my appetite for life, just when my exile began to seem more and more like a scandalous and hateful crime. How could I be happy while all around me the death knell of human butchery was sounding? And yet I succumbed to irresponsibility, to the warm, comforting atmosphere isolation offers. I was not forgetting the war, I denied it with all my strength, with all the foreign bodies that had entered me and were undermining me and that, under the circumstances, had become my allies in transparency. But my comfort was fragile, sensitive to the slightest gasp of emotion, to the least memory. . . .

And then machines and manipulations and doctors' tests took over, showing me how inconsequential I was. After tasting the tart pleasure of solitude, I was engulfed by a rage for contact with the patients I had previously avoided. I systematically took every chance to develop this sociability. But games and meetings were abortive acts, superficial contacts that barely cut into the dense layer of solitude that covered my entire being. There were men who sometimes gave me the illusion they might replace Franz, Stefan, Maximilien, and Hugo. There were women—two or three—whom I conversed with, who excited me and led me to believe that I might discover another Julia, another Cosette. In vain. What was real was the inevitable return to myself—to writing and masturbation. I engaged in both with a fury that would never be matched in my later life. I was smothered by them, possessed, and they wouldn't let go: I had gone *inside* and could only disappear. Steadfastly, selflessly, I developed my own destruction, while my physical energy increased daily. I could sense the paradox, I could even see it, but I couldn't shake it off. The closer I was to being cured, the more I told myself that it would be ephemeral, that I must prepare for the disease's return. And the best way to do that was to hurl myself at the *external* aspects of the disease.

I even thought of organizing my fellow patients. At some foolish meetings, I made remarks that aroused a flattering echo. What if this temporary haven were to become a privileged place where totally new human relations could be established, what if we were to announce from our mountaintop the birth of a new society with no war, no army, no hierarchy? An ideal place, the sanatorium. An asylum of beauty and love. From it we would build Utopia. And now the hour of revolt had come!

I dreamed of speeded-up time, of free sexual relations that would pull down the walls of the prison in which we were all confined. Consumptives, TB victims, syphilitics, to your stations! Attack order, attack death! The Liberation Army of the Sick would invade parks and highways, roads and villages, climb to the summit of the highest mountain. From there, as space expanded beyond the frontiers, a wave of pleasure would bring down the last hurdle between them and the horizon. And I, the Hero, would fling open the gates of dream: Eurydice would nestle in my arms and slowly we would glide toward the dawn, with love to guide us toward the corrupted tabernacle which in turn would open on the flanks of the sanctuary beyond which glowed the resplendent vision. . . .

My deep urge to die from forcing desire to its limit was what gave me the strength to bear the emerging destruction, the rising apocalypse.

Such was my state when Father's letter about Mama arrived. The news greatly increased the chaos, the fever pitch, in which I lived. And I was completely unable to distinguish between a return to health and the pangs of self-destruction.

Signs of both states mingled in a jumble of confused thoughts and contradictory emotions. I was at once drunk and sober, freezing and burning, virile and impotent, feverish and lucid, lunatic and sane, lover and monk, writer and mute. . . .

I knew I was cured. Refueled with vital force. And this time my mother, from high in her shameful tower, from the depths of her prison, sent me some nonsensical signs to indicate that I had played the illness game long enough. She invited me to contact reality. And reality meant my father.

I wrote to tell him I was coming home. My English doctor had confirmed that, at least for the time being, I was free of the disease. He signed my release slip. Everything was back to normal, nothing would ever be normal again! I also told Father everything I hadn't said during my three and a half years at Semmering. I told him of the books I'd written, and that nothing would make me change my intention to be a writer. I wrote that I hated him. Because of Mama, of course, but also because I held him responsible for the unbearable times we lived in. I didn't realize then that blaming him was too easy a way to excuse my own behavior, to wash my hands though they were stained with blood, lymph, and bile, though they were soaked in sperm and excrement, steeped in desire and evil acts, bathed in cowardice and radical theories.

It took pages and pages to cover all that, along with everything I'd never dared to say about Judaism. Did the Torah not condemn the consumption of meat? Thou shalt not kill. "*And God said, Behold I have given you every herb bearing seed, which is upon the face of the earth, and every tree, which is the fruit of a tree yielding seed; to you it shall be for meat.*" And it took a cataclysm for man to be authorized to kill and eat animals. We, too, have our cataclysm. Today, we are all Noahs drifting by the continents in an ark of misfortune, never to find welcoming shores or a world to rebuild. "*And the fear of you and the dread of you shall be upon every beast of the earth, and upon every fowl of the air, upon all that moveth upon the earth, and upon all the fishes of the sea; into your hand are they delivered. Every moving thing that liveth shall*" *be meat for you; even as the green herb have I given you all things. But flesh with the life thereof, which is the blood thereof, shall ye not eat. And surely your blood of your lives will I require; at the hand of every beast will I require it, and at the hand of man; at the hand of every man's brother will I require the life of man.*" And from you, Father, I require an accounting for the blood that has been shed, for all the blood you have drunk, for the soul of Mama (and my own) that you have devoured. You see, I believe after all that I am the real Jew.

12.
Bestiary of the Yellow Notebook (IV)

❧❧❧ As the crow flies, the earth is not round but a scant ellipse, pressing on infinity.

The cage is circular, a grille closed safe and sound upon itself.

He has allowed them to lock him up. To put him in irons. And his head struck the bars before he fell, stunned, onto the smooth ground. A giant hand approached and scattered a few seeds. Its forefinger pushed the inert body, and flicked the creature over and ordered him to eat. But the beak does not open fast enough for him, so, thumb pressed against the heart, forbidding it to beat, he forced the beak open with his middle finger and inserted a seed.

The bird struggled. Dusty wings. Powerless. And when the fingers loosened their grip he hastened to a corner of the cage, the one he thought was farthest, safest from prying eyes, although in fact the flat surface is exposed on all sides. Then he vomited.

Once his stomach was empty and the shadow was no longer there watching him, he resumed his flight and constant collision with all the bars of the cage, one after another, until exhaustion makes him founder in the night of a world that turns and turns and never stops.

13.
Blackie's Notebooks (VI)

❧❧❧ Once I was back in Vienna my first move was to go see Mama. Vienna had changed; the frantic life had given way to the calm and silence that stamp times of upheaval. There were no cars on the streets; carriages were more common again, more numerous now, as at the turn of the century, but the horses seemed tired and half-starved, and the few travellers preferred to use their own legs. Everywhere, at every street corner, there were long lines outside shops where merchandise was scarce. Milk, butter, sugar, and other essentials were rationed. It was whispered that defeat was near. Emperor Franz Joseph was dead and Emperor Charles had only to wait for events to settle things for him.

I walked to the asylum. When I got off the train at the Western Station I checked my trunks and arranged to have them brought to me the next day. Without stopping at "home"—a word I could no longer say, it felt so hollow and meaningless now—I began to walk along the Mariahilfer-strasse toward that other "home," prudishly described as a place for "health" and "rest." I myself had just left a similar place and expected to find my mother in an environment as pleasant as mine had been. Violent and conflicting thoughts slowed my step, as I vacillated between the desire to run away and the desire to rush into the arms of madness.

The world in which Mama lived was impossible to describe, if indeed living was the proper word for her state. I tried to do it several times, in my books and in the diary I was keeping at the time, but I failed. It went far beyond the bounds of my imagination, and by its existence gave me the strongest sense of my inability to write. What is the use of stringing words together if the most mysterious, most powerful forces that control us remain elusive? It's not like that here, with Clockwork, where everything is illuminated by a bright light that cuts you up, that enters you and tears you into as many fragments as the passing days, but is still perceivable and describable. Clockwork cannot take that ability away from any of us, from Pattie, Snuffie, Garry, Linda, Lola, or me . . . does he know it? I don't think so. For him, as for us, the questions and answers are elsewhere.

Mama was in the middle of an attack. She was brought to me on a wooden stretcher, bound into a straitjacket, foaming at the mouth, her face ravaged by hatred and pain. She didn't recognize me. They had to hold me back from throwing myself on her. The guards' suspicion was understandable; the emotion that had overcome me could have resulted in my embracing her, in weeping over her poor torn body—or in strangling her to put an end to her suffering. I sobbed hysterically, like a child, until I was exhausted and they showed me to the iron gate of the asylum. I was told to come back the next day, because Mama was usually unconscious for no more than twenty-four hours, and once she'd come back to herself she was perfectly normal—depressed, of course, but able to express herself and behave rationally. I didn't have the strength then to respond to these observations, which seemed to me totally irrational. Nor did I have the strength to talk to Father when I got to Bäckerstrasse. He just told me, "Tomorrow is the party for cousin Brod's circumcision." And without a word I shut myself in my room.

Mama hadn't changed much. Her features were as gentle as before, despite a few faint lines and a pallor increased by confinement. She was lying exhausted in her chair, with a characteristic air of exaggerated humility. "Mama." She looked up, startled, unclenched her hands, and opened her arms as if she were about to expose herself once more to cruel blows. "Anton." But she kissed my brow, my eyes, my cheeks, and my lips, with an appetite I'd never felt before. She was dreaming that I'd come back. I held her tightly in my arms and felt that the pain had ebbed from her for the moment, though I suspected it was lurking nearby, ready to pounce on her and overtake her again. . . .

We talked and talked, of everything and nothing. We had so much to say to one another, to try to erase the months, the years that had separated us. With a flood of words, with hugs and kisses, we tried to wash away the specters that haunted us both, ghosts we suspected we shared. The only difference is that I made my madness the motive, the excuse to withdraw from life. It gave me the strength (or the weakness!) to invent worlds even madder than this one where the apocalypse was being played out. Mama, on the other hand, had let herself be overcome by the excesses of a life she had previously repressed.

I wanted to talk about Father, but she laid her finger across my lips, begging me to be still.

"Shh! Tell me, tell me instead about the mountains. . . . What matters, Anton, is your health. The books, did you receive them? And see, I've kept all your letters." (She took from her smock a bundle of envelopes clumsily tied with butcher's cord.) "So I have some idea of what you've written. I'd love to read your novels, Anton, you must publish them. . . ."

"I intend to, and there's nothing Father can . . ."

"I also know," she interrupted, "who you were living with there, who your friends were."

She sighed, and then with an offhand smile that contrasted with the gravity of her remarks, she said teasingly:

"And what about women? You must have met some! They say there are beautiful women in those mountain lodges. And you've always liked them pale and skinny, haven't you?"

"Mama . . ."

"Come, come, don't pretend. Do you think I've forgotten that French girl, what was her name? Catherine? No, Cosima, wasn't it? Cosima, that's it."

"Cosette, Mama. Please, don't talk about her."

"Why not? Why must you always avoid reality? Why should I be the only one to suffer, to shoulder your anxieties, and your father's? I always had to sacrifice myself. For you two. Both. That's why it's so much better for me to be here. I don't have to watch him selling himself to the highest bidder, and I escape you and all your nonsense, as if you'd forgotten how to live. . . . You shouldn't have let Cosette get away, you should have followed her to the ends of the earth. Because you did love her, didn't you? You loved her."

What could I reply? I was shocked. Mama had never discussed such things with me. She had been discreet, of course, but also concerned not to encroach upon the scrap of freedom Father left me. So now she regretted having protected me. She would rather have seen me thrown to the lions.

I was too disturbed to tell her about the strange conflict that simultaneously attracted me to women and kept me from them. And how could I explain that I'd quickly forgotten Cosette, cast her into obscurity, in the fantasies that drew me into liaisons, either sexually rewarding or simply so useless that, at Semmering, they forced me to ignore my weaknesses and stage extravagant rituals where everything was permitted? In the peculiar, everyday universe of people who know they will die soon, every sort of pleasure, even the most depraved, becomes the natural order of things. How could I talk to her about debauchery when I realized from her next remarks that she wanted only one thing—to see me married, settled down, out of my deadlock? How could I confess that for me there was no clean route, only backyards, blind alleys, dark lanes, untraveled roads, underground passages, and precipices?

I reassured her instead by talking about my writing plans. No more half measures, I told her, I was going to get down to it seriously. I was going to work.

The word was magical. She smiled. Kissed me. I hugged her again and realized that I had to leave. Before the trembling in her hands increased, before her features stiffened, before her body grew restless. . . . The bastard had arrived, I sensed him slip under her dress, pinch her till she bled, corrode her speech, so quickly fragmented, interrupted by pitiful sobs.

"Anton . . . be careful . . . your father . . . don't let him get his hands on me . . . on you . . . again."

The guttural song rose up, swirling over the participants like a swarm of flies drawn by the odor of fresh meat, by the prospect of a wound oozing blood in which they could hatch eggs that would proliferate endlessly, then go and nest on other haunches of meat stripped bare by expert and obliging hands.

The prayer swelled, filling the room with a muffled yet supreme hum. All were spellbound. The covenant was absolute. Smiles grazed lips, attentive and admiring gazes followed the Circumciser, whose every move prepared for the coming of a mystic newborn.

The child saw nothing, but was the only one who saw, who understood. His body, imprisoned in white linen that positioned him, offered up like a martyr to the priests' daggers, was waiting. And the song—a joyous, heartrending chant, alternating lush low notes and high notes that glittered like blades—the song enclosed him in timeless time that tied him even more firmly than his bonds.

Only the little penis emerged from the tide of bandages. Frail, yet proud, isolated, a slender spire, a small islet submerged in a storm of bewitching words and sounds. It mocks them, damp-eyed parents, uncles, and aunts who cluck as if a hen were having its throat cut in the kosher ritual, even the *mohel* who is overdoing it, with the precise and careful movements of an ancestral ritual, always the same, down to the last detail. And I too, I am moved at the sight of this morsel of pink flesh shuddering in the chilly autumn air (the room is unheated, the war has just ended, there are restrictions). I imagine that this tiny glove, folded at the tip, is mine, that my skin too must have shuddered slightly when it was set free, on that day when big hairy hands with long, grimy nails took hold of it and turned it into a piece of human debris.

The knife gleams. The fingers flutter. One last little start. And the blood springs out. The *mohel* works expertly, moving surely with a perfect approach. The operation is over in a flash. There's enough time for me to look away, to avoid seeing that piece of myself end up in the trash. I felt a sudden pain, very strong. But sudden. Very quickly, it passed. I swallowed. My tears, my fear, my hatred. I know that in spite of myself, I have found a family. I am they and they are me.

We all sing together. My eyes flood and flow with shameless tears, prompted by an intoxication that burst from some unknown corner of my being. My eyes do not see the faces now, do not see my own body; they are blinded. But already the group is absorbed, not with the Torah, but with thoughts of schnapps the Brods have kept for the occasion, and of the elegant dishes my father has been able to provide, in spite of the situation, thanks to his connections and his personal position. Amid the greedy clamor of the guests, I hear only the furious meowing of the cats wrangling over the piece of meat in the trash.

"You're going to work in the factory."

The remark was expected. Derisive, punishing, and ugly. Hermann knew his son had no choice now, that history had cleared a path for him. After the truce illness provided, which had kept him from the battlefields where other boys his age hadn't had the privilege of considering the quality of entertainment, Anton found himself among his own ruins, with nothing to rebuild but a past he had wanted to escape forever. . . .

. . . I was cured, but I was suffering from an inexhaustible disease, a spiritual gangrene that would rot my life before I could make the slightest move to prevent appearances from conquering reality. They'd got me, the beasts! Hermann didn't even have to participate, he just stood by and watched a flat and neutral, almost virgin situation develop. I had promised myself I would resist. But my first move, in spite of my disgust, was to be pushed bluntly to my work table, behind a file-laden desk, in an office next to those dominated by Father. My ultimatum was pending. The offices muffled the noise of machines, the animals' cries, the perpetually running conveyor belts, which the room's elegant upholstery distorted comfortably. Hermann was well aware I must be handled gently. He wanted to show me from the outset that the employer's position had nothing to do with that of the workers, whose dirty hands were soaked in oil and blood. Hermann's conscience was clear. And when he made me tour the factory, introducing me to one employee after another—"Herr Stirner, my son, my son who is going to succeed me"—the feeling I'd repressed earlier increased, the sensation of being quite literally displaced; my conscience, unlike Father's, was easy, but I was in a world that did not in any way belong to me.

For several weeks I read files, pretended to take an interest in the running of the business, shook hands, visited shops, inspected foul canteens, tasted vile food, watched beautiful young workers slowly change into sinister shrews, grimacing with fatigue and pain. I tried to conceive of the social laws that would put me in a benevolent position—and I despaired at so much hypocrisy.

Hermann was jubilant. Despite my disenchantment, my passivity, my lack of interest in the firm's success, he had the satisfaction of having me there, under his hand, at his side, shut up in an office where the writing I could do would never be considered indispensable to humanity. He promised I'd go to work in the factory. And there I was. Or rather, I was pretending to be there. But it didn't matter; he asked no more of me. He just needed me to play the part, even if that part was devoid of meaning, or dramatic power, even if I never stood up to him again.

As a matter of fact it suited him for me to take my duties

lightly, as an anticipated retirement, an unconscious extension of my stay at Semmering. He cared that I was present, on time, there every day, playing the part of the boss's son.

It took me some time to realize the real connotations of the expression "the boss's son"! I was still too drowned in the passionate labyrinth of my mountain stay to realize that the role my father created for me brought to light a Pandora's box of prevarications and baleful influences I'd never knew I had. I was greatly preoccupied by Mama's fate, and in the months following my return to Vienna I had one purpose: to see her, speak to her, console her whenever her monsters released her. So I extracted every advantage from my privileged situation, leaving the cursed office for the clinic, where I would shut myself in with her for hours, until the supervisors had to tug my arm and extract me from my daydreams or strange conversations and show me to the door. My position was no longer a problem, it had no meaning compared with the urgency and necessity to be close to my mother. The university, Maximilien hounding me with invitations to join the staff of a literary periodical or follow the lively debates on the political destiny of the newborn, fragile Austrian republic, my novels, which I had put under lock and key in my bedroom cupboard (who knows what Father would have done with them if he'd discovered them!), I buried it all, flung it into the limbo of hibernating memory. It slept more strongly than ever in the face of attack from the present, trying desperately to uncover facts that eluded it.

Never had I been so cold and inconsistent. I was making a living, but it took no effort and it gave me the vague but persistent feeling that I was losing my life. *To win* my life, that was what everyone wanted. What cost me most was that even Mama spoke of nothing else, though the expression didn't have the same meaning for her as for Hermann. For her, it was a way of reassuring herself that I could still escape from the dungeon where she had gone of her own free will, a way to tell me that real life was somewhere else, that my present situation—though uncomfortable—was transient, an opening onto something else, onto a future of which I would be master. But I was far from sure. . . . These discussions were much more exhausting than my days at the office. I felt as if I were still at school, having to prove myself, to resolve those false ethical problems that rhetoric taught us to turn upside down, so as to draw from them reasonable balanced conclusions, harmonious lessons, honest, measured wisdom. I didn't even try to defend myself to Father; if I had, only one solution would have been possible—a complete break. With Mama, it was harder; I didn't want to cause her pain, to enrage her, to give her reason to summon the demons that would grab her by the throat the minute the atmosphere grew tense, as soon as an argument arose involving new ground, unusual elements.

She would simply say, "Of course, writing also is a way to make one's living." And she then would kiss me, clutching my arm until her fingernails clawed my flesh, leaving deep marks.

She knew how to evoke my rationality.

"The factory workers have no choice."

I agreed. But rebelled as well.

I told her about girls who were debased, soiled, destroyed. These girls, once desirable, whom I sometimes in confusion caught myself wanting, though I looked away to avoid meeting their eyes, which seemed to mock: "So the boss's son can't find it anywhere else! He needs subservient tits and ass and skin too! And everything else, all of life. . . ."

Mama couldn't help noticing the change in me, affecting even my attitude, my clothes. Before the war, when I came home from the sanatorium, in spite of my generous social ideas, I dressed like a bourgeois, a young intellectual dandy, a member of the privileged classes of *ancien régime* Vienna. Cravat, morning coat, white silk scarf, and gloves were my normal attire. Today, I dressed simply: charcoal-gray suit, barely decent shirt without a starched collar, black necktie. I wanted to dissolve into the darkest anonymity, avoid standing out from all the other bureaucrats who were part of the administration of Huka and Son.

Vienna too, overcome by misery, had changed considerably. The imperial capital had become a city, active and productive to be sure, but still just the largest city in a very small mountain state. As if wanting to somehow retain a previously exceptional destiny, Vienna had new aspirations to set her apart from other European cities. Now Red Vienna gave itself the insolent luxury of being governed by socialists at a time when the majority of the country remained under the sway of bourgeois peasant conformity, tied to the traditional values of an autocratic heritage. This ought to have given me a way to emerge from the lethargy I'd allowed to imprison me. But I did nothing. Becoming a militant would, of course, have been one way to shed the fleeting spiritual tribulations that were extinguished in me as soon as they were born by a storm of contradictory and inconsequential feelings. These were what I had, for a long time, called my vows. I could take up the torch of politics which had stirred us young revolutionaries of the Museum Café, but the (painful) reality was that I understood nothing of what was taking place before my eyes, the events—decisive for my country and for the rest of this twentieth century's cursed history—that were unfurling there before me, within my reach, malleable to my thoughts and action. I wasn't even trying to shirk responsibilities; no, it was as if I were dead. I had left the sanatorium. They said I was cured; but I was only in a state of remission. It would have been better if I'd never left . . . or so I thought at the time. Experiences to come would totally banish that self-pitying attitude, which stemmed, after all, from sheer irresponsibility.

Later, yes, some years later, Vienna the Red, Vienna the Rebellious would ignite me with enthusiasm. But it needed Milena at my side, all around me, a fertile seed planted deep in my heart. . . .

But during the darkest, most troubled period of my life, which, in the end, mattered really very little, it was Mama who roused me from passivity. It was she who, between two crises of her own, showed me the truth I knew was also inscribed within me, though it was hidden under a thick swath of self-satisfaction.

"I know, Anton," she said during the visit only a few days before her death (her mental and physical state had deteriorated rapidly, and on each of my visits the effects of her decline seemed ever more brutal, which also had much to do with my persistent alienation), "I know what you want. You want a society of literature in which each citizen could speak and live as a writer."

I looked at her, surprised, while her eyes gazed out the window toward a gray sky that seemed to seep into her. She smiled twistedly. I railed at her:

"Why tell me that now? What do you know about writers? Where do writers come into it? Are they of any use? Do you know that too?"

She had stopped listening. Gone somewhere totally safe from the violent words I wrenched from myself, as though trying to wound myself by proxy. And my anger was released proportionately to the distance Mama moved from any pain I might cause her. In reality, she was tearing my guts out, forcing me to see and accept her as she was—bereft, innocent, and mired in unfathomable solitude. And that hurt, made me suffer all the pain I had conscientiously spared myself for months by constructing a rampart of indifference. Her leaving—which I knew instinctively would be final, irreparable—signaled the end of my mind games, enough proved that continuing to believe in a world free of dream, neurosis, and cruelty was truly mad.

I suddenly took fearful measurement of the consequences of my words. I committed myself, once again, and with more force and determination than ever. If you have to accept your limits, if you have the courage to declare yourself an impostor in the face of everyone, why not *be* a writer? Totally. Forever.

That was our last conversation. During her lifetime, at least . . . for it would be difficult indeed for me to explain the dialogue that continued (and will perhaps still continue) to tie me to Mama.

She died. They told me at the hospital that she hadn't suffered, but I knew the opposite was true. January 17, 1920; that, yes, that I remember. Perfectly, as if it were yesterday; with the icy clarity of deep winter it flayed my soul, removing entire swaths of memory. The transport of the body to the cemetery seemed endless. I hadn't spoken to Father for days; he was locked in a silence I could not identify either as disapproving or resigned. In the car that inched along behind the hearse, neither of us uttered a word. We realized that Mama's death, far more than the war, far more than all the defeats that descended on us in just a few years, her death had rung the knell for an epoch, etched in stone the differences that had always set us apart, and selected the roads that would separate us forever.

The drive to the cemetery took so long! What peculiar reasoning had decided to keep Vienna's dead so remote? At that time I couldn't have cared less that my mother was buried near Beethoven and Schubert! In the Jewish sector, it's true, at Gate 4. . . .

Smoothly, with little fuss, I had settled my accounts with myself. My mother had shown me, perhaps unintentionally, the path I must take. I had seen Maximilien the night before the funeral; he had offered me a job proofreading at the newspaper where he worked. It was a part-time job that would leave me enough time to write. Maximilien also suggested publishing some of my stories in the paper, and recommended that I show my novels to a publisher in Berlin.

"I'm going there next month; come along, if you like."

A few days later, after reading my manuscripts, he repeated his proposal, but this time with an enthusiasm that I confess made me feel good.

"They're fantastic, Anton, you're a great writer! You *must* have these published!"

I didn't have to be asked twice. I accepted the job at the newspaper, from time to time they would publish my short pieces, and I'd go to Berlin. There was another immediate consequence: I would leave Father to his meat. I left him for good. With the money I'd earn I could take a small furnished apartment. Maximilien had helped me track down the secret haven that I'd wanted for so long but until now—lacking of courage or sincerity—had refused to admit was within my reach. It was a modest studio, nicely kept up, at 30 Berggasse, just a stone's throw from Freud. A bed, a table, a chair, bookshelves . . . everything I might need. Maximilien also lent me a lump sum to get me started.

I reached an agreement with Father quickly. He'd probably been expecting it. I learned later that to avoid losing face he had told them at the factory that my disease had struck again and I'd returned to the mountains. He didn't even argue with me, just told me to go to hell. He threatened to disinherit me, then carried out his threat. Not only was I scarcely affected, I felt an unexpected relief. It was he who was cutting the umbilical cord. He was responsible, but I didn't care. By doing so, he saved me.

14.

Clockwork's Notes (IV)

❦❦❦ I'd have liked to have solved the Blackbird case before I left for Paris. I even thought that a paper on the subject might create something of a stir, or at any rate change the routine hair-splitting sessions on theoretical matters. At the risk of seeming behind the times, still engrossed in outdated notions of pioneer romanticism, I hoped to substitute for my paper on nonverbal languages a case study which, though traditional, provoked reactions so keen, so intense, in me—whose cause and effects I couldn't control—that my colleagues couldn't help but be interested.

That was why, instead of putting the finishing touches on my talk, I focused all my attention on Blackie. I had decided to start from scratch and carry out my investigation as a detective might do, not trying for too many interpretations, but simply organizing the facts. The truth was that I didn't give one sweet damn about the conference. I was being paid to attend, but I thought it would be much more interesting— primarily for the discipline I'd specialized in—to recreate Blackbird's trail in Paris, to track down the story he'd covered over like some shameful tattoo, to follow step by step the drama he'd done his best to forget, by assuming another identity, lying, and silencing the remarkable voice he carried within him, a voice that never should have been extinguished. . . .

I didn't know where to start. Needless to say, as I suspected, there was no Blackbird in the telephone book, and no one I asked had ever heard of Anton Huka. I questioned my few friends and acquaintances in Paris and polished up my college French in order to place random calls to various cultural magazines—*Les Nouvelles littéraires*, *Arts*, and *Les Lettres françaises*—as well as to various music publishers. Luckily, an old friend of mine was then the Associated Press correspondent in Paris. We'd been at Columbia together. I had no trouble finding his number, and called him as soon as I arrived at the Hotel Lutétia, where the American contingent were staying. Bob Fall (he was later killed in Vietnam, while reporting from the front) and I arranged to meet at a bistro a minute away from his place, Le Rouquet, not the famous Fouquet's on the Champs-Elysées but a typical simple little Parisian café on the boulevard Saint-Germain with a bar, hard-boiled eggs, Côtes du Rhône, *croque-monsieurs* and strong black coffee. We hadn't seen each other for a good ten years. Bob greeted me, as easygoing as I remembered, age and experience had given him the constant serenity that often marks great reporters accustomed to the most incongruous or dangerous situations. He responded to my nervous excitement with some entertaining observations on the state of contemporary psychiatry between puffs on his pipe. To fortify and soothe me, he ordered us two kirs, an odd drink combining white wine and black-currant syrup popular with the French. After the third glass, and the inevitable reminiscences, I couldn't hold back and posed the question I'd been dying to ask. Did he know of Anton Blackbird?

Bob had never heard the name, of course, but he listened carefully to my story, then gave me valuable advice. "If you think the crux of the problem occurred somewhere between 1934 and 1938, there's only one thing to do—go to the Bibliothèque Nationale and look up the newspapers of the time." And he gave me some names.

The next day I went to the periodical room, flipping through old copies of *Le Temps* and *L'Intransigéant*. I didn't know what I was looking for, but I had a hunch that if I did find anything, it wouldn't be some little item tucked away on the back pages, but a banner headline plastered across the front page.

It took three full days to go through 1934. On the fourth, just as I began to lose hope, my efforts paid off. Did they ever! Here's what I found:

PIANIST ANTOINE CHOUCAS

MURDERS FATHER

Lengthy statement found in apartment
on avenue de la Bourdonnais;
murderer disappears without a trace

The headline on *L'Intransigéant* for July 10, 1935. And in *Le Temps* on the same day I read:

ANTOINE CHOUCAS

SOUGHT BY POLICE

Famous virtuoso murders father,
wealthy industrialist Louis Choucas

I was exhilarated. I knew Blackbird at once. He was *obviously* the man. There was no doubt about it. Besides, the photographs provided incontrovertible evidence: Though the man was younger and thinner than the Blackie who arrived at Bellevue Hospital in 1945, and he had a thin mustache, the features were the same—that aristocratic boxer's face I knew so well.

I scanned the remaining articles and pounced eagerly on the following days' papers. I had discovered the first vital elements that would put me on track, lead me to the source. The newspapers traced Antoine's career and his father's, priceless information on the case. Soon I knew everything there was to know about his concerts and recitals all over the world. And I read the opinions of his contemporaries, musicians and musicologists. Showers of praise, floods of amazement. . . . As for the father, Louis, there were references to his political past: a disciple of Maurras, he had been active in Action Française, and it was said that proceeds from his foundries had extensively underwritten the extreme right. But the press didn't play up that aspect of the story. Choucas senior had probably been granted the anonymity that big shots tend to get—kid-glove handling from the French press. In the end, though, no matter how it looked to American eyes, it didn't add up to much. I was still in the dark. Antoine's letter had been seized by the public prosecutor and then, according to the papers, had mysteriously disappeared. So the press had been reduced to making guesses which, considering who I was dealing with, struck me as rather risky. If only I'd been able to get my hands on that statement. . . . Approaching the police got me nowhere, nor did support I requested from some big deals in French medicine. My investigation lost steam. As a matter of fact, I wonder if Blackbird ever really confessed in this statement, since from what his sister would tell me, it was pretty short.

I knew I'd uncovered only a fraction of the truth. Day by day, the articles shortened, moving from the front page to the obscurity inside the paper. At night, in my hotel room, I turned over the different pieces in the puzzle. I lay on my bed and chain-smoked, trying to fit each detail in place. Old Blackie wouldn't let me go! And it would be some time before he did! Who knows—taking notes on the "Blackbird case" a few years after the trip to Paris could have been my attempt to rid myself of him, to exorcise him, in a sense . . . as if getting him down on paper could put me back on top, enable me to turn him into a mere case study, make him see that I, too, could invent a fate for him. . . . Blackie's tragedy is that he's always considered himself a genius, a genius endowed with all the powers in the world, especially the power to create and to destroy. In his deranged mind the act of writing, of keeping a fictitious notebook, was no different from killing.

At the time, though, I had to push on, not let myself rest easy with the notes I'd scribbled secretly at the Bibliothèque Nationale; they only made me warier than ever. Had my bad French misled me? And how much could I believe of the newspaper stories, of funeral orations by friends and personalities from the world of arts and letters? Cocteau, Breton, and Aragon had known Antoine in the 1920s, particularly Cocteau, who, it was said, asked his advice about *Parade* during a conversation in a bistro (before Erik Satie committed to compose the score). I'm sure it's all terribly fascinating for contemporary music historians. Antoine Choucas wasn't just a master pianist; in his youth he'd been the only surrealist composer worthy of the name. After taking all the prizes at the Conservatoire de Paris, he'd flung himself with boundless energy into the dadaist hullabaloo, presenting a few pieces for piano that later won him a couple of lines in most honors theses on the subject, but according to contemporary witnesses, they were generally considered to be unacknowledged masterpieces. Too unusual, too idiosyncratic, it was said. At a time when glittering orchestrations were admired, Blackbird—sorry, Choucas—was composing pieces that were disconcertingly simple, childishly naive. I was able to verify this after his sister lent me some 78s he'd recorded in the 1930s, when I discovered, with stupefaction and admiration, music that, at the time, must have seemed utterly crazy. It was like Stockhausen, with chords and harmonies so audacious not even Debussy or Stravinsky had suspected. . . .

No, I had to uncover Antoine's true life, to discover why, at the peak of his career, he had sacrificed everything, lost everything, by making an attempt on his father's life. The newspapers and even the weekly and monthly magazines I examined so closely could tell me nothing, or almost nothing. It was most urgent—I had only two full days before returning to New York—that I find Antoine's family, if anyone was still alive. Was Blackie the sort of man to have a mother, a brother or sister? This time the telephone book produced results. Only one Choucas was listed. Bob, to whom I'd told the whole story over dinner in Les Halles, assured me that the name was uncommon enough in France. "You shouldn't have any trouble tracking this one down." The Choucas in the directory was listed as a widow. The mother. . . .

When I woke up next morning I rushed to the telephone

and excitedly dialed the number. It rang twice, three times, five. I imagined the worst. A recent death. A trip abroad. Or simply a country house in the south where the Choucas family had some property, near Grasse, if you could believe the press. I was about to hang up, sick at heart, when I heard a man's voice asking, "Whom do you wish to speak to?"

"Madame Choucas, please."

"Who is calling?"

His tone was dry, unwelcoming. Open dialogue seemed improbable. Suspicious, I decided to fake it, and under an assumed name I introduced myself as a Harvard professor briefly in Paris, at work on a learned paper on French music between the wars.

"One moment, I'll check."

I waited for almost a minute, and then the same harsh, inhospitable voice returned to tell me that Madame would not speak to me. I was daunted, but about to protest when I heard the fatal click ending the conversation, if you could even call it that. Annoyed, I could think of nothing to do now but order breakfast. I usually enjoy continental breakfast, but that morning the croissants tasted stale, the black coffee too bitter, and I had no appetite for the buttered bread, though it looked quite fresh and crusty. (I'm getting bogged down in useless details. Dammit, I'm trapped in my own ambition: I want to write like a novelist, but I just circle around what might have been. At least Blackbird, in his notebooks, knows how to get to the heart of the matter!)

After an hour, five or six cigarettes, and another summary of all sides of the case, it was time to make a move. Instead of waiting for the truth to come knocking at my hotel-room door, I must jostle it, rough it up, cut it from whole cloth if necessary.

I dialed the number again. The man answered. I said straightoff that I knew where Antoine was. This time he hesitated, briefly. Then he said dully:

"Wait."

A few seconds later he was back on, saying:

"Madame will see you at five o'clock sharp."

It was eleven in the morning. I had six hours to kill, six hours in which I could make absolutely no progress in my investigation. It was all right—I was scheduled to speak at the conference early that afternoon, so I put in an appearance at lunch with my colleagues. It was the least I could do to justify the trip, though I secretly felt I had enough material to satisfy the hopes and dreams of the most demanding psychiatrist. But I didn't intend to breathe a word of that to the other doctors, at least not for the moment.

I was on time for my appointment. I'd hardly rung the bell when the man I had spoken to showed me in. Surprised, I didn't say a word—he didn't give me time to, but asked me at once to follow him. The hall was large and dark, and smelled strangely stuffy, with a peculiar underlying odor I couldn't quite identify. At the door to the large salon the man, who was severely dressed in black—a servant or a member of the family? No way to tell—paused briefly, then flung open the door and receded. Inside, it was even darker. All the curtains were drawn, not one lamp was lit, and only a thin thread of light slipped through the fringes of the velvet draperies. I advanced uncertainly, not knowing how to proceed next. The fellow on the phone had mysteriously disappeared. Step by step, I groped my way through the dark. My eyes slowly grew accustomed to it. I could make out, in order, a large sideboard, a low table covered with objects which, judging by their gleam, were probably silver or brass, a standing lamp, and, finally, pictures—portraits. The heads were indistinct, but I felt they had all been brought together there, clumped like a wall in a crowded museum, the better to observe me, to catch me out in case I committed some faux pas. Suddenly I stumbled against what must have been an armchair or sofa, and probably groaned in pain, because a voice in the gloom said:

"This way, Mr. Myrer." (That was the name I'd chosen, out of the blue, perhaps because it sounded like the name of the author of the book I'd read on the plane.)

And the Widow Choucas—for she could be no one else, the voice cracked by time, quavering, but decisive and abrupt—added:

"Take three steps to your left and you'll find a chair where I should like you to sit." (It was an order.) "With your permission, I shall remain in the dark. I'm not anxious to show you my face, and it's none of your business. . . ."

I sat down. She went on:

"So, Mr. Myrer, you claim you know where my son Antoine is. I hope you are right. You've come and disturbed a very old lady in her solitude, her oblivion, her illusion. Some phantoms, you know, are best not awakened."

"I know, Madame, and I'll tell you the truth. I am not a scholar conducting research on the history of music. I'm a doctor."

"Whoever you are, you must be well aware that Antoine Choucas has been dead for a long time."

Then the man in black slipped into the room, without my hearing him. I started when he brushed against me while setting a tray on the low table three feet away. I'd gotten used to the dark and now I could just glimpse the motionless silhouette of Madame Choucas. Naturally, her face remained hidden, but I could see her wrinkled hand with its long nails as she gestured, or asked me to pour. I was being invited to take tea with her. I felt as though I were undergoing some improbable ritual, a product of the desperate imagination of a writer who'd run out of unusual situations. And yet I was really there, stuck in my chair like an idiot unable to present a neat history, to plead his case convincingly enough to be taken seriously by an interrogator uninterested in small talk. Antoine's mother would not be satisfied with the short version.

I could now name the odor that hit me on entering. It was the one you get in a Catholic church: incense and holy water. I was in a temple, a sanctuary. And at the altar, Madame Choucas presided over the funeral rites for her beloved husband—eternally. She had taken herself out of time. I realized this when she spoke again, after taking a sip of tea—or so I assumed from the faint sound.

"About the music, I've nothing to say. My husband and I always hated the barbaric fantasies of the person who was our son by blood, but who ceased to be ours—through blood as well. Louis used to say that in every family, even the most honorable, there is always a black sheep. He became accustomed to the idea, though he regretted that it was his eldest son who suffered such a calamity. Happily, after the fatal day, he was able to see his hopes and dreams fulfilled through our younger daughter. . . ."

She sighed and fell silent again. I didn't know what to say, where to begin. I couldn't care less about the sister or about Antoine's social gaffes. But I should have taken advantage of the situation to push Madame Choucas into a corner. I'm sure that if I'd done so I could have forced some information from her. But instead, remembering the magic formula that had worked the first time, I said again, thinking I'd set some spectacular revelations, "I know where your son is."

"Balderdash, young man. I've already told you that as far as I'm concerned, the person named Antoine has been dead for a long time. There still lives—close to me, in this furniture, these carpets, these paintings, these objects all around us— someone of whom France need not be ashamed, despite the lies invented by posterity to sully his memory."

I had no idea what the old lady was talking about, but dared not interrupt or ask any questions lest she decide to stop talking. So I just drank my tea, slowly and quietly. I hadn't thought to refuse it, though I didn't really want it.

"That man has no business here. . . . He was banished long before he carried out the disastrous plans he harbored against the family—against us, who had cherished him and brought him up to respect the best of France's traditional values."

I was completely lost. Then I played what I thought was my trump card:

"Antoine isn't dead, he's insane. A patient in Bellevue Hospital in New York."

"Insane! I don't believe you!"

Madame Choucas straightened up in her chair, crying out with a vigor surprising in such an elderly person, one who for some reason (perhaps the sound of casters) I thought might be crippled. As she moved she flung her left arm violently out to the side, striking the curtain so that it opened for a fraction of a second. That flash of light enabled me to see her face. I saw Antoine, Anton, my Blackbird as he is today, who was probably at that very moment covering the pages of his peerless notebook or vigorously coloring bestial images with all the dazzling pigments of his sick memory. Unless he was taking advantage of my absence to play the piano, to compose, who knows . . . to thumb his nose at me from afar, assuming I hadn't succeeded (yet) in penetrating his secret.

There was an amazing resemblance between mother and son. And I sat there, so stupefied I didn't realize just how upset she was.

Now she was screaming:

"That's impossible! You're just another horrible liar!"

"But . . . Madame," I stammered, setting down my empty cup and scrambling to my feet.

"Out! Out! I will not allow a fanatic from the anti-Choucas cult to remain in this sacred place a moment longer!"

And in a penetrating voice she called:

"Louiiis!"

The man in black was instantly at my side, asking me to follow him in a low but compelling voice. I was ceremoniously ushered to the door. It slammed behind me; a key turned twice in the lock, followed by the sliding of three superimposed bolts. The elevator hadn't even been called for me. I was so flabbergasted anyway that, without thinking, I'd taken the stairs. As I was mechanically descending, my footsteps muffled by a heavy carpet, I told myself the woman was insane. For the moment that was enough. It was comforting. But deep down I knew I was using it to mask my dismay, my

total lack of control over the situation. Would I ever truly
know Blackie? Doubt pounded through my chest, in rhythm
with my watchful heart. Combined anger and weariness
made me resolve to drop the case. I was scarcely outside the
building when I spotted a café on the avenue. I needed a good
whisky—even a bad one—and I needed breathing space in
order to reflect calmly about everything.

And now, as I write and rewrite these lines, I realize as well
that I must put some air into my factual account. I see that it
is definitely beginning to wander in a labyrinth of incomplete
information, poorly constructed phrases, badly connected se-
gues. And I have to discipline my thoughts, aim for the bull's-
eye. What right did I have to say the Widow Choucas was
insane? I think instead I heard a cry of pain from deep in a
mother's body. This woman had been unable to bear the
horrible truth that her son was worse than a murderer—a
madman. A killer could be punished, exiled, kept at bay with
rituals and chants, he could be drawn and quartered,
lynched, disemboweled, left bloodless, lifeless, amorphous,
obliterated. But a lunatic affirms his right to exist too loudly,
protests too vigorously the theft of the inheritance others
covet. Antoine dead was taboo, but redeemable and redeemed. Mad, he turned back into the son both loved and
hated; he escaped the category of mystery and passion to
become once more an unmarked, unmartyred individual—
especially because his madness released him from judgment
according to the rules of the society that had condemned
him.

I should have been able to see and hear and reconstruct
this at the time. Only Blackie himself could have done so. I
should have listened more attentively to peripherals; the
name the Widow Choucas called the man in black: Louis.
Strange coincidence. I was a miserable detective. . . . So
there I was examining myself in the glinting gilded surface of
my single-malt whisky, wondering if all my research was
worth it. It may be of interest to mention that just then, or a
moment later, I remembered that the American library was

close by. Bob Fall had told me when I mentioned the avenue de la Bourdonnais. We should learn to avoid such traps in school! Is it possible? In the United States they even offer courses in creative writing, but the more I write, the more I wonder if they *really* teach people how to write. Go on! Faster! Get to the point! Library closed. Opens at 9:00 A.M. I'm there the next morning. Look things up for two solid hours. I read French fairly well, but it's so much faster in my own language. There it is! Got it! I call Bob with the good news—and he puts me on to a friend of his, an ace reporter with the *Journal de Dimanche*. The guy's been everywhere, he's seen and heard everything. He was just starting his career when my case was breaking. He confirms that Antoine's sister did indeed become the Marquise of F., that she still lives on her husband's ancestral property, some fifty kilometers out-side Paris. I rent a car. And step on the gas.

Whew! And here we are, with no transition, no paraphrase. The next voice you'll hear is that of Claire Choucas, wife of a marquis. Typical case of money marrying money. French history. I'll reread Balzac, Maupassant, or Georges Ohnet—get back to the rigorous style I should never have abandoned. After all, my role is just to collect the facts and analyze them later on, not to wrap them in some fairy tale tissue that may well produce twisted, distorted, even suspect meanings. That I leave to Blackbird. It would be unbearably ironic to find myself unconsciously parodying him!

The rule to obey: physician, not novelist. Policeman if necessary. In any case, stick to that identity. Proceed one step at a time through the dossier.

Claire. Physically, not at all like Antoine. Takes after the father. Warm welcome. Most cooperative from the start. Shows me pictures of her brother performing at concerts, posters for recitals at the Pleyel and the Albert Hall, various autographed scores and other sacred objects. And to crown it all, the maestro's piano, placed with care in the front hall. She is the true guardian of the temple. The widow adores Louis, and Claire has poured all her admiration and worship

into the genius of her unnatural brother. She puts on a re-
cord. "Would you like to hear it?" I don't hide my enthusiasm.
I'm musical, of course, but above all here to detect. That's it.
I'm on the right track. I won't get caught again. I leave Claire
her emotional recollections, filled with a warmth and love I
could never describe here. You imagine it.

She speaks (I thought of everything this time, including a
tape recorder, that tool so helpful to all those unimaginative
word-eaters and hack writers who pride themselves on presenting the "real" truth).

Claire says:

"My brother Antoine . . . Antoine was always a very gentle
boy, affectionate and hypersensitive. He was especially vulnerable to the outside world and couldn't bear violence or
aggressiveness. . . . He got upset when people, especially
Father, raised their voices. His eyes would often fill with tears
for no particular reason. He took everything to heart and if
frustrated was hard put to swallow his bitterness and forge
ahead. Antoine was without a doubt one of the last romantics, one of those uncommon, offbeat individuals who was
irritated by everything about contemporary mores, who saw
no way to cope with the future but to leap into the unknown—and he was frantically preparing to take that leap.
Because, you must understand, unlike our father, he was not
a man of the past. He believed in progress, in civilization,
illumination, in all those republican, humanistic values that
soon—he could sense it—would founder in a hideous apocalypse. Despite everything he was a man of his time, who lived
life passionately and didn't want any absurd rules or social or
religious boundaries to block his emotional course. Antoine
lived only for emotion. To him, everything was raw material
for feeling. Superficially, but spiritually too . . . because he
was first and foremost an artist. I always wondered how my
parents could have given birth to what, for them, must have
been a monstrosity. Antoine was always labeled a monstrosity. A child prodigy. From every point of view. A brilliant
pupil at the Lycée Henri IV. Ultimately too brilliant for the

family's taste. At first Father was proud, but he soon came to
fear that such intelligence, such spirit, would only cause this
son to betray his, Father's, ideas and interests. Which is what
happened. Antoine was always at odds with his social peers.
. . . You don't know what really happened, Mr. Myrer. The
newspapers, yes, the newspapers . . . but their version of the
story was whitewashed in comparison with the cruelty of what
really happened. I don't know why I'm telling you all this, Mr.
Myrer; after all, your interest is the music of the twenties and
thirties. The Choucas tragedy isn't part of that history. It
springs from myth. . . . Father was a traditionalist. For Antoine, everything led to some ideal of freedom. They were
constantly arguing. When Antoine was at the lycée he was
already friendly with the socialist crowd, and he'd come home
with anarchistic declarations that would turn into furious bat-
tles. Father took a rigid position against those he contemptu-
ously called 'outsiders,' the very ones who, he said, had corrupted his son. It's true that in high school and later at the
conservatory Antoine had many Jewish teachers and friends.
When he joined the avant-garde, particularly when he became an outspoken pacifist, Father kicked him out and cut off
his allowance. At the time, though, Antoine was developing
an international reputation. His deliberately open mind made
him receptive to all kinds of outside influences, and his inter-
nationalist theses unleashed our father's fury. The final break
occurred one day just a few weeks before the declaration of
war, when Antoine decided to go and live in Vienna. He'd
been offered a concert series, and he intended to continue
advanced studies there, under the masters Austria harbored
at that time. Father swore he'd never see him again. And he
kept his word—I mean, it was inevitable. He backed the anti-
Bolshevik, anti-Semitic movement. Then Antoine returned
to Paris in 1921, for a series of recitals, with a reputation as a
deserter that for a time compromised his career. And to make
matters worse he brought a woman, Vera her name was, and
they weren't married. She was, according to Father, one of

those Eastern European Jewesses who embodied all the seven deadly sins, all the faults, all the dangers of the unknown. . . . I saw Antoine then. Without, of course, telling my parents. He'd changed a great deal. He told me he'd been sick (without ever specifying the illness), and he had visibly suffered the indirect consequences of being poor and doing without. Year by year, his fame diminished. But he was relentless. He was working steadily on some compositions that, unfortunately, have totally disappeared. At least, that's what I always assumed; maybe someday an enterprising researcher will track them down. Vera? No, wrong track. I met Vera once or twice. She was a splendid woman, and I was very pleased to see my brother so happy with her. She was strong enough for both of them. I mean, her personality complemented Antoine's perfectly. And I'm sure that with her help, if luck hadn't turned against him, he would have triumphed. I knew that Antoine had to give music lessons to pay the bills. And one day I went to their place—a little two-room apartment in an old blue-collar neighborhood—when I knew Antoine wouldn't be in, and when I went away, I left them as much money as I could scrape up. What else could I do? Antoine wouldn't accept anything from me, knowing that the money was Father's. Vera would understand better. Some months later, I learned that she had found a job. I knew she planned to do so. She didn't want to burden Antoine, to interfere in any way with his art. She was liberated, strongly independent and unafraid of any rebuffs she might suffer because of her background, in the chauvinist France of the day. She was talented, too; she knew several languages, and was able to play up the medical diplomas she had obtained in her native country—was it Hungary? I don't remember now—to find work as a nurse in an insane asylum just outside Paris. She could have done better, but as I recall there was some problem about accepting her qualifications, something like that. . . . In any case, she wasn't afraid of hard work, nor did she stand on ceremony. Her goal was to save Antoine.

And perhaps that was why she lost him. I mean, because of the distance, she didn't come home every night, and her desperate love for Antoine suffered. She was neither a flighty nor faithless—the opposite—but so sure of her feelings for the man she loved that she wasn't afraid to indulge in brief affairs that broke social convention. And that gave Father the winning hand! I don't know how he found out—he probably had Antoine's whole life spied on. Because he wanted to disinherit him; decided, as he said, to 'have his hide.' It is certain that, disgracefully, he began sending Antoine anonymous letters. Or so I found out, when it was too late. I would have tried to stop him. It was especially unbearable because Vera—she had confided in me—wanted to have a child with Antoine. Perhaps that was what really made her find a job. Antoine just curled up in his shell and submitted to the blows. He, who had always believed in nonconformity and rebellion, let himself be carried away by irrational jealousy. He grew silent and composed less and less. And as if trying to clear his name, to escape his weaknesses, he increasingly relied on his role as neighborhood piano teacher. The great Antoine Choucas was finished—or almost! For one day—and oh, how our evil father rejoiced!—Vera disappeared without a trace. Perhaps back to Vienna or somewhere else. . . . Antoine went back to composing harder than ever, and succeeded, driven by a passion fiercer than before, in making a name for himself again among the pianists of his time. His salvation came from London, where his talent had not been forgotten and where an influential music lover gave him a chance. The critics were wildly enthusiastic. The great Choucas was reborn . . . for a few more years. After my marriage, although it ended the independence I had gained when I turned twenty-one, I was able to follow him on some of his tours in France and abroad. Listen to his recordings—they speak for themselves. I have never heard Tchaikovsky's First Concerto in B-flat Minor or Schönberg's Five Pieces for Piano— Tchaikovsky and Schönberg were two of his favorite composers—played the way Antoine plays them. I think he found in his own resentment and helplessness the strength, the power, the breath he needed to become a genius. The rest came quickly, suddenly, during the year 1934. Father continued to harass him. But Antoine had learned to defend himself, and his talent was more powerful than all the base accusations brought against him. There were the dramatic political events in February. The right-wing attack on the Chambre-des-Deputés . . . Father played an important part in that. Antoine blamed him for the dead on both sides, who fell during confrontations with the police. And finally their fatal interview. Antoine learned, I don't know where, that his father was the true architect of Vera's departure. . . . For the first time in ten years, Antoine sets foot in the apartment on avenue de la Bourdonnais and heads straight for Father's office. There is shouting. Accusations by Antoine in a vengeful tone I've never heard him use. And finally, on the threshold, the ultimate clash: 'But of course I'm a Jew.' And from within the room, curses, death threats. Some days later, whether because of political positions he had taken, openly favoring the left, or because of another of Father's vile operations, Antoine was beaten up in the street, on his way home from rehearsal, near a Métro station. He was attacked by four masked men who obviously weren't looking for money, which he didn't have anyway (even during his wealthier periods, Antoine rarely carried a lot of cash), and virtually left for dead. The whole thing was hushed up; there were only a few subtle references in the press. Even the papers that shared Antoine's views didn't agree about the case; they could have come up with motives for a scandal, made my brother into some kind of martyr for the cause, used the opportunity to denounce the fascist gangs rampant in the capital. In their eyes, though, Antoine wasn't a good example, he was compromised in spite of everything because of Louis Choucas, that notorious extremist. Too bourgeois as well, most likely, and only dubiously committed. Perhaps too artistic also . . . by definition capricious, uncontrolled and uncontrollable in his acts and thoughts."

I listened, speechless, to this astonishing account, which, I confess, I only half believed. Once again something was missing, part of the mechanism that would bring it all together. So I asked the question that had been burning my lips: "But . . . the act . . . Madame . . . I mean, the murder?"

At that, Claire Choucas, the wife of Marquis of F., became more withdrawn. She mentioned a trip her brother had taken to Eastern Europe some months later. She said she thought that it was a reunion with Vera. She mentioned a child who had died, or perhaps been kidnapped. In short, totally fantastic, vague statements recounted helter-skelter. Should I believe any of it? At the time I was so impressed I didn't even think of questioning the story. But upon reflection, after I left, certain questions bothered me. In the airplane while I pretended to sleep, I tried to organize everything I'd learned in this brief time, material of supreme importance that—why not admit it—contained elements which would upset the most stable man, which was, undeniably, what I thought I was at the time. . . .

There was Vienna. Vera. Yes. That cleared things up a little. . . . But I was struck by the fact that Claire Choucas had made no attempt to find out what had become of her brother. She had swallowed my Harvard-professor story, or seemed to. As for Antoine, I thought she accepted his disappearance too easily, along with the official account of his rather disconcerting end. Now, having weighed everything carefully, I realized that conspiracy or not (and Claire might well have taken part in one—in which case she would have just continued to play her role, the better to take me in), I realize I hadn't been playing fair either. Why was I so brave, or rather so cowardly, that I said nothing about the present situation of the man who had become Blackbird? I kept my conscience clear at first by telling myself that my silence stemmed from a humane concern not to upset anyone, to leave the "sanctuary" pristine in its innocent virginity. As if anyone or anything in this story were *innocent!* I can say it now (what do I have to win or lose?): the truth is, unconsciously, I wanted Antoine *for myself.* I felt that having taken him in, analyzed and finally rehabilitated him (although on that score I was so wrong), I could refuse to turn him over to anyone else. In any case, why *should* he belong to anyone but me? Antoine Choucas was dead. Blackbird was mine, only mine.

I took a few notes on the plane. Here is the gist.

"A. seems to have no childhood. Why? Strange nobody talks about it. Not a trace. A nuisance for me. Where to now? Was it happy or unhappy? Can't tell either way. Assuming the first hypothesis was correct . . . Widow Choucas + Claire = too melodramatic. Hard to believe. Grand opera. But I have to believe them: I've made myself their faithful interpreter. I'm not cheating there. Whatever literary theorists may think (and may they forgive my brief incursion into their territory), there's a novelistic paradox that consists of *reducing* what is real in fiction as a way to avoid being criticized for implausibility. But in all my years as a doctor, I've known many cases (starting with Blackie's, naturally) in which the truth was somewhat melodramatic. What can I do if reality is grotesque and baroque? . . ."

That's it. I came back to New York with this dreadful, unfinished story. For what I, like everyone else, still didn't know was what became of Blackbird after the fateful date of July 10, 1935. . . . Glory is fleeting indeed. The research lasted several months, the journalists' investigations barely two weeks. Then the case was filed away. Since there was no Anton. . . . I couldn't figure out what happened during the ten-year gap between July 1935 and August 1945, when Blackbird came into my life. And I wouldn't be satisfied till I'd closed that gap.

I had a hunch I'd find the end of the story in Vienna. And I was right. By a happy coincidence or a stroke of luck (though the reasons for the choice are obvious), the next international conference of psychiatrists was to be held in the Austrian capital two years later . . . so I'd have all the time I needed to go on observing Blackbird, try to make off with a few more fragments of his notebook and his bestiary, and to try to enter into a nonverbal, I mean an "oral," relationship with him.

One piece of the puzzle in particular was missing, and it haunted me for a long time: a remark of Blackie's that went back several years now, but that I remembered perfectly. Why had he said he'd met Toller in Spain, in 1937? What did it mean? I read all the biographies of the writer in vain; not one detail stood out. Very little was known about the time the famous playwright spent in Spain. . . .

Still, without his having told me anything or demonstrated any change in attitude toward me, I was sure Blackbird knew I'd found out something about him.

Immediate result: he suddenly began to make things easier. In particular, he deliberately left his notebook lying where I could get my hands on it. As if he wanted to deny historical reality, as if he wanted to destroy the few certainties I'd acquired, and corrode the therapeutic conclusions that I'd reached.

I admit that *his* version still throws me into a state of confusion I rationally refuse. My own scientific training knows this is a dangerous trap. But how can you deny the evidence? The existence of a piece of writing that stands on its own with its own laws, its own boundaries—a closed universe that contradicts the Paris story and asserts another that is equally terrible and even more tragic. The physician shouldn't say it, but I think more and more that I prefer Anton Huka to Antoine Choucas. . . .

. . . ever since he's known that I know, Blackie's been playing the piano again. He shuts himself away in the concert hall and spends hours pathetically tinkling away. Now and then, in a tremendous burst, he'll play some great melody; his fingers seem to have rediscovered their former agility. Apparently only the exceptional circumstances of the concert I put on for him had enabled him to perform at his best. These days, after some marvelous lyrical flights, his fingers will suddenly slip and skid as he tries over and over to get back the thread of the melody, leaving him tired and depressed. I tried, with what I thought to be good, timely advice, to help him find his center, so he could resume his work on a "healthy" basis. . . . As if such words could touch a creature who operates, inside and out, in rhythm with a sleeping volcano that roars though there's nothing to suggest it's about to erupt!

. . . over the years, it's true—especially as the notebooks become increasingly voluminous and broader in scope—Antoine Choucas's musical vocabulary diminished. For five years, for example, he would or could play nothing but Satie's *Gymnopédies*. Tirelessly, interminably. . . . At first it was beautiful, very beautiful, but eventually the phrasing became insipid, the attack languid, the fingering uncertain. It was as if the process of writing were eating into the musician's talent and abilities. . . .

The question I ask myself today (am I in any position, do I have any right to do so?) is this: Did Antoine Choucas become, *in effect*, the writer Anton Blackbird? Or am I imagining it, allowing myself to be taken in by make-believe, letting myself be surprised by appearances or simply by my own inadequacy?

15.
Bestiary of the Yellow Notebook (V)

☙☙☙ We did not notice their arrival. Then all at once. A vast number. Clustered like an excited swarm of bees. Alone, in the lead, the scout or leader trained his nose, wrinkled with excitement, on the victims that had taken refuge on the other shore. They had appeared out of nowhere, and were all the more disquieting because neither their origin nor their goal was known.

The rats were very hungry.

After the customary conferences, their people had decided to leave the cavern that sheltered them behind the wall fretted with mazes.

There were brown ones, russet, gray, white, black, red. A teeming mass that shook the earth as it moved. The column advanced, devastating everything along the way. Only a pestilential smell lingered long after the clawed feet, the shaggy bellies, had traced tangled paths toward the river. There, they knew, they could sense it—squeals of contentment—was assembled the small population of birds.

The invasion had been scrupulously prepared, masterfully planned. The elders, who were the wisest, had explained the deployment techniques, the commandos' stratagems, and the proper uses of siege and assault. The youngest ones, fidgeting from too much inactivity or unhappy at having been detained by the arguments of the fearful or cowardly, were sharpening their teeth on stones set aside for the purpose. And the females were giving hasty birth to new broods of warriors who, after they were properly trained, could take over if necessary.

At nightfall the vanguard went into action, taking the entire troop with it on the journey that would end the following day, in death or victory. From every hole came a cluster of moving flesh, from every chink flowed unbroken lines of slimy bodies. The rats were thoroughly coated with a fatty excretion that occurs before attack. War masks. Proud ornaments. Marks of infamy.

They had ruffled each other's fur. And the strongest, those who had already shown their mettle during brief but fierce incursions into enemy territory, had the loftiest ruffs, which emphasized the powerful, elegant muscles of their necks.

They scorn the first victims, the feeblest, those that haven't fled in time, leaving them for those at the end of the procession, who can feast at leisure on the half-smothered corpses, crushed by the elite of the caravan. No, what interests and fascinates them, like one body guided by a single instinct, is one specific prey. More than hunger, what leads them through the dense night toward the light of day about to break on the horizon is a curious creature that by itself embodies all the tastiest viands they have dreamed of from time immemorial, even before man appeared on the earth—man to whom they deign to pay attention only occasionally, en route to other conquests, for his flesh is quite insipid compared with that of the sole object of the species' desires. O glorious day! The King of the Rats, sensing their goal, has raced ahead of his troops, to take on in single combat a prince who is worthy of him. . . . They will have driven him to the precipice, and the encircling army of invaders will sound its victory cry. He must take up the challenge.

And yet, as the horn sounds, the bird sings, with no concern for the rumbling that swells all about him, balanced on a slender branch, facing the rising sun.

16.
Blackie's Notebooks (VII)

✎✎✎ Clockwork's gloating is ridiculous. He *thinks* he knows. A writer, an artist, has sworn to disappear, to deny forever that he might once have "lived" (sic) by proxy, through acts he has not committed but that he might have wanted to do—or, conversely, through acts he has committed but that he might wish he *hadn't* done. And now, with the pretext that uneasiness, ambiguity, and confusion are disturbing honest souls, I'm expected, out of the blue, to give in to pressure, to award stars, to gratify with a no or a yes—in short, to settle my own hash. A likely story! When my goal has always been not to count chickens, or draw up a balance sheet but, on the contrary, to flow inexorably into a system rendered infinite by its implacable logic. . . .

Take the year following Mama's death in Vienna. The amount of time it took me to figure out an escape, to accept the idea of resurrection.

I dealt with my ties to Hermann. I told him so. (Well, almost, for after the passionate years of freedom that followed—perhaps the only time I would ever feel truly alive—came Dora, to blackmail me into reconciliation, illness, and death's temptation. . . .) But there was still Mama. In the blind euphoria that follows life's dramas, I thought I would escape the harsh grief that had previously assailed me. My sorrow remained abstract, closed up inside a bubble of untouchable malaise. . . . Indifferent torpor soon gave way to an emotion that I attempted, with all of my mind and body, to analyze and reduce to an appropriate or, at least, justifiable

104

feeling. For several days I was unable to eat or drink or sleep or write. I would be hard put to say what I *did* do. My attachment to my mother left me in a stupor from which I would emerge for demented moments only to be plunged into fearful anxiety. Sweating, cramps, delirium, a broken heart. . . . Until the morning when I got up, half-conscious, and looked at myself in the mirror on the back of my bedroom door. I was haggard, unshaven, uncombed. I ran my hand over my face, through my hair. I recognized myself. And then the image of my naked body appeared, and it didn't startle me excessively. My rumpled clothes were scattered around the room. I looked about. Within me, silence had returned. And all around me, the vacuum was slowly filling once again with familiar forms and things. Within reach. . . . Tired and red-eyed. A teeth-baring grimace for a smile or inspiration. The better to remember by. One is alive. Here. To agree. To see onself from the other side of the mirror. Neck craned. Arms held slightly away from the body. The hairy chest, looking firm, but trembling, because behind the forest, enemy troops are on the march. Ah, the call of the senses! My hand caressing my stomach. All the muscles stretching, from head to foot, from thigh to nape, from groin to fingertip. Skin pierced by wild features. I stop dreaming. Leave the nightmare. Life rises from my lower belly. It rears up, resists briefly, quivers, and at last emerges from the imprisoning matrix. I massage. Gently. Head thrown back. Eyes open. Toes reaching toward the center of the earth. Let me take root! Bury myself in the present. Everything in me is vertical. To feel, to know that I can move without fear of falling into shadowy abysses. I forget my childhood, the past, force my way to the point of no return, from where I can look back. Forgotten are the butchery, blows, blood, the sanatorium, the mountain . . . yes, even the mountain, where there were only shadows, only attempts to mimic a state of shock, of grace from which I was wrong to expect miracles. What happened to me that day, before the mirror, my body in desperate plight, my limbs and head wrenched with mingled fatigue and pleasure, was far worse and far more beautiful. Life seized me in every pore. I exploded, annihilated. From now on I belonged to myself. And in a long gush of semen I hurled myself fearlessly, unreservedly, into the unknown.

Examining my body had always been a sort of occult rite that I held as one of my deepest secrets. Observing a hair, a crack in the skin, the bend of an arm or leg, the folds of my belly or penis, had always been part of a daily exercise I performed, without really knowing why. It was theoretical, rigid, forced, affected. Now I knew that Clockwork's beloved *ego* had nothing to do with vague palpitations or ideological giddiness. No, it was the law of blood. Visceral heat. The weight of the genitals between the legs was enough.

When I lost the person who had until then been dearest to me, I found a balance I never had before. And I prepared to live a little, for as long as I could. Yes. I was going to live so intensely that with every passing hour, every event, no matter how insignificant—did I have even a chance?—I would catch myself saying that I was happy after all. That was also the time, remember, when the novel I'd written at Semmering was accepted by Goldstein, the Berlin publisher. Maximilien had suggested taking me there to submit it; I sent it by mail. I let Max go alone, promising to join him if the opportunity arose, if my book was accepted for publication. I waited for the letter that would either wipe out my newfound confidence or give me the strength to continue on the route I had traced for myself—with such anxiety! It came. . . . At last I would be able to emerge from my shell and experience, if not success, then at least some payment for the days and nights of toil that had cost me so much, body and soul. My friends would be able to see firsthand that my life had not been an empty web of words. (I will try, if possible, not to say another word about my father until circumstances force him to reappear, to beleaguer and pollute my thoughts.)

In the evening, I usually found Maximilien leaving the university, where he was giving courses in the history of religion. He was able to supplement his salary from the newspaper and, more important, provide a context for the articles he was writing. His reputation was starting to grow among those who counted as the intelligentsia of Vienna in the early 1920s. I was still a humble scribbler who hadn't yet proved himself. I had a lot of ground to cover. . . . Maximilien dragged me once again to the cafés I'd abandoned before the war. The atmosphere was no longer quite so carefree (they were having too much trouble bandaging their wounds), but the incomparable charm of this Viennese Mecca seemed intact, with rituals that not even the worst disasters seemed to interrupt or change. To please Maximilien, I also agreed to attend some Zionist meetings with him. The speeches, the excerpts from books, the precepts left me cold, but I was interested in the discussion for its own sake. Then their association organized an evening of Jewish popular songs which I attended, somewhat nervous and edgy, but still not unhappy to give in to the music, to mark the beat of melodies joyous or sad (always beautiful), clapping or stamping my feet with the rest of the audience.

Mornings, I would go to the newspaper. By eight o'clock I was at my desk, where I read the insipid copy, correcting, rewriting, cutting here and there. Because the articles I was asked to shape lacked any genuine meaning, I treated my work as a sort of free-for-all which couldn't cost me too much. There was no apparent relationship between my work as a writer and the "writing" I was playing with here. I just had to keep cool, know where to place my bleacher for a good view of the show, while remaining distant from it. A sidestep situation. . . . I didn't notice the subtle effect of maintaining such diffraction: Underneath exchanges, accumulations, permutations, seesawing motions, clusters were buried—far too deep to be visible to the naked eye, but no less real for that, as I would learn later—a little too late.

I spent the afternoons writing. In theory. That was what I'd promised myself, the plan I'd drawn up, the procedure that had seemed, when Maximilien proposed it, to make sense and be totally gratifying, providing an enviable balance between my job and my vocation. It was quite straightforward. Almost too much so. Because, following on the heels of my first fumbling efforts—and nourished by the fact that some of my stories were published in the newspaper—came the bad habits, the truancy, the vacuum.

Everything would have been perfect, miraculously arranged, if the problem of writing hadn't cropped up again (certainly not for the last time) as acutely as ever.

I needed desperately to write, because I felt that I *could* write. This was when the words chose to escape me, leaving me lax and insecure, without respite. My time at the office—and this was the big problem—consoled me falsely, because my confidence disappeared as soon as I faced a blank sheet of paper, returning once the proofs, black with printer's ink, were delivered to my work table. . . . Endless process, no way out. In the afternoons, after a lunch that I cut short, made as frugal as possible all in vain, I would sit exhausted until sweating, aching, dog-tired from sitting still, unable to write a few lines, even a few words, I would lie on my bed. There I'd muse and dream in hopes of creating visions I could write down, but they took flight the minute I tried, to be transformed between my numb fingers into dark phantoms I could see only as formless shadows, as washed-out versions of what might have been said.

I would rush in despair out to the street. I walked, I haunted the bookstores where new titles made my head swim, then I would escape to the parks, only to be driven away by memories. Finally I would seek out Maximilien, the balm of friendly words, the warmth of familiar places. But still, there was the night, all the nights. . . . My last hope, which I would follow up during the hours of sleeplessness, was that the gloom might turn out to be more merciful, more commodious to the secret movements of creation. During that period I was never more aware of the strange romantic deception of belief in the power of shadows. . . . Oddly, with the passing years, the night would prove to be the optimal setting for my anguish and exaltation. Exhausted, with pains shooting through my heart and lungs—sharp aches that forced me to straighten up and catch my breath—I struggled against the headaches that more and more frequently accompanied my nightly journey while I slowly wrote books that were never published. When at last I fell asleep, I would be stormed by dreams that left me in the morning with a bitter taste in my mouth, as if they had washed away some essential substances, and I would never know what they were. I remember, once dreaming of my father, and waking with a start just as he was preparing to stick a big knife in my chest.

Fortunately, Maximilien would draw me from these dread miasmas, though he knew nothing about them. For during the day I worked conscientiously, with no sign of the night-time horrors I would undergo. And this dearest friend was the opposite of me: He was positive, aggressive, self-confident. It was good to be around him and knew I could rely on him absolutely. If the day ever came when drastic measures were called for, I knew I could count on him. Goldstein announced the publication of *The Hollow Man*. Maximilien offered to come with me to Berlin, as he had to see the correspondents of *Der Zeit* and meet some colleagues from *Aktion* in Vienna. "Afterward, we could take a side trip to Paris," he said. "A vacation," he said enthusiastically. "We've earned it." He arranged all the details, especially at the newspaper, seeing to it that I was given leave.

During this happy detour I would forget about illness, nightmares, and failure, and clutch instead at other illusions. Even if Berlin and Paris did not provide the salvation I craved, I could test out my brand-new armor by exposing it to the bursting life in the two capitals. I would write nothing at all, aside from a few paragraphs (or "poems," as critics and posterity deemed it proper to label them), really very little, in any case nothing compared with the fever that was seething inside me, a desire for tangled worlds, exploded suns, bare ruins, illuminations, the constant attraction of languages— fleeting visions of an organic whole. Little enough, but it was something compared with my helplessness in Vienna. My compulsion to write was becoming painfully evident, and not in my spare time but according to a fixed schedule. Waiting for the afternoon, with no surprises. Hoping for a weekend, without disappointment. I was being transformed—and I realized it but didn't know how to stop the terrible process—into an official writer.

What irritated and exasperated and completely exhausted me was the absence of a woman. I'm not talking about abstinence, which cost me little more than some healthy itching; no, I mean *absence*. After my mother's death, all women—Cosette, the ones on the Kärntnerstrasse, the ones at Semmering—disappeared behind a dense fog curtain, where I left them, impervious to the entreaties of their graceful passage, their flimsy dresses, their airy footsteps, their heels clattering on the paving stones of the old streets. In Berlin, I would discover another kind of woman—a new-world woman would draw us out of our paralyzed frames and invite us to act at a speed swifter than impulse itself. The era of the waltz was over, long live the jazz age! And I would discover the embodiment of this renascent woman, Milena, on my return to Vienna. Milena, who would make me feel that I was striking out in space with the force of lightning; Milena, who would wash away flaws and blemishes, who would guide me through the maze of new passions; Milena, from whom I would learn again, who would teach me again (before the fall) about living and creation. . . .

Berlin, the Berlin of the 1920s, was synonymous for us with regeneration and hope. How different from Vienna, which had fallen, after the war, into a sort of stunned doze, as if still blinded by the past! The prevalent mood was no longer one of sensual pleasure, but of atonement and guilt. My generation of young Viennese intellectuals was fascinated by Berlin. Maximilien had described the action there, talking excitedly about all the innovations that would overthrow traditional criteria, providing wide-open prospects for the sensitive men and women who, until now, had been kept within borders always thought to be impassible. How do you describe the impulse that carries you along and convinces you, from the start, that you must possess the present? I expected the impossible, but did not dare believe in the sudden burst of hope that arrived at just the right moment, to comfort my brand-new state of mind. The least I can say is that I wasn't disappointed.

We arrived to the clatter of streetcars and automobiles. The streetcar was common here, whereas in Vienna it was still a somewhat disturbing sign of modern times, outnumbered by horse-driven hackneys and berlins which were not then the picturesque relics they would later become. The buzzing of the central train station. The commotion of the streetcars, the sight and sound of motor-driven taxis humming impatiently . . . all the way to the pension where Maximilien would get off, which was swarming with artists, students, journalists. Berlin gave an immediate impression of a crossroads for new and visibly nonconformist ways of thinking. I wasn't quite at that point, as you can imagine, but the warm welcome I received intoxicated me. They knew my name, they had read my work, they hoped to hear me speak. I was a member of the brotherhood, even a privileged member.

Goldstein, my publisher, had arranged for me to give several talks to mark the publication of my book. I was surprised and told him so: I had nothing prepared, and felt quite incapable of holding my own for more than five minutes before even the most attentive and most kindly disposed audience. The written word came to me relatively easily, almost too easily while breaking free of the crises I mentioned, so that I had to be constantly on guard against it. Until then I'd always written in a sort of burst that enabled me to work up to a considerable rhythm and performances that I knew were unusual—I wrote ten or fifteen pages in a stretch, and I didn't need to reread or correct, but let myself be guided by an intensity of purpose I had meditated on earlier and at length. But speech was forbidden ground. I was barely capable of stammering some incredibly awkward prepared remarks that always left my audience in a state of embarrassed expectation, as if they were unwilling to admit that a writer could be such a bad speaker. How could I transmit, reinterpret, go over what had already been expressed in a worthy form that stands on its own? Repetition could only send the work veering off into the void.

Goldstein insisted. In the end I agreed. I was so pleased at his enthusiasm for my book.

"You must show me more, the rest, all the rest," he said, clapping me on the shoulder.

Goldstein was a typical Berlin publisher. He was fair and looked a bit like Richard Strauss. A Jew like most of the people I met at the pension, the newspaper, in literary cabarets, a Jew like me and unaware of the perils beginning to awaken in the still bland depths of the Germans' clear conscience. He would burst out laughing when he heard the word *Kulturbolschewismus*, which the right was starting to use to stigmatize and even harass everything that came close to the new sensibility, whose fertility I valued. *Kulturbolschewismus* included, helter-skelter, Jews, Communism, nonconformity, free love, and the artistic avant-garde. Goldstein was what would be called today a happy left-wing intellectual, open, brilliant, incisive, jovial, a *bon vivant*—but naive.

"Come now, my friend," he said to encourage me, "surely you can come up with something to astonish these puffed-up Berliners who think they know everything and have nothing left to learn! Stay away from the classic debates on psychoanalysis and literature, or the avant-garde and creation; they won't listen to that anymore. No, tell what it is like to be a writer today, in Vienna, in Paris, New York, or Honolulu. No more rhetoric! Go straight to the heart of life, show them their own weaknesses, suggest a little less smug certitude and self-importance, and a little more truth. . . ."

"But I put that in my novel."

"All the more reason. . . . Anyway, don't worry, everything will be fine. Right now, let's enjoy ourselves. We won't waste your visit here. We'll dine at the Schwanecke. It's amusing, you'll see, everyone's there, people who will heap praise upon you or run you down, without really knowing why. You must appear in public. I'll introduce you to a couple of influential critics. Today it's not enough to have written what I consider a masterpiece, you have to pay in person, go fishing for friends, use every wily strategy to make people notice you. It doesn't matter what they say or think, what matters is that they talk about you, that you're on the firing line! Courage! We'll go to Schwanecke, then we'll have a look at the nude revue on the Admiralpalast. It's splendid, you'll see! Tonight you're my guest—and Berlin is yours!"

At the restaurant there was an indescribable crush. Handshakes, congratulations, condolences, hugging, hand-kissing, murmuring, shimmering, altercations, scrimmages, friendships, jealousies, proprieties, smutty stories, opportunities, subterfuges, caresses, unraveling, equivocations, toasts, addresses, speeches, snickering, winks, inopportune greetings, pranks, exchanges of fine remarks, of fine behavior, weighty silences—it was all there. Goldstein knew I was uncomfortable in these noisy, glittery surroundings where I didn't know all the rules and laws, and he went out of his way to make matters easier by doing most of the work himself. I was in his shadow and asked for just one thing: that he keep performing, that let me alone, that this dinner—excellent, actually, but for my inability to enjoy it—be over as soon as possible. One event too brief for my liking interrupted this babble. Goldstein waved Karl Kraus over, saying that he wanted to introduce his new "discovery." In Vienna, I had always hoped, without succeeding, to meet the famous poet and satirist whom I so admired, both for his newspaper, *The Torch*, whose position on compromise and decadence I agreed with, and for his play *The Last Days of Humanity*, which I considered the most radical work of the postwar period (in it Kraus denounced, with a courage and pugnacity I envied, everything I hated: war, money, the army, corruption, the rotten press, every form of contemporary lying). I wanted to express my admiration. I stammered something, he replied amiably, and I was grateful that he didn't interrogate me or pretend to know who I was or what I wrote. From his expression, from the way he shook my hand, I knew at once that Kraus was the real thing. What was he doing with this bizarre crowd? That's another story. As is the account of how I finished off the evening with Maximilien. My friend had arranged to meet me in a small cabaret on the Tauentzienstrasse: He'd been to see Cilla de Rheidt at the Admiralpalast, and I knew he didn't want to get involved in my duties with Goldstein—or perhaps he deliberately left me alone and helpless in a cage with wild beasts, as if it could serve as an ordeal or purification rite.

Nonetheless, I was happy to see him as I entered, sitting at a table in the wretched little smoke-filled room where a magician was putting on his act. The audience applauded, and I took advantage of the distraction to slip over to his table. The magician disappeared. The curtain rose and an orchestra bathed in soft lights started playing soft, languorous music of a sort I'd never heard before. Maximilien poured me a glass of champagne and urged me to describe my evening so far.

I was about to describe Kraus when the brass played two resounding staccato notes. Six girls appeared on the stage, as an impersonal voice announced through a loudspeaker: "The Fuzzy Girls! The sexiest girls in Berlin! Performing here exclusively, straight from New York!" The sight of six almost naked bodies—sequined panties and brassieres—had me dumbfounded. You never saw anything like that in Vienna. I knew that America was sweeping Europe and that in Berlin, especially, everything cultural from across the Atlantic was viewed as the sacred expression of a new world still healthy and pure. And that was my state of my mind when I arrived in the Promised Land some fifteen years later, only to learn very quickly that the terrors, the apocalypses I was fleeing, had taken refuge on this continent as well.

The next day Goldstein had arranged to meet me at a boxing match where some American champion was to fight. The newspapers were full of the event, and seats fetched huge prices on the black market. Goldstein was full of incongruities. But when I told Maximilien, he said I shouldn't be surprised: Being progressive was synonymous with being athletic. Indeed, at the pension I'd noticed that the boys wore odd-looking trousers that came to mid-calf and ended in a bulge of fabric they tried to make as puffy and conspicuous as possible. I discovered they were golf knickers. I was still sorry I'd accepted Goldstein's invitation, because such spectacles horrified me. Jack or Jimmy, whatever his name was, would turn out to be one of those big oafs Hermann was so fond of. As the Fuzzy Girls started to sing, kicking up their legs under our very noses, Maximilien sold me on the popularity of sports: The next morning, after my talk, we would go to the swimming pool. I agreed to, happily, for it was one activity I didn't scoff at: I loved to move through the water, where I could feel my whole body working, alternatively flexing and relaxing. I'd just expressed my pleasure to my friend when my eyes locked on one of the Fuzzy Girls, the second from the left. I couldn't say why she seemed more beautiful or more interesting than the other five, who had the same sculpted figures. To say that Lili, or Carlotta—I don't exactly remember her first name, though I know she wasn't American, but as German as her sisters—to say that Lili, let's call her that, possessed a flawless beauty would be an extravagant trick of memory or senses. Her body was endowed with every feminine enticement, but there was something intriguing about her face, as if the makeup didn't altogether conceal the uneasiness I thought I discerned in her eyes. I felt, at once, ready to do anything to get close to her, to know her, to love her. No doubt my reaction stemmed from certain reflexes typical of people like me who, in those days, considered such occasions a chance for slumming, as we used to say, a way to justify a condition, a sort of adequation. The strength of my reaction was probably the result of excitement brought on by slumming. At that time, men like me found great satisfaction and justification in situations like these. I usually despised and rejected that attitude and should have avoided falling into the trap. But I knew at that moment that meeting her was the only thing to do. It was as if Lili had turned up just when I needed her, a perfect example of the woman-as-object. I usually found that icon horrifying and repugnant, but this time I was snared by this raw sexuality that justified only itself. The streets of Berlin were filled with tempting sights. Women had changed, greatly. They wore tight skirts to their calves, whose curves were accentuated by stiletto heels that replaced the old-fashioned low boots. Apart from the strictly sensual excitement this produced, I saw a sort of poetry, difficult to define, to grasp, in these women with their short hair and cloche hats, smoking American cigarettes in endless holders. In the bars. . . and in the streets, during that spring of 1924, their slender silhouettes wrapped in short, clinging fur-collared coats . . . their long necks glowing with sparks from chunky multicolored necklaces . . . and Lili fit the model perfectly.

In the gaudy easy virtue of the time, Lili became my mistress that very night. The circumstances of our meeting were so typical that anyone could have invented them. But the few days the affair lasted warrant an exploration of the memory, somewhat blurred but still capable of enriching these notebooks with some authority, some truth.

And so I experienced the unique combination of health and disease that characterized the lush times we lived in. I spent my days in the company of the intoxicated and intoxicating young crowd discovering the attractions of radio broadcasting, flocking to swimming pools, tennis courts, sailing and rowing clubs, as well as to dance halls: cinemas, theaters, exhibitions of painting and sculpture, avant-garde performances, even taking to the air, where Zeppelins were streaking across all the skies of Europe. With Goldstein and Maximilien I went to vernissages, expressionist shows, literary receptions, editorial offices. In apology for having dragged me to a boxing match, a torment I endured with a less than ecstatic expression, Goldstein took me to Josephine Baker's *Revue Nègre* and to Hasenclever's play *Der Sohn*, which had been running successfully for some years. He thought highly of it, as a sign of the young generation's rebellion against the tyranny of their fathers, who had led them into the butchery and slaughter of war. Goldstein said:

"The subject is right up your alley. You'll like it."

To my great regret I had to admit, after the show, that I didn't share his enthusiasm. I was right to be wary of the antipaternal literature then in vogue. The fathers were too dirty, too spineless, too vaporous. I told Goldstein, without worrying that my sharp reaction might lower me in his eyes.

"Don't you think it's ridiculous for the father to have a heart attack at the mere sight of his son waving a revolver under his nose? In real life, I suspect these people are more sturdy, harder to knock down."

"I thought you were fascinated by the theme of parricide."

"Yes . . ."

"Didn't you say in your talk that you consider the expressionist Georg Heym a great poet?"

"Because of one sentence. Which he wrote in 1911, a year before he drowned: 'I would be a great poet if it weren't for that pig—my father.' His wish was never granted. . . ."

"Anton, I don't understand you. You're so baffling, so unpredictable, always looking for punishment!"

"I can't help it, I've never liked the sort of art that consists of saying shit to people who then applaud you because their pleasure is in their own destruction. There are better ways to rebel. . . . But that parody of the evil father is too pathetic, too melodramatic. . . . I want the discipline of blows dealt, not to the most sensitive parts of the body, but to those that offer the most resistance. Otherwise there's neither rebellion nor art."

I had taken a position, on principle, supporting all forms of modernism then breaking the taboos and rules of art and society. At the same time, although I drifted along with the exhilarating superficiality produced by the isms of the day I personally didn't feel involved. I was alone, in the background, following nocturnal imperatives.

Yes, the night . . . the night was purposeless and fascinating. Post-theater, post-performance, post-pretenses, post-speechifying . . . with Lili. I would call for her at the cabaret, then she'd take me to some run-down dance hall and drag me into tangos or fox-trots, new dances she tried to teach me, that left me demolished, exhausted, entranced. When I touched Lili's body, her skin, her arms clung to me like an octopus, her belly writhed against mine, and I could feel myself in a new body, a new skin, with arms that assumed different poses, with a belly no longer driven wild by the heat of frenzied rhythm. I threw myself wholly into a mad race for pleasure, where Lili and I indulged in excesses I didn't know I was capable of.

Lili didn't give a damn about my speechifying, my *a priori*, all my sentimental and sexual evasions. She laughed, laughed. And her laughter would bring me to her couch more readily than the most persuasive argument, the boldest theories or the most subtle specters of my past inquiries. And Lili wouldn't let me go until I was exhausted. Destroyed.

Dancing gave her a natural freedom of movement that could take on any combination or position, without seeming either complacent, venal, or perverse.

At night, Lili would draw me from my daytime lethargy (broken only by outings to the swimming pool) into the false illumination of her spotlights like a moth that flings itself, wings beating, onto an electric heater. I took pleasure in letting myself be burned. Not content with giving my body everything hers had to offer, Lili wanted to introduce me to the very particular circles she moved in, which were beginning to take over Berlin.

"You're being ridiculous," she would say.

I could boast of having seen a fair amount already—in Vienna, in Semmering, or in my imagination—but it was nothing compared with the films being shown in the German capital. Lili seemed so familiar with them that I wondered if she'd taken part in some of the pornographic scenes I found so fascinating and repugnant. "Made in Hollywood," the posters declared in English; but the most sought-after were those marked: "Special: Made in Germany," where I kept expecting, as I looked away from a curving breast or leg, to see the sensual mouth, the open thighs of Lili. . . . Those rapid, jerky movements of the films, sticky and damp with silence. The entranced bodies shook all the more vibrantly, abrupt and violent, because their movements occurred in luminous silence. The absence of the sounds of lovemaking turned these erotic spectacles into depictions of action much like the athletic events in the newsreel playing before the movie. Like the rest of the audience, Lili seemed scarcely affected by the actors' quaint motions; she savored muscular rites and gestures that resembled the sprinter's leap from the starting block or the diver's plunge from the six-meter board. Lili thought sex was healthy, not beautiful. And the minute we crossed her threshold she stripped down, all set for her own version of similar exercises. I hardly had time to ponder the philosophical implications of this new cult: Excited by the revels on the screen, I would throw myself at my dancer for a ballet in which it mattered little that the positions had been decided in advance.

During those few days I asked myself no questions. Only later, half asleep during the journey from Berlin to Paris, was I haunted by the thought of venereal disease. I'd heard some rather alarming remarks in Berlin about fresh outbreaks that could of course be traced to the recent moral liberation. But I didn't even think of my dangerous slide, every bold or excessive act. I knew, for instance, that Lili saw other men. This didn't provoke my usual jealousy; on the contrary it added spice to a liaison I knew from the start would be especially transient. On the other hand, I firmly resisted anything that seemed like a call to group activity. Once or twice, Lili took me to parties that gave me the shivers. I went along with current fashion and took some cocaine, but merely shut my eyes when Lili briefly disappeared into the next room, where I knew some very bizarre ceremonies were taking place. Don't think unhealthy timidity or misplaced decorum had me in an eternal clasp! I didn't abstain for moral or religious reasons that would bar certain forms of sexual activity. No, my appetites had led me, rather, in the opposite direction. In fact, I think I alluded earlier, without actually describing them—would it serve any purpose?—to certain exotic practices at the sanatorium. To tell the truth, I was familiar with this stuff; it held no surprises for me. What I had with Lili was a sort of preparation for what I unconsciously felt coming: Milena. . . .

As for Lili, she would tailor her behavior to what she thought were my desires or peculiar habits, depending on my mood. She had no illusions about me—how could she?—but took what she could from an experience that, though it wasn't unique, at least had the advantage of introducing her to a sort of man she'd rarely met. I had no illusions there; I knew I was material for her to examine, as much a subject for reflection, an object of pleasure, as she was for me. To a certain extent it was a perfect agreement, a providential meeting. But overall I didn't think so when I came home from Berlin.

Everything was on the verge of collapse, it's true. I had finally learned how to make many of my aspirations direct and concrete. Sometimes muted, assuming the most varied forms, they culminated in an image of liberty incarnate. There, against me, upon me, within me, were burnings, attacks, outrages, deviations. People were breaking free of old precepts, restrictions, half-measures. Hypocrisy was in retreat. The field was clear. On with it!

And yet I felt an irrepressible loss. I had everything that I could wish for, but the ultimate effect of this acceleration of time, this agitation of space, this tangling of forms and thoughts, was merely discomfort, diffuse suffering, an odd suffocation. As if behind the luxuriously lit facade there were secret fissures, and crevices, hidden abysses. . . .

More than expressionism or the Bauhaus, which I could view objectively, more than all the other artistic and social expressions of the time, my malaise was fueled by the cinema. It confirmed my loneliness and distraction. One film in particular, which I hadn't been able to see in Vienna, marked me deeply: Fritz Lang's *The Cabinet of Dr. Caligari*. The 1830 fun fair in that movie became for me the fair that was Berlin of 1924. Cesare, the sleepwalker, was me, Choucas the jackdaw. I saw myself killing the student—the one who enjoyed certain liberties with Lili—abducting a young girl (Lili, or was it already Milena?), and then being taken prisoner, condemned to die of exhaustion as indifferent spectators looked on. Unless—as happened in several dreams (at the time, or since?)—I was Caligari himself, escaping from prison and taking refuge in a lunatic asylum! An asylum of which I would become the director! Too ironic. . . . But I didn't know then that far from Berlin, far from Vienna, there existed in flesh and blood the brilliant inventor of Caligari, of Cesare and of Anton Blackbird, alias Choucas. The madman who described the director of the asylum as a man with Caligari's features bore a strange resemblance to Dr. Clockwork. He *was* Clockwork!

Beneath its joyful surface, a wonderful world was working its own destruction.

I had a single respite from this lengthy mild vertigo: rereading Lenz—*The Soldiers* and above all *The Letters*, an old edition I found in an antiquarian bookshop on Budapester Strasse, only a few steps from the famous Romanische Café where Goldstein kept dragging me. Lenz, dead in Moscow, exiled, in total financial, physical, emotional, and intellectual misery. Deranged, mentally ravaged, and destitute.

Maximilien and I arrived in Paris, at the Gare de l'Est, on June 4, 1924. The day after Franz Kafka's death in the sanatorium in Kierling. I found out on the train, through a brief article in *Der Zeit*, which I'd bought before leaving Berlin. The death, virtually unrecognized, of the man I considered to be the greatest writer of my generation.

(There's one for Clockwork!)

We spent a week in Paris, a city that in many respects reminded me of what we'd just been through across the

Rhine. No need to cover Montparnasse or the surrealists or the museums here (oh, but the Delacroix in the Louvre . . . *The Massacre at Scio, The Death of Sardanapalus!*), or the publisher Goldstein had persuaded to bring out my book in French, or the nightly parties that took off at a rate we could have continued nonstop, if we hadn't been so broke. The ransom for all this life and novelty was incredibly high. Maximilien and I had far exceeded our budget and dipped deeper than we'd expected into our savings. Goldstein had given me a fairly substantial advance on the first printing of ten thousand copies of *The Hollow Man* (which at that time was considerable), but I prudently transferred that money to my account in Vienna. I wasn't a man who worried about tomorrow, and I'd always believed in living according to the impulse of the present, but at the time I was dicing with fate. Squeezed between a past that refused to be mollified and a future that had to be built upon a very unstable present, I had to prove that I was a genuine writer, from a strictly professional point of view. That was the first step. The rest, all the rest—struggle, assault, climax, the marriage and divorce of words—couldn't be touched or cashed in no matter what happened.

Of Paris, three episodes stand out: Cosette, the landlady from the rue Haxo, and walking through the neighborhoods of the Commune.

Cosette, of course. I hadn't forgotten her. How could I find her in the teeming city? Of course: her father. His name was still famous, I hadn't forgotten it, and I had no trouble getting his address. He greeted me courteously, I explained who I was, that I'd known Cosette in Vienna—though I didn't confide the extent of that knowledge. He told me she had married, but that I could reach her at an address which he jotted on a sheet of letterhead from the Ecole Normale Supérieure. After some commonplaces about my trip and a few questions about the political situation in Austria, he showed me to the door.

I wrote a brief note to Cosette. Without going into too

much detail, I asked to see her, requesting a prompt reply sent to my hotel. I didn't wait long. The next day I received an equally laconic response suggesting we meet that afternoon, in a tearoom on the rue de Rivoli.

Cosette hadn't changed much. Physically, I mean. For as soon as she came in I could tell from her clothes, hair, and makeup, from the way she moved and greeted me, that she had become another woman, totally different from the one I had known. Cosette had settled down. She was married to a provincial deputy (I don't remember what province he represented, but it was one of the great wine-growing districts), had abandoned her studies and career, and spent most of each year on her property. She told me, with a smile I found a trifle too chilly to be genuine, that I was lucky to have found her, since she rarely joined her husband in their Paris apartment, once or twice a year at most.

Our visit was not uncomfortable, but rather empty. I didn't push it, observing with growing bitterness that any attempt I made to bring back a shred of the past we shared was neatly sidestepped by Cosette, who had become a virtuoso at parlor chitchat. Beneath the veneer I still sensed her quick-wittedness, pride, and independence, which hurt me even more. Had I been so wrong? I didn't want to accept the facts; I didn't want our past, my love, reduced to an ingenuous, naive illusion; I was denying that my early thoughts, actions, and emotions hadn't been serious, solemn, or honest! I refused the evidence, refused to play the part of the reasonable, healthy adult separated from events that, in the end, are unimportant. So I took the initiative and cut short the awkward tea which I regretted having set up. Cosette would have been glad to keep chattering, to envision herself in an amiable social dialogue. Delighted with my success, she asked me to send her an autographed copy of my book. I promised to, but in fact I never did. . . . Perhaps it was true, maybe she was right, and I was only foundering in the smug and morbid tricks of old loves.

But I wouldn't find the answer to that question in Paris.

Cosette's ghost was replaced in my imagination by yet another upheaval. A woman, again, and this time I would let myself be utterly seduced. . . . Along the way, I have to point out some details that, to me, are practically meaningless, though I know people have always asked me about them. I don't think I was ever particularly handsome or particularly ugly. The origin and development of my relationships with women, throughout my life, have always been anywhere other than on the well-marked grounds of charm and seduction. I honestly feel that is true for most men and women. So you won't find special privilege, exotic or romantic effects, here: only the ordinary forms of life, and if their accumulation suggests that there was an extraordinary experience or a deceptive account, shine a bright light on it and it will prove unquestionably false.

So this was exactly what happened with the owner of the hotel on the rue Haxo. She was a woman close to forty. Despite her full figure you could see that in her youth she must have been beautiful. An oval, fine face, sparkling eyes, a broad mouth, satin skin. Delicate features. Her neck was still slender, though the prominent ledge of a stiff bodice revealed that the same was not true of the rest of her body. Huguette was divorced and lived with her two young children. The eleven-year-old boy and five-year-old girl were the most fresh and mischievous children I'd ever met! The boy would insult us every chance he got; he called Maximilien and me "dirty Huns," which a clout by his mother didn't silence. And the other clients came in for a litany of offensive remarks too. His sister had the disconcerting habit of grabbing hold of what men's flies were supposed to conceal, whenever she could. And try to make her let go! Maybe she picked up this unfortunate practice from her mother. For Huguette was a specialist in lusty jokes. As soon as we arrived, she insisted on giving us some samples from her repertoire. (Imagine which ones. . . .) She wasn't vulgar, no, that's not the word; on the contrary, she emanated a typically Gallic sort of health. There's a word the French use which sums her up perfectly:

rigolote. But I was really taken aback on the very first morning in the modest room where breakfast was served. She greeted Maximilien and me with a particularly salty joke. I wasn't sure when to laugh, wary of any tricks my French might play on me; it was good, but no match for Huguette's Rabelaisian refinements! But as if to confirm her story, she came up to us, whispered something in Maximilien's ear, laughed heartily, sat opposite me and pretended to grab my penis, saying: "The naughty boy! He's been having dirty dreams again!"

And she laughed! Once our initial surprise had passed, Maximilien and I would laugh whenever we talked of it. It became a ritual. Daily. Now with Maximilien, now with me. But it was my room that she entered one night, without warning. . . . I was impotent. I should have just regretted what was, after all, a minor incident, a chance mishap, but my inability to have a bit of fun, *rigoler,* upset me far more than my failed reunion with Cosette.

Having said that, and without being grumpy (how could I be?), Maximilien and I were happy with the hotel, which we had heard about from a journalist in Berlin. Located in a working-class neighborhood in the east of Paris, its prices matched our tight financial situation. And even though we were far from the splendiferous center of Parisian life, we had the privilege, yes the privilege, of visiting the important sites of the Commune. Père Lachaise, the Mur des Fédérés, Belleville . . . even the rue Haxo itself, where—Huguette had told me, in bed—the last barricade was taken away from the people of Paris during their massacre by the Versaillais. Thanks to our walks, and our long discussions of history and politics, we recaptured some of the elation that had stirred us in Vienna before the war. I took advantage of it to reread Kropotkin's *Memoirs.* Maximilien wanted to introduce me to Vallès, whom he admired, but I didn't like what he told me and the little that I read of *The Insurgent.* Too didactic, too mechanical. For me, literature need not *become* militant, it *is,* by definition. . . .

Ah, Vienna! Yes, I was starting to miss Vienna. I who

prided myself on my internationalism, I who had greeted the prospect of this journey so fervently, I who had seen in the amazing ups and downs of this escapade a sort of symbol of the radical change that could extend even to my personal life, here I was caught in the futile net of vague melancholy and homesickness.

I longed to get back to work at the newspaper. As if the late-night proofs were a drug I couldn't do without . . . unless, as I hoped, I was swept away by the desire to resume my writing. But for that, for my second published book, Milena was responsible. My entire body, and all my energy, were even then reaching out to her.

17.
Clockwork's Notes (V)

A. is infecting me.

He's turned everything upside down. Every which way, back to front. Or else his way of fitting things together, his personal sense of order, is beyond me. . . . Can it be? Is he trying to mislead me, or simply to lose himself? What I'm really asking is this: Has Blackie cooked up this mess deliberately, or unconsciously? The answer will determine the verdict, a diagnosis of writer or madman. . . .

I look for references. I'm wary of clues that seem too easy. I know Blackie won't miss a chance to pull what I call his "Kafka syndrome trick."

At first I was dizzy and constantly thinking about it. For ballast, I reread all of Kafka. I noted in *The Metamorphosis*, *Amerika*, *The Trial*, and the short stories any details that echoed something Blackbird had said. In the *Letters* and the *Diary* I did, in fact, spot certain names and phrases that seem to have rubbed off on the author of the *Notebooks*. But that's all. They're very different. Once you get past the harsh style, you realize there's a whole world separating the two men, the two writers. And it helps to know that the name Blackbird conceals Antoine Choucas. . . .

Maximilien might be Brod. Okay. But Stefan, Hugo, Robert, all the others—who are they? Kafka means Prague, not Vienna. But Vienna is synonymous with K.'s Milena. The real one. While for A. She is actually Vera, the Hungarian or whatever. . . . But we'll find that out later. Maybe.

You'd have to be blind to miss the cross-references, the connections. But it's also true that only a panic-stricken insect bangs into doors that are shut or painted in trompe l'oeil. A. was able to take me in, to string me along with his little tricks, but at least I know now what masks he wore for his comedy.

K.'s *Diary*, which I've scrutinized, possesses a number of passages that I'm certain A. would be happy to pass off as his own without batting an eye. Old devil! But who's copying whom? I just have to cite one passage (don't worry, only one)—for an example, to show that I know what he's up to, as an instant reminder. And I have forgiven myself for the lapse, since it's only the result of an innocent desire to understand Blackbird's writing.

"Max's objection to Dostoyevsky, that he allows too many mentally ill persons to enter. Completely wrong. They aren't ill. Their illness is merely a way to characterize them, and moreover a very delicate and fruitful one. One need only stubbornly keep repeating of a person that he is simple-minded and idiotic, and he will, if he has the Dostoyevskian core inside him, be spurred on, as it were, to do his very best. His characterizations have in this respect about the same significance as insults among friends. If they say to one another, 'You are a blockhead,' they don't mean that the other is really a blockhead who has disgraced them by his friendship; rather there is generally mixed in it an infinite number of intentions, if the insult isn't merely a joke, or even if it is."[*]

A joke perhaps, a mixture of intentions certainly. Exit Kafka, then. Before I even started making these notes, I knew the digression was hardly worth the trouble, but it was like a crumb in my throat I had to worry, to get out, if I was to feel entirely free of it. I will be more thrifty later on.

There remains the salt in the story, the bite of the insult, the sting of the invective. I say, "That's right, Anton, you're crazy." Then he laughs at the good joke I've just made till the tears come, and replies, between hiccups, "What about you?"

[*] From *The Diaries of Franz Kafka* 1914-1923, translated by Martin Greenberg, Secker and Warburg, 1976

18.
Blackie's Notebooks (VIII)

🐦🐦🐦 I'm afraid. Memories erode, my clear-headedness grows suddenly dim and stares at itself, appalled, while the words that might define it flee. I fear I no longer know Milena. Or I know too well how tempting she can be.

How many months, how many days of life do I have left? Will I have the strength, the courage, the time, to explore the period of my life that was the most surprising and concentrated of all? In spite of all my work, I should settle now for some other disguise. Not to mislead Clockwork, or play with modern ghosts, but simply because this time I don't want to distinguish between the actual events and the visions they inspire in me, visions that never ceased. Splinters of my life float in them even as they blend permanently into this opaque narrative. I am afraid because, for the first time since I began this journal of my life, I am repeating a situation I suffered when I was a novelist, one I have tried to forget. To turn not only me but Milena as well into a fictional character disturbs the serenity I thought I had in this asylum. But I see that an account of these events, even a fragmentary one that moves too quickly through the eternity of time past, could tear me from its embrace. What still hurts is the knowledge that I will only betray Milena again. I seem to take some perverse pleasure in rushing to reconstruct the labyrinth where I lost her. . . . I know full well that I'm tempting fate, that I'm sliding into the madness I've done my best to ward off. The stakes are high, but I'm willing. I've agreed to share the same life as Garry, Snuffie, Pat, and Linda, but not to retreat from the ordeal at the last minute, to face the death I constructed to my own specifications. I have to sort out why, whether through lassitude, through cowardice, through contempt or holy madness. . . .

Our first meeting took place on June 15, 1924, a few minutes before noon, at the newspaper, where Milena held a senior editorial post. My junior position had not allowed me to meet her until then, but I'd noticed her, when she came down to my cubicle once or twice to settle some detail concerned with proofing copy just before deadlines. I had been struck by her determined look, by her free way of moving and her ambition. Along with her spirit and resolution, she had a very feminine beauty and sensuality that were enhanced by her hair and dress, which stood out in that very masculine setting. At the time it was unusual for a thirty-year-old woman to be assistant editor-in-chief.

So I was surprised when she sent for me on my first morning back at work. She asked me to come to her office at noon. I wondered what I might have done wrong. Was I going to lose my job? Were they going to fire me because I'd taken off for several weeks to roam through Germany and France? The newspaper didn't need parasites. It wasn't a charity for failed writers. . . . I could already hear her and pictured myself silent, blushing, not daring to meet her intense gaze, head drooping, ready to dive under the chair, ready to quit, to acknowledge all my faults, to plead on bended knee, to pray, to die of shame. . . . In this state of mind I knocked reluctantly on Milena's office door a few minutes before the hour, minutes I hadn't been able to endure in front of the wavering lines of copy on my desk.

"Come in." The voice was firm and sweet.

"Ah, Mr. Huka." (There was a pause that seemed to last for hours, while I felt she was literally undressing me with her eyes.) "I'm delighted to meet you. Do sit down."

I thought she was making fun of me, shamefully savoring her victory and her superior position, and I found myself stupidly reproaching her, cursing all women who owed everything to their husbands' influence. Like everyone else at the newspaper, I knew that the banker Joseph Weiss was one of its principal shareholders. To the small-minded, I among them, this fact said worlds about the abilities of his wife, Milena.

But then, to my great surprise, she said in a warm voice that left no doubt as to her good intentions, "I've read your book, Anton. It's extraordinary. . . . I'm glad I trusted you instead of listening to the poor fools here who had no idea of your literary skills. You are surprised—is it what I say, or how I say it? Well, you haven't heard the last of my words, dear man! And I'll have you know that I was the one who *insisted* your short stories be published. The influence of your friend Maximilien alone wouldn't have been enough—far from it! He explained everything to me—that you need time, financial security, and independence in order to write. And I understand your not wanting to debase your talent, even if it means staying here, doing relatively menial work. Am I correct?"

I stammered something incredibly stupid about the condition of the artist and the impenetrable paths of creation. I was making a fool of myself.

Milena smiled. A straightforward smile devoid of affectation, but still elegant. She was an exceptional woman, it was quite clear. Even Cosette didn't have her unique way of investing an ordinary conversation with so much conviction, and power to seduce, without ever making you feel that she was granting you some privilege, yielding an inch of ground, or tolerating any harebrained ideas. Milena was the real thing.

"As for your job, no problem," she said, "but I'd very much like to have a few pieces on your trip to Berlin and Paris. With no restrictions. *Ad libitum.* A *writer's* pieces. . . . Will you do them?"

I was beginning to gather my wits, fascinated more than impressed by the behavior and look of this woman. The distinction is subtle, but important. . . . I agreed to her proposal, outlined what I would say about Berlin (sports and culture, health and politics, creativity and decadence) and Paris (I thought one article on the neighborhood of the Commune and another on daily life in a small working-class hotel).

"Fine," she replied. "We understand each other perfectly. I'm not interested in a particular literary or artistic experience, or society news that others have already reported. I'm interested in *you*. Yes, you."

I noticed then, with growing confidence, that she was marking time as she pretended to examine the stacks of files spread out before her. She was slightly flushed, embarrassed at the vehement tone of her last words. The words blurred in my mind, so that I could not distinguish clearly between her personal unease and her interest in some new form of journalism. It doesn't matter, the fact remains that Milena had, consciously or not, caused a remarkable innovation, one that would change the direction of my career and my life. The articles created a furor: sales of the newspaper rose considerably, and they generated massive enthusiasm for *The Hollow Man* and resulted in personal glory that allowed me to give up my job as a proofreader and devote myself entirely to writing. In this respect, as in many others, I owe Milena almost everything. She not only ran my articles in the newspaper once a week, she also encouraged me to write my second novel, the one that would make my reputation.

But on that first day in question, she pulled herself together after her momentary agitation and said steadily:

"Come, let's celebrate over a good lunch. And we can continue our conversation."

She took me to the Rauchfangkehrer, a traditional old gasthaus just five minutes from the newspaper, at the corner of Weihburggasse and Rauheinsteingasse, the dark and narrow street in which Mozart had died at number 8 (I couldn't help thinking of him, imagining him in the harsh winter of 1791, dancing an impromptu minuet with his wife in order to get warm, to forget hunger and ill fortune). I had never been there before, perhaps because of the crowds that flocked there, or prices that were previously beyond my means, and no doubt too because of my lack of interest in food. That day I did uncharacteristic justice to a huge plate of goulash and even enjoyed the pianist playing some fashionable jazz tunes. Milena chose goose with cabbage, which she insisted I taste. I didn't recognize myself as I went along with it, and even joined her in a pastry feast. I don't usually play word games either, but I must admit that it was as if I'd rediscovered an appetite for life and now was digging in! Milena was responsible for this sudden intense appetite—Milena with her hunger and thirst for life, for free words and actions. She had swept me from the hollow of the wave up to the crest of renewed hope and inspiration. She laughed and talked enough for two. Elated as I'd never been, I even told her stories, of Goldstein and Huguette. She laughed, but for once I knew that I could keep going, that she wouldn't make fun of me, that her laughter was honest, without ulterior motives. From the very outset, she invited me to share all my secrets, to bury the past, turn it into raw material for my literary work, for what she called my destiny.

We washed down our lunch with a great deal of wine. And my fears about the bill—I didn't know how I could pay it— evaporated when Milena regally asked for the tab and signed it, reminding the maître d'hôtel to have it sent to the newspaper. He nodded, with a businesslike "Of course, Frau Weiss" that completely relieved me. To tell the truth, I didn't really understand what was happening. It was all so unexpected, so instantaneous, so baffling. I wasn't used to such attention as a writer, or to such solicitude from a woman—and what a woman! As we left I panicked again. What should I do? Throughout our lunch, it seemed to me that Milena had surpassed the bounds of simple courtesy, and her lively interest in me had quickly taken on the appearance of a regular courtship. But she had taken the initiative and given the directions; and I was far too impressed to display the feelings and sensations that everything about Milena aroused in me.

She was everything I had dreamed of. It was too good to be true, but it was happening. She was beautiful, as I've said, but I don't want language and memory to misinterpret her, to suggest some sort of ideal, fatal beauty. No, she was an attractive woman, like many others. What made her unique were her intelligence, her vivacity, her panache, her self-assurance. Milena didn't play on her physical attractions; they were there, that was all. She never gave in to the slightest weakness of the woman who wishes to be desired. Unlike many women of the time, who sought approbation or gratitude, flattery and praise, who feigned helplessness, fragility, and susceptibility to being conquered, she behaved in a completely independent manner, asserting her personality, which was to be taken as is, with no fuss or complacency. I had loved or thought I'd been in love before, as you know. But I was overwhelmed with desire for Milena. I say desire, because love is a very feeble word to describe the storm that took hold of my entire body and mind. I may have experienced passion earlier through preconceived notions, ready-made ideas, relying on a meaningless syntax. With Milena, to speak of being thunderstruck would be to say that thunder and lightning are mere physical phenomena that can be explained and identified. To say that I wanted to possess her would be equally false, equally limited: how could I imagine "possessing" a woman when everything about her showed that she could never be possessed by anyone or anything?

On the sidewalk outside the Rauchfangkehrer I didn't know what to do. Should I suggest that we continue the conversation, should I follow the instinct that told me Milena, too, would like to spend the afternoon with me? Or was I being swayed by my incorrigible imagination? I was about to suggest that we take a walk, not daring to consider a visit to my apartment, but I told myself in time that undoubtedly a woman like Milena would let me know if she wanted our meeting to develop beyond merely good professional relations. And I'm glad I did, because she held out her hand and, looking me straight in the eye, said:

"I'm going back to the newspaper. Work hard and don't forget, I'm looking forward to your first article! I'll see you tomorrow night, after the editorial meeting, and let you know then how we've defined your new duties. You'll be able to fit in a drink with me between paragraphs, won't you?"

I agreed eagerly, and she shook my hand. I noted then that contrary to the custom still prevailing among Viennese women of the best society, she did not wear gloves. The touch of her soft, warm skin was electrifying. I probably held her hand a little too long, for as I recovered from my rapture I could feel her pulling it free. With one last smile she said, "Au revoir," then disappeared into the crowd on the Graben.

I headed home on foot, trying to get my wits back during the long walk. But when I got back, my mind was still in turmoil. I opened my bedroom door and threw myself on the bed, overcome by excitement I thought would lead to a familiar fit of crying. Not at all. On the contrary, I suddenly felt calm, breathing freely in a peaceful rhythm that filled my whole body with comfortable warmth. I got up, slowly undressed in front of the mirror, peering at the part of my body each garment unveiled. And once naked, I took a long look at my reflection, then went right to my desk and sat down, not to get up until well into the night. Ordinarily I would have masturbated.

The next day Milena met me at the Museum Café. I gave her my first article, which I'd entitled "The Lights Go Out at the Berlin Fair" and subtitled "When Will the Fire Rage?" Milena read it through silently. When she had finished, she laid her hand on mine and simply said, "Thank you." Then, with her arm around my neck, she brought her face close to mine, until her lips grazed my own. That night, Milena became my mistress. And so began a liaison—why must I put it so stupidly!—a passion that lasted five years and was extinguished only when a powerful and devastating counterattack had been launched by criminals we could not reach or control.

All Vienna was quick to learn that Milena Weiss had found

a "new lover." I didn't gave a damn what they said, or if they marked me out for jealousies, bitter remarks, and sly snickers. I was well aware that I was neither the first nor the last; Milena was determined and open about the freedom she intended to preserve. And I wasn't jealous. I should have been: Everything forced me in that direction—my own nature, my education, even my somewhat old-fashioned notions of love. But I was incapable of feeling such a narrow, imprisoning, suffocating sentiment with a woman who was like fresh air, a source of endless coolness or like a living torch burning with the oxygen she avidly inhaled. She wasn't worried about the ripples that stirred the fetid, stagnant swamp of public opinion. Milena taught me, above all, to laugh at "What will people say?"

One day, though, Maximilien came to see me, saying: "Anton, I must talk to you."

From his tone and expression, I knew at once what it was about, and I almost sent him packing. He stopped, with his hand up, adding:

"I know, I know . . . you do as you like, and that's fine with me. But be careful, Anton—what I'm going to say has nothing to do with idle gossip. After all, if Weiss the banker can make cabaret singers rich, it's not a bad thing. No, my friend, I want to talk about something completely different. About you. I never see you anymore. You pass me like a comet, and I wonder if you still control your own trail. Look at yourself. You've lost weight again. You're pale, gaunt, haggard. How long can you go on like this?"

"Till the end," I replied.

"Yes. To the end. What are you waiting for, to get sick again? You're working like a madman. Till the end of time? You see what I mean."

"Maximilien, if you don't mind . . ."

"I know, it's none of my business. But I was the first to encourage you to write, I always knew that you'd be a great writer, and I'm worried. Things are going too well, too fast, Anton. Will you be able to hold on?"

"I don't give a damn. You don't understand. Listen."

And I told him then about the fever I'd been living in for some months now, with Milena. I told him almost everything. How at first I'd been literally "stunned" by Milena. I'd been frightened, very frightened, like a child in the presence of an animal preparing to throw itself at him. Petrified, I had waited for the Amazon warrior to charge, and I'd allowed myself to be taken. The first time, yes, the first night, I hadn't escaped the vise that still held me and heartbroken, I found myself impotent. If my penis had been torn off, mutilated with a knife, the suffering would have been no more intense. But Milena realized that she was pushing too hard, and she reassured me. It was she who taught me, with timely words and gestures, that love was not a test of strength, a combat from which a victor and a victim must inevitably emerge. Milena taught me equality.

Calm moves from the outside. And on a bed of ferns, the heat expands on either side. One wing flutters free. A beak has bitten, tenderly. Behind the foliage is the rustling breath of spring. Nearby, a stream gushes and its purling forms a symphony that accompanies the caresses of the entwined lovers. The forest folds in upon itself, the vines embrace, and giant flowers open, offering bursts of perfume to the air, which is set aflame with all its millennial gold. All is life.

"Do you understand?"

I don't know if Maximilien did understand. But he never badgered me about my seemingly real life again, at least not until the climax of the storm that was sweeping me away. And Maximilien was the first to come to my aid when things went wrong, to understand me without a word, to help me without sermons or reproaches.

"Yes, I understand."

From that moment, I knew how it would be. I could count on him alone. Everything, everyone else, was pandemonium, a huge joke, a *rigolade* as the magnificent Huguette would say! Maximilien's next question was about my work in progress. I smiled and clasped his hands. He understood. That was why, later, I could appoint him the trustee and incinerator of my "posthumous" writings.

I was then in the final stages of my novel *Death of a Desire*. I confess that the subject originated with Milena. She thought Adalbert Stifter was one of Austria's greatest writers. I too admired the author of *Indian Summer* and *Witiko*, admiring the granite purity of his style, but not as much as Milena. Stifter's notions about beauty and humanity seemed naive to me. Milena urged me to reread him. This reading did yield something different from the first one: His writing was dominated by an intolerable sense of propitiatory terror. It was fascinating! In context, the author's own life was surprisingly interesting. When I gave Milena my impressions she said:

"Why don't you write about Stifter? There's a need for a good biography of him. And it would help you take stock, have a close look at what you want to accomplish with your life and your writing."

She didn't realize how timely her words were! I set to work on the life of this man who was born in Oberplan, Southern Bohemia, on October 23, 1805. Soon I was deep in his childhood and adolescence and had no trouble reconstructing the main events. Adalbert had lost his father at age twelve, and the quest for a father that runs through his work inspired me to develop themes that because they touched me so closely, proceeded beyond the evidence provided by the facts. It wasn't long before I was identifying with Stifter too closely to confine my efforts to a conventional biography. I put myself in the place of the thirteen-year-old who had gone to take refuge and study at the Benedictine Abbey in Kremsmünster. I became the student in Vienna who had to support himself by tutoring young society girls. The young man who was forced to break off his engagement to his childhood friend Fanny Greipl was me. And was I not the man who hesitated at the gateway of life between painting and literature? It was I who married, in terror and confusion, the little milliner Amélie Mohaupt, who despite my desire for paternity, could not give me a child. She had a child from her first marriage and tortured me by pointing out that it was I who was sterile! And my pain when that child died, who wasn't mine but for whom I'd developed a boundless affection, as if he were my own. . . . I found myself able to confront and express things I'd never dared before that I knew were buried within me, that Milena's presence helped me reveal. But after three months' work I came up against an obstacle I couldn't pass, although I tried many times. Stifter was a writer, granted, and his intense struggle resonated for me and informed what I wanted to say. 1848 was where the block occurred. I wasn't too interested in Stifter's political equivocations, his uncertainty about what side to take in the face of national revolutions and loyalty to the Empire. The wretched man became a school inspector, in the service of Metternich's pedagogy—very discouraging! So I got bogged down in digressions, emerging from them for only a few more successful passages, such as the long flashback in which I set out to retell—or should I say to reinvent—an adventure of the adolescent Stifter, when he and some friends traveled down the Danube from Linz to Vienna on a raft.

I told Milena of my problem. On that late December afternoon, I remember, we were walking in the gardens of the Belvedere. It was very cold. Milena had taken my arm and we walked close together, huddled in our furs. In the distance, on the heights of Leopoldsberg, we could see great expanses of fresh snow. The wind was icy, as it often is in Vienna. But we walked briskly and our animated conversation took the place of physical warmth.

"I can't do it, Milena, I simply can't. Stifter's eating me alive. He's taking more out of me than *The Hollow Man.*"

"Yes, but in that book you lied a little, didn't you?"

"Yes, yes . . . but don't you realize, he almost forces me to take his place. When his own words are insipid, I catch myself putting words in his mouth, trying to say what he couldn't or didn't dare express."

"Exactly! His contradictions, his hesitations, his lyrical illusions! You have been there, haven't you?"

And Milena started to laugh, a long cloud of mist escaping

from her scarlet mouth. She knew she was hurting me, but she knew as well that I needed to confront my ghosts. She was pushing me somewhere I had always refused to go. At those moments my heart filled with rage and resentment. I don't know what I would have done to her. The urge to strike her . . . But Milena had taught me that such desires, too, could be turned to another purpose, that intimate violence wasn't something to banish with shame, but a delicate fuel to be used with circumspection and dexterity. The first time, I was horrified when she asked me calmly one night if I would whip her with my belt.

"Tie me to the bed. Tie my hands. And above all don't listen if I cry out or weep or ask you to stop. Do as you please. Only one condition: no questions, not a word. Silence. And the last blow must be struck between my thighs . . . but only the last one."

I want to set one thing straight immediately. Milena was neither a nymphomaniac nor a masochist. I have every reason to believe this. She was a woman. Like any other. Except that she never walled off her desires from her actions. Her way of loving had nothing to do with what was then called lax morals, with approval or disgust. Milena couldn't have cared less about the fashionable dictates from Berlin or across the Atlantic. She wore her hair and her skirts short, but that was just fashion. In general she kept an amused distance from stylish dictates. No, Milena simply loved. She loved as I have always dreamed of it, with no restraints, unceasingly. Every moment, every breath of air, every beat of her heart was love. Descended from a good Catholic family in Linz (where Stifter came from, in fact, and she gave me many details about it), she had been able—just in time, as she liked to point out—to shake off an education others might accurately call excellent. Milena, too, had come to Vienna to study; we probably sat on the same benches at the university in Cosette's time. One day I told her I was sorry I hadn't known her then, and she replied:

"But don't you see, I would have had to put up with you as long as I did my husband!"

It is not the right time to talk of him, the banker Joseph Weiss. When the time arrives I'll say what must be said. For now, briefly, Milena met him when she was finishing her education, and, goaded not by ambition but by her taste for pleasure, which she had consciously decided not to curb, she took him as one of her lovers. And when she discovered she was pregnant and not too certain who was the father, she stopped resisting the proposals of the banker, who, though a good ten years older, would no doubt be the best possible father and provider for her child. Nothing cynical about it. Milena told me everything. She neither gloried in the event nor pitied herself, let alone regretted it. She could have raised the child on her own; she was prepared to make any sacrifice, do anything necessary. "No matter what," she told me, "I'd have made a life for myself. I decided to become a journalist, but that's not why I married Joseph. For Marie"—that was the name of her daughter, who was a little older than six at the time—"if I had to—and despite the corruption surrounding us—I'd have acted as if everything were normal, I mean the fact of having an unmarried mother. But then there were my parents. My father and mother, who had finally accepted me completely, even as they prayed for my folly or sins. Until then, I'd only driven them a little deeper into their religion or, at most, during one or two violent outbursts, almost incited my father to curse me. But they still loved and were proud of me. Deep down they knew I was right. My father kept telling my mother, not to console her but because he truly believed it, look, our daughter has done what neither of us—especially me—was able to do, and so don't worry about whether or not she succeeds in the unlikely career that she's chosen. What's important is that she is being herself. Because he failed as a violinist, my father spent his whole life as an inspector in the music schools of Linz. Yes, like Stifter. . . . No, I knew it would kill them if I became what they called in a terrified whisper an 'unwed mother.' So I set myself that one limit. I wouldn't be the cause of the only sorrow I knew they'd never get over. I decided to marry Weiss. But on one condition. The deal I offered him, that I forced him to accept, marked the end, forever, of our liaison. I would never again belong to him, restoring my freedom, my total freedom. Joseph probably thought he could make me reconsider. Nothing of the kind. But I give him this: Although in every other aspect of life he thought his money and power could buy anything, he has never tried to make me break our contract. He knows who my lovers are, and how many. He knows that I love you, Anton. But that has given him no right to control my life. You know, he had nothing to do with your position on the paper. I fought for that on my own. He's always trying to cut the ground out from under my career. I've worked hard to prove my competence, and if I hadn't, the men running this contraption we work in would never have let me through. They would have liked to grind me under their boots at the first chance, at my first sign of weakness."

Milena didn't give a hoot about malicious gossip, especially what was being said about us. Only one thing drove her wild and brought out her claws: If anyone dared to insinuate that without her husband . . . then the claws came out in earnest, as I saw myself one night when we were having supper after attending a performance of Richard Strauss's *Rosenkavalier*. Milena was expressing somewhat strongly her lukewarm reaction to the opera, and an influential old drama critic sitting at the next table said to no one in particular, but loud enough to be heard by most of the room, "Ah, women! Think they can get away with anything nowadays! Especially if they have a powerful husband to protect them!"

I saw Milena's face freeze. She was livid. Before I said a word she rose and headed straight for the man who had spoken. I thought she was going slap him, but instead she dug her fingernails into his face, severely scratching him. Taking advantage of his surprise, and of the silence that had fallen in the restaurant packed with a holiday crowd, she shouted at the petrified man, "That's what a woman can do nowadays! Especially when she has a protector!"

The critic began to howl in pain, and probably from spite as well. He took his napkin and theatrically wiped his cheek, where, as a matter of fact, a few droplets of blood now stood out. Before he had time to provoke a widespread riot, Milena had paid the bill and motioned for us to leave. . . .

But back to the Belvedere. Milena had pushed me ahead of her and started racing to the exit.

"Come on, get moving! It's freezing!"

I ran up behind her, delighted to see her leaping and shouting with joy. But when I caught up with her on the sidewalk, I was overcome by a violent coughing fit that took my breath away and lasted too long. Milena gently patted my back, saying tenderly:

"Now, now, what is it? Dear Anton . . . is that better? My love . . . take a deep breath . . . I love you, Anton . . . here, let's go to your place; it's freezing out, you'll catch cold."

Until then I'd never dared to speak of my illness, which, though it seemed to have disappeared, was still at work inside me. Milena, without knowing it, had observed the signs.

At my place we made love in front of the fireplace, where we had lit a big fire. It was long and intense, live a lava flow that left us flat on the floor, side by side. When, as usual, Milena tried to arouse me again a few minutes later, her efforts were in vain.

"You're tired . . . you work too hard."

No reproach in her voice. It was the first time in months that I'd been unable to respond to her caresses. I said nothing, but knew that work had nothing to do with this; it was the first sign of my reawakening illness. The logical continuation of my coughing fit. . . . I pretended to ignore the pain I expected to return to the base of my rib cage, on the left. I dressed silently. Milena, wrapped in a heavy blanket, was sitting on the bed.

"Will it bother you if I smoke?" she asked, lighting a cigarette without knowing the ironic content her question had for me.

"No, not at all," I replied in a falsely casual tone, sitting beside her.

"You know," she began, "you should drop that business of the school inspector. Why don't you simply write the end? You know, the suicide and everything. . . . Once you've done that, I bet you'll be able to write the blocked section."

"That's an idea."

Indeed it was an idea, and for almost two months it cast me into one of those crises I thought I was rid of forever. If Adalbert Stifter had been truthful, what about me? But this time, probably because it took a while for the catarrh to start up again and because Milena helped me with all her persuasive power, I won. During the first days of spring I'd written about the death of Stifter, who had slit his throat rather than face slow and horrible death from cancer of the liver, undoubtedly one of the finest pages I've ever written. But there was that hole in the middle, gaping like an open wound on the flank of my unfinished account. How would I fill it in— and must I do so? I was casting about for a solution when my cough became so pronounced it was impossible to hide the truth from Milena any longer.

Her reaction was totally in character. But she put so much heart, so much of herself into it, that my passion for her soared. Calmly, as tears poured from my eyes, she said:

"You must be looked after. We'll stop everything. We'll go to the mountains. You'll see, it will be beautiful. We'll love one another. I'll show you where I come from, we'll go to Oberplan, you can see Stifter's birthplace, and it will give you the inspiration and the strength to finish your novel." (She used the word "novel" as if it was quite obvious that the biography had been changed into a culmination of my limitless anguish. And indeed it was. For in the calm of Marienbad where we went to take the waters, on the other side of the Bohemian forest, on the Czech side of the mountains, in the place where I was born, I completed the final chapters of *Death of a Desire*, dropping the school inspector and writing instead about the suffering and happiness of a writer. And the writer was Anton Huka. Now that the book has disappeared (unless some curious or tortured soul has unearthed it in the

back of some library and presented it to the eyes of the world
as a treasure of some vanished civilization), I'm sorry I wasn't
familiar then with Franz Kafka's diaries, which I read much
later; otherwise I would have used the following as an epi-
graph: *"The sweetness of sorrow and of love . . . Always only
the desire to die and the not-yet-yielding, this alone is love."*

Death of a Desire was published in September 1925. The
novel was a success. Milena (and Goldstein too, I'm not forgetting him!) worked wonders to give it a good launching. She
wrote the strongest and most perceptive observations that
have ever appeared about my work in *Der Zeit.* Although
certain dusty historians have felt they had to "reveal" our
relationship in their studies of me, she did nothing for me out
of kindness. She spared me no criticism. Her criticism! It
went straight to my heart, to my belly, my lungs, my genitals,
it pierced my whole body with arrows that were not poisoned,
but showed me the pain of voluntary martyrdom. I was invig-
orated, far more stimulated by them than by the splashy
praise.

The journey to the mountains had been good for me; it had
given me strength not only to finish the novel, but to get
through the feverish period before my book was published
relatively unscathed. Once the excitement of facing the public and critics had passed, I found myself again at the gates of
winter, with a fresh bout of symptoms. Nothing violent, but
the muted, sustained, regular, oppressive presence of disease.

Milena was still there, of course, and our love was as strong
as ever. I knew from certain subtle signs that Milena had two
or three affairs that allowed her, no doubt, to forget for a
couple of hours the intensity of our relationship. Our thirst
was so great, our ardor so strong, that I understand quite well
how she might need to quench her thirst at a fresh spring,
take a few sips of new water before plunging back into the
stormy sea that continued, unabated, to hurl us against and
into one another.

Needless to say, all sorts of envious and petty people kept

* Kafka, *op. cit.,* page 740

trying to sow trouble between us (yes, we'd become a couple, not in any traditional, institutional sense of the term, but in the sense that we couldn't live without each other—nothing could come between two people who had given themselves utterly to one another, body and soul). Once a brave hack whispered to me unctuously:

"Did you hear Milena Weiss is a lesbian? Somebody saw her French-kissing a little redhead in a beer hall near the Prater."

I couldn't drum up the expected reaction. On the contrary, I was certain the story was true. That was my Milena, the woman I loved.

Milena did all she could to make me forget my lungs, to force me to live as if nothing had changed. She successfully brought me to love at a pitch, a delicious intensity, that surpassed the ravages brought about by germs. I remember Christmas night—no not that night; Milena's one sacred principle was spending Christmas night with Marie, her little girl, whom I'd met no more than once or twice, for she thought it unnecessary. She was probably right, it would have been enough to make me want a child with her someday. It was later, on New Year's Eve, the eve of 1926. Maximilien had invited us to his house (he was the only person in Vienna who fully accepted us together). We ushered in the New Year with forced enthusiasm, as though we knew the night was damping the last fires of our youth. I'm speaking for Maximilien and myself, of course. Milena lived for the present. It was as if, without having to say a single word to one another, we realized simultaneously that we'd turned a corner and now were heading downhill. We were over thirty. He was an established and recognized university professor. I was a famous writer. Having reached the top, we were amazed to learn that on the other side of the summit there were more peaks, many more, as far as the eye could see. The race was far from being over. I think we wanted to know what fissure, what hazardous rock face, what deadly glacier, what trap would ultimately kill us. That night our only answer was booming laughter, lively table talk, and childish jokes, punctuated by numerous glasses of champagne. Milena, however, suspecting something, was able to intervene in time to tilt the good humor we'd donned for the occasion into out-and-out madness. When we kissed, as the last stroke of midnight sounded ponderously from the big bell of nearby St. Etienne's Cathedral, she cried out:

"Let's have a carriage race!"

We sped to the Heldenplatz, where, despite the late hour, we knew there would be harnessed horses. I had taken Milena's hand and breathlessly did my best to keep up with her frantic pace. Maximilien ran beside me, egging me on. My body was inwardly shaken by painful spasms and laughter.

Finally we got to the horse-drawn cabs. It took some time to persuade the drivers to go along with our mad impulse, but a wad of bills from Milena's purse convinced them. Maximilien chose a lean, well-muscled chestnut; Milena insisted on a dapple-gray whose powerful hindquarters augured well. She took the reins with determination, and I sat on the coachman's seat beside her. Still muttering but amazed, the owners of the cabs sat in the back, where the passengers usually sat. Maximilien drew up beside us, and Milena handed me her white scarf for the starting signal. I stood and waved it above my head. The whips clattered. We were off! I was thrown off balance by the lurching movement and fell heavily onto the seat, one hand clutching the reins, the other Milena, who shouted, "You're crazy! Look what you've done! You'll make us lose!" After we turned right onto the Burgring—for we'd decided to take the ring road all the way around the old city— Maximilien had gained slightly on Milena's cab. The horses were just trotting, for we knew we had to pace them carefully. Their rhythm was steady, and as we were passing the Parliament, Milena said, "Let him go on with his Arabian. We'll catch up with him later." This seemingly accurate decision took me by surprise; she wasn't usually so restrained, so prudent. At the time, I said nothing, abandoned myself to the pleasure of driving along a deserted boulevard on this cold and festive night which the Viennese had chosen to spend indoors, in restaurants or their homes.

"Aren't you cold?" Milena asked.

"No, no."

"Here, take the coach blanket. Cover yourself up."

Milena's soothing words concealed our shared anxiety. As if this absurd, irrational race was a good way to exorcise our everyday fears. Besides, she was having fun. I loved to hear her laugh as we rounded a curve and she leaned toward me, her whole body swaying as if to guarantee that the cab could maintain speed and direction without slowing down. We lost sight of Maximilien's carriage, which had disappeared into the darkness of the broad Schottenring. Then, as we were descending the slope to the Danube, Milena, using the whip with surprising dexterity, speeded up even more. The dappled horse straightened his neck, mane drifting in the wind, and I could see his hindquarters stiffen, shudder, and respond to the driver's call.

I looked for the black water of the canal. By straightening in my seat I was finally able to catch sight of it, and briefly forget the object of the race that had us speeding along its banks. I glimpsed the distant acid moon gleaming on the surface of the shadowy abyss that always made me inexplicably uneasy. I was probably the only man in Vienna who had never responded to the so-called poetry of that artificial arm of the Danube. A stinking stump that reeked of poisonous fumes. Bowels of death, hallway to hell. . . . A brisk neigh roused me from reverie. Our horse sensed his nearby companion. By the light of the street lamp I could see Maximilien's cab some fifty meters ahead of us, its lantern swinging wildly from left to right.

Milena shouted in my ear:

"Hold on tight. Remember, I told you. . . . Watch out, here we go!"

And she whipped her horse into a gallop. Behind us, the coachman yelled, "Hey, what's going on? This wasn't part of the agreement! You'll kill him! We'll crash!" Milena said nothing, kept looking straight ahead, staring at the goal she'd promised she would reach. I turned and tried to reassure the fellow with a smile. He was clutching the post that held up the roof as best he could.

We were gaining on Maximilien. Now I could clearly see his back, guiding his steed expertly but with restraint. He must have heard us catching up, because he turned and waved. Milena just cracked her whip again and again, and, the dapple-gray galloped even faster, pulling the carriage at full tilt with much jolting and creaking of axles. At the Aspernplatz we were practically abreast of Maximilien. Side by side, wheel by wheel. Just as we turned onto the part of the Ring that would lead us to the Stadtpark, Milena saw to it that the two animals were flank and flank. Then, attempting the impossible, in a reckless and potentially disastrous move, she suddenly swerved right as she came out of the turn, cutting off the chestnut, which, with Maxmilien holding him back, had to move aside—neighing, nostrils foaming—to make way for us. I said nothing. Nor did the coachman. Everything was happening too fast. Milena had launched us on an insane course. We couldn't possibly understand it or even imagine the outcome. It was better to be silent. To listen to the night, the speed of the wind, the clatter of a chariot from hell. I was enthralled. Milena too, but for a different reason. She suggested the race, so the goal was to win. My own victory came from trusting her completely, forgetting her even as she was displaying the vital dictatorship of her presence. I was beside her. Elsewhere . . . it all had to end. With an accident, a wound, a kiss, a smile, even death. . . . I wasn't even thinking about it. Today I tell myself it would have been better if we had ended there, arbitrary, impromptu. But no, we still had to mimic death, to follow the trails blazed by the living dead who are never exhausted by imaginary races.

Several lengths ahead, we passed the monument to Johann Strauss that had been unveiled just a few days before. I turned and saw that Maximilien no longer accelerated. It was as if he'd accepted defeat—unless he was fed up with the dangerous game which, a few moments earlier, had nearly cost us so much. Besides, the horses were tiring. Their breath melted into the icy air in broad spirals. And Milena, who must have realized that she had slowed down too, slowed to a steady trot that felt like the calm following a storm. I was about to tell her to spare our horse, but it was unnecessary. On the Schubertring everything seemed back to normal, a lighthearted outing for bold night owls. We passed or met three or four other cabs traveling scarcely faster than ours. But I knew the respite would be brief. We had arranged to meet at the Opera. If Milena was giving her dapple-gray a chance to get back his strength and wind, I was sure it was only to improve her own chances once she was on the straight line of the Kärntner.

I looked at Milena. Her hair had come down, I mean the braids she'd deftly arranged at the front of her cap of hair had come undone, so her enraptured face was surrounded by wispy sparkling curls. Her little nose was pinched, not from the cold but, as I could see, by a sort of pleasurable tension that contracted every muscle in her face and body. She was rearing, stamping impatiently, vibrating with the hooves that pounded the cobblestones. She followed the steady rhythm of her horse with every breath and internal shudder. She no longer guided him with the reins, she was out front, bracing herself to pull the carriage and maintain speed. She was a mare, a filly, beastly and thoroughbred as I'd never seen her before, not even at the most intense moments when our bodies met. I caught myself feeling jealous of the dapple-gray, whose rump streaming with sweat seemed to fascinate her, her eyes riveted on the movements of the skin, betraying her deep excitement. Muscles, flesh, blood, lymph . . . scalding sap, stirring in the hollow of the testicles, throbbing against leather straps, murmuring, sudden grunting, fingers' pressure, clenched fists, shuddering belly, aching groin, open thighs, moist and tensile in contact with the cold, the dark, the unknown. . . . Milena did not belong to me, never would belong to me. How could I have thought, have dared?

The life she lived, her share of humanity, was precisely what was missing from mine, and my own, conversely, was probably unknown to her. What odd coincidence had brought us together? Or did our bond, stronger and deeper than it appeared, have its roots in this radical difference. . . .

I laid my hand on her arm. She flinched as if it were a red-hot iron. She turned her head and stared at me blankly. Then suddenly her expression relaxed and she burst into strident laughter. I didn't know if it was a sign of that bond or, on the contrary, whether it delineated the terrible precipice that still came between us. Without giving me time for questions, she flung an arm around my neck and, drawing my head toward hers, kissed my mouth with such violence, such intensity, it hurt, and left a taste of blood on my tongue and gums. When she loosened her embrace and got her breath back she said: "All right, watch, this will be the real thing!"

How I wish it had been "the real thing"! But when she said it she wasn't thinking about the same thing as I.

We accelerated again. Between the bare branches of the trees I was able for a moment to catch sight of the gymnasium. On that night in particular I wished I could recapture the order of memories that often came, piecemeal, to remind me they hadn't disappeared. To go all the way back to the school in Prague, Oscar, the race through the forest, that other race and the self-discovery. . . . But no, everything was tangled together in my mind and before my eyes: the boulevard, the back streets of the old city, bridges, gardens—a labyrinth where contradictory feelings isolated the past from the present . . . and the future, which I could sense close at hand, immediate, swept up at the speed of the wind, beneath the wheels of the carriage, then striking me again like a boomerang, against the tide, inopportune. . . . Time speeded up. I knew now that years could pass by at a dizzying rate and no deed, no breath, no act—not even an irreversible one—could assuage their passing. I was carried along. And the chariot tumbled down hills, lances at the ready for repeated, signature acts of aggression. War had been declared.

All that remained was suffering, death—or flight. Milena uttered her battle-cry. And the troops flung themselves into the
assault.

Horses harnessed, plumed, led vigorously to torture. Exotic massacre. Vision clearing. The gates part. In surge
sounds of rifle cracks, bugle calls, the muffled thump of
drums. On stage, blaring music of destruction. I disintegrate.
Take shape in the tableau that floods my eyes. I am an actor. I
am myself, in a picture dripping blood. And everything roars
in my ears as if wild beasts were hurling themselves, claws
exposed, at my naked body exposed like an offering. I need
only seize the moment, fix for eternity the curdling present.
Sickly, exhausted, drained, stretched out on the ground,
trampled by hooves, uprooted by the fury of the elements, my
chest bursts. And the woman, her bodice indecently exposed,
hastens to join me. To kiss me. Comfort me. Suckle me at her
cold and deadly breast. Bile of disheveled mornings, bitter
drool of vainglorious morrows. There is no more time. Only
carnage. Scio is violated. Scio is ravaged. Scio is dead. Cold
light of the Louvre. Cosette's passion. Huguette's ass. Frills
and flounces and smirks and smiles of Semmering. Oscar's
cock. Lili's cunt. My life flies past, there on the Kärntner
Ring. Reflected in the eyes of unseen passersby I can still
sense, hiding behind their walls, by the curtains at their windows. They laugh. Enjoy themselves. *Rigoler.* Mock me.
Maximilien has burst from the night like a comet. He too is
laughing. Because he is catching up with us. Milena whips,
whips again, until she loses control of the reins. Now there
are only two mad horses running down a deserted avenue.
Maximilien will win. Now he is abreast of us again. His horse
seems less tired than ours. Head erect, proud. Nostrils steam-
ing, but not torn and bloody like the dapple gray's. His chestnut wasn't in Scio's battle. He belongs to another world, other
lands. Nor does Maximilien belong to my country, to my
prison. Any more than he is part of Milena's galaxy. He's
something else again. . . . Suddenly I feel irritated by my
friend's honesty, his calm, his reason, his restraint. He could

have run his race more intelligently. And I don't want him to win. So here I am railing at Milena, demanding more speed, more cracks of the whip, more ferocity—take the bit in your teeth! Go on, Milena, kill him, kill us, have done with it! Now we stand like Ben Hur driving his chariot to victory. Like Apaches, we howl. The Opera isn't far now. More than a hundred meters. Fifty. Maximilien has passed us by a neck. We can do nothing more. Unless . . . Milena makes a frightful neighing sound. As if he has heard her, the horse lunges ahead as if taking a leap into infinity, the crowning touch of folly, his unnatural effort justifying the madness of the act. We cross the finish line a few meters out front.

I don't know why, but I had the impression that during those last seconds, Maximilien reined in his steed. . . .

The night has closed in. Safe in the down-lined nest, male and female look at one another. Their eyes try to absorb the warmth that is all about them. Outside it is very cold. The silence is frozen and darkness lingers on their vulnerable but satisfied bodies. They sense, they know they are defeated, even before the fight begins. The rain that fell has soaked their plumage, and they struggle to laugh as they shake the icy dampness from their wings. They hadn't even thought of taking cover! What is a shower compared with the dangers lurking in every corner of the forest! They have decided to love one another at once, straightaway, no matter what. And their bodies are inseparable, their cries mingle with the rhythm of the cruel, tender spasms of love.

At the first howling of the moon they moved apart, but barely, as if to question one another. What wild beast would they nourish, tonight or tomorrow morning? To hear their bones crack between sharp teeth . . . to be crushed, shredded, swallowed. To dissolve, together, inside a sticky mouth, and feel and know they were digested by a single stomach. The birds desired to be lions, panthers, pumas, even hyenas perhaps, so that suffering and pleasure could make them understand their fragile savagery.

For a long time they loved one another, huddled together, coiled one inside the other, clinging together with harmless claws. And when life flowed into them like a shudder of scarlet plumes, dream animals they had always heard of but never seen appeared in the dawn sky. Yellow octopi embraced the sun, which swayed like a pendulum. And on the seventh stroke of morning the Phoenix shattered its scarlet shell and, like a ball of fire, shook off the celestial crust and finally took flight while the exhausted lovers looked on, amazed. The green dragon sent its scalding breath in pursuit of the fantastic bird. And all the earth resounded with one tremendous, hideous flat note, as if the belly of the shadows were opening again to swallow up the day. The hydra craned its multiple necks, lured by blood. Gigantic snickers. But suddenly the unicorn loomed on the horizon. The fabulous animal kicked off its iron shoes and slashed at the howling, drooling heads with elegant rage. The frightened birds who had hidden under each other's wings emerged to witness the monstrous contest. They held their breath, hearts in their throats, as they tried together to retain the sight of this mythic confrontation on which hung the fate of their own lives and death, the balance of day and night, and the preservation of the universe. These birds crane their necks outside the nest, within reach of tooth or horn, the better to take part in the show! They do not know what they do, or perhaps they are fueled by their love for each other, a tempest as powerful as the celestial cyclone. . . . The unicorn has donned the colors of their passion. Proud and pure, he enters the lists. Trumpets sound the charge.

The united bodies strive to keep each other from falling into space.

Trees are uprooted.

All that remains is the echo of the sea. Slack. It has inhaled everything, gulped everything down. Under virgin water swims a narwhal from the Arctic. An exile.

Yes, time has speeded up, until I feel I have neither the right nor the desire to assess the years. Anyway, it doesn't matter if the twists and turns of fortune, scrambled by memory lapses or lost in the torrents of history, have lost their proper place, since the result—abandonment, the final leave-taking—has been clearly established. Only one chance, one wan light remains: As we accelerate into high drama, the essence of the tragedy that put an end to us all bears down harder on this sidetracked tale, sodden and inane and too busy listening to itself hum under cover of illusion.

Milena herself had changed. Physically, first of all. She was no longer the mirror of perfection in which I had melted and merged with so much pleasure and pain. Her black eyes had lost their glow. Her face, well rounded but firm, was marked with two or three wrinkles at the lips and eyes. And her hands, above all, had lost their impeccable balance of strength and elegance; her fingers were heavier now and her nails, if unpolished, no longer had that fragility, at once innocent and sensual, that is the prerogative of very young women. I don't know if you're familiar with Egon Schiele's *Sitzende Frau* in the Prague Museum (Clockwork must know it; he's been there). I first saw this portrait by a man I consider to be the greatest Austrian painter (so much more powerful, more tormented, more real than the gilded affectation of the far too famous Klimt) when I traveled to Czechoslovakia for one of my books. I was struck by its resemblance to Milena. The complete Milena: ordinary and lunar, venal and virgin, open, but on guard. Milena with her auburn hair which she'd allowed to grow, knotting it in the back, with wisps drifting freely around her face, in untamed ringlets. Milena sitting on the floor, at the foot of the bed, half naked, legs spread, head on one raised knee, looking at me—a reproachful pout, a look of love, glowing eyes, icy lips. . . .

I remember that tremors began the day I took Milena to a movie. It had disastrous consequences for me in more ways than one. The Burg Kino was showing G. W. Pabst's film *Street Without Joy*. Greta Garbo plays the daughter of a ruined bourgeois family who is forced to work in a nightclub to support herself. I don't know why, but during the first part of the film Milena kept muttering, pinching my arm, distracting me from my fascination with the images. But the point where I literally jumped was when the poor woman is raped by a butcher. Who, though lacking Hermann's features, had the same bestial face, the same brutality as my father. At once, I believed it all: the pessimism, the fine feelings, and the forced expressionist lighting. Outside, on the sidewalk of the Ring, Milena exploded:

"How ridiculous, the American arriving miraculously to save her from prostitution!"

"But the rest—the despair, the unhappiness, one man's money, another man's lust—that's us. . . ."

"You really think life has those happy endings! You believe that women are prepared to pay for men's damn foolishness."

"On the black market . . ."

"All the markets are black: mine with Joseph, with you, even with myself. . . . I'm not stupid, you know, I realize what I'm *worth* to you."

She gave the word the weight of a butcher's ax on the neck of a lamb. That night, for the first time, we parted without a kiss. Lately, Milena had seemed less eager when we met. I hadn't dared admit it to myself, or face up to the truth. I'd let myself be dazzled by the mirage of the "feasts" she would still bestow on me. But I should have seen how her tolerance ebbed during the ritual crises that cast me for days at a time into unbearable, obstinate moods . . . weak in soul and body. Milena threw herself frantically into work, leaving little time for my litanies and complaints. She devoted the time to her daughter, Marie. One day she told me, "There's Joseph and there's you, but Marie is Marie." Seemingly commonplace words, but they made me stop and think. I didn't want to hear the truth she stated so clearly. I gave makeshift speeches, I invented reasons for not giving up hope, for continued faith in Milena's ability to protect me forever from creative impotence. This blind belief would cost me Milena. But not before Joseph tried to take her back, not before disease tried to take hold of her, not before death had started to dance about me a seductive ballet that almost carried me away altogether. . . .

For there had been a reprieve. One I measured from the day after *Street Without Joy*, which, after all, was only a passing episode, the kind of vague quarrel experienced by most couples, whether they are happy or not.

The day was an eternity for me. All at once I was free from the violence that had led, since birth, to deep dejection, and to the gut-wrenching fear that racked me, an apparent adult. It was the day the rioting broke out. The blessed dawn when my father was murdered.

. . . a few days earlier an unknown hand, awkward and even childish, had written on my door in chalk the word JUDE.

One morning, three men lay in wait. Waiting for him, sure of themselves, and what they would do. They had been spying on him for weeks, and had a detailed knowledge of his habits and how he spent his time. They allowed him to go out. Just as if . . . To take his morning walk. And they did not interfere. No, they waited until he entered a dark, narrow street that led him, every day, to the original butcher shop where he had superstitiously insisted on setting up his own office, though his factories and warehouses could have provided a larger, more prestigious space. Hermann was still the same. Despite his inordinate appetites, despite his lyrical suffering, too affected to be real, they called him Huka the Tiger. Workers and employees were frequently exposed to his fury and his raving.

All three fell on him at once. They flattened him against the wall, and two of them pinned him there while the third gutted him with a knife. With broad, precise motions. Panting. From bottom to top. Right to left. Like a pig.

Hermann, the windbag, slumped to the ground, deflated, psssttt! A pool of blood.

They wrote in black on the wall: NO MORE BLACK MARKETS! KILL THE KIKES!

That day, at the same time, I found myself in the middle of

the riots, without knowing why. The night before, I had silently, apathetically, witnessed the socialists' demonstration from afar . . . alone, on the sidewalk after Milena left. Then it started to rain and I went home and, strange for me, went to bed very early. I fell asleep almost at once and did not awaken until dawn. It was rare for me to be up at such an hour, to watch from my balcony the struggle between sun and shadow. Bewildering . . . until I realized that something important, something extraordinary was happening outside. I was impelled to go out, throw myself into the street as if it were the sea, to find, after a painful crossing, the lighthouse, the harbor, the sunny beach—or the shark's teeth, the monster's belly, the putrid fumes of the Leviathan. Who knows?

Milena had not said when we'd see each other again. Did it mean we were separating? Unthinkable. And yet . . . it would have to be . . . now I was on the "street without joy." And suddenly the silence of the avenues was broken by a surge of cries and slogans, the chilly cobblestones frozen in the night were slapped awake by thousands of feet marching in rhythm toward a unknown destination, my stunned soul mingled with the multicolored noise that floated in festive streamers as we advanced toward the abyss. . . . They were singing. My heaving guts, shuddering bowels. A little farther, on a street corner, I managed to move away from the crowd and vomit. I emptied myself. Completely. Turned inside out like a glove. Torn apart, shouted hoarse, back broken. Harakiri.

Then came the first confrontations with the police. Violent, rapid, frightening. I wept with shame. And joy as well. I recognized Milena, unreachable but definitely out there with stone-throwers. Found Milena again. Imbued Milena with all the misplaced desires, all the craving gathered in morning's hollow belly. I tried to reach her for more than an hour. In vain. Struggling against the human tide that swept through light and shadows, fear and confusion. I clung to sticky bodies, lashed myself to fatty buoys, threw myself at jagged reefs. Jolted left and right. Dashed down and tossed up. . . .

I saw Milena running from a counterattack by men in helmets. I saw her wave a placard, I saw her throw homemade fire-bombs. . . . Set fire to the courthouse. Then the troop fired. Massacre. The first rows fell. We moved aside, opened like the roaring Red Sea before Moses. The madness, rage, distress that united us, a single body welded by calamity and hate, gave way to the concrete violence of the law. Milena fell. I cried out, "Milena!" Powerless, too far away, too weak, too cowardly! And the birds flew into the clouds, or perhaps some celestial ogre inhaled them in one gasp. . . . The square is empty. Ten, fifteen bodies remain on the ground. Over there a woman is still moving. Milena? Yes. Is she wounded? Dying? Fear bursts in my head and my guts. I am no longer myself. I dart forward.

She smiled up at me. For a split second I thought I was seeing Cosette's smile again, under the arches of the university. But it was Milena, *my* Milena who clutched my neck and said, "Anton, take me away from here, come on, let's go!" I helped her to her feet. Despite my fears, she wasn't hurt. She'd been overwhelmed, knocked down and trampled in the scuffle.

We ran. I don't know how we escaped the charge of mounted thugs wielding blackjacks. But after the rout, the mob regained their self-control, and the boldest of them quickly began re-forming ranks, spreading out across the square to block the policemen's way. When they saw me run up, with Milena leaning on my shoulder, they parted slightly to let us through, and immediately closed up the chain again. We were protected, safe. Then Milena stopped, flung herself at me, and kissed me violently, as if at any moment death would tear us apart. She said, without taking a breath and looking me straight in the eyes, "You came. Nothing else matters. Anton, take me. Now. Make love to me!" In a dream, I took her to a nearby hotel. Seedy, grimy, the sort that rents rooms by the hour—a memory of Julia from the Kärntnerstrasse, perhaps. . . . As the tide of blood and fire, rioting and repression washed over Vienna, we made love with equal violence. She opened a path for me, gave me everything. I took everything. I gave everything. She took everything. For the first time, she wanted me to sodomize her, in response to my blind desire. We destroyed one another, in order to be reborn.

By night we were at peace again. Outside, life had resumed some semblance of its normal course. The ravages of the morning were certainly visible, gutted before our eyes. But the return to calm and everyday life kept us from imagining what had really happened while . . . We went to a café and ordered large cups of hot chocolate and pastries. We ate and laughed like children, until I saw the newspaper headlines. They snatched the sugary pleasure from my mouth and filled it with bitter blood and bile. Three headlines on the front page. Spread across five columns. "THREE DEAD, 150 WOUNDED." Underneath, in smaller type, across two columns: "Hermann Huka Murdered." And in the right-hand corner: "Meatworkers' Union Protests Screening of *Street Without Joy*."

Without looking at me, Milena said:

"The bastards, they sent in Starhemberg's fascist militia!"

Tears poured down my cheeks. Milena wiped them away with her hands. She said nothing more. Nor did I. Then I collapsed, my face in my hands, my body shaken by terrible shudders, legs trembling. I couldn't hold back the sobs, the wailing that rose from deep inside me. Happiness had disappeared too soon. Right to the end, Hermann came and called me back to reality. His death, instead of freeing me, now bound me ever closer to him, to everything he stood for, to a nostalgia for an ever-present past rapping at the door, reminder of utter defeat. How many times had I prayed for my father's death? It was done. Suddenly, his existence swelled, took over everything, all my sleepless nights and loveless days.

I went home alone. I begged Milena not to come with me. The police were waiting at the door to question me. As if I had any idea of how the deepest fear left me after Mama's death actually came to pass! They asked their questions, all wrong of course, then made me follow them to the morgue. For the identification. For the sake of appearances. I didn't cry again ever. My eyes were dry, burned forever from contact with white heat. All I had left to see was endless night. I knew it would soon come, it was hidden, billowing at the corner of the first road we might take.

Milena, Maximilien, and the few friends I had left came to Father's burial. I have few memories of that day. I do remember that it was livid, cold, that Father was put next to Mama, in the Jewish sector of the central cemetery, at Gate 4. . . .

Later, there was a painful interview with the notary. In the end Hermann had not disinherited me; it was probably the only promise that he didn't keep. I said I didn't want his money but they told me this was impossible. Fortunately Maximilien took care of this unpleasant business for me. For some years I would be the Huka heir. It would hasten my ruin, until I decided to leave everything to a woman I didn't love, to use however she wanted.

Then everything speeded up. Inside as well as outside. I was attacked on all sides by urgent unsatisfied dreams.

I shut myself inside this calamity. I was bad-tempered, surly, sniveling, self-satisfied . . . but Milena didn't leave me. Not right away. Not brutally—perhaps less brutally than I might have wished. We still loved each other in an echo of the old extreme passion that no longer corresponded to what either of us was living through, *for himself.* The ultimate paradox: Even as outside forces urged us to unite more profoundly, we were permanently walled in our separate solitudes.

I started to smoke heavily. Until acid distaste for it filled me. And I buried all thought of my disease, pushing it away into the fertile gloom of alcohol. At the same time—or a few days after the demonstration and the intense session at the hotel—my obsession with syphilis returned. Tenacious as crab lice, it crawled through my nocturnal anxiety, swarmed across the blank pages at which I stared in vain, all day long.

When Milena wasn't there. Yes, she had come back. We promised one another things we knew were impossible. It didn't ultimately matter, we didn't know we were hurting each other.

I told her I wanted to marry her. She didn't refuse. Another day, I confessed the desire that had obsessed me since Father's death. "What if we had a child!" I feared her reaction, but no, she threw her arms around my neck and kissed my cheeks, my mouth, my forehead, my eyes, while crying out words of love. As if we'd won. . . .

I didn't have, I never had, any ancestors. I felt that my life was getting away, like a whirlwind, leaving nothing behind. That was why I suffered an attack of paternity, the way other people have a heart attack or come down with cancer. Or so I say today, when there's no longer any doubt about my rootlessness. At the time, though, I felt so empty that my longing for descendants was all mixed up with the other morbid instincts that shook my daily existence. I forgot all about my cough and its possible consequences. For me, for Milena, for the child to be conceived, to be born, to be raised. . . .

Clockwork has entered the room. Stealthily. Without a sound. I know, I sense that he's here. Watching me. As if he suspects something. He would be delighted to see me stumble. It won't happen. I won't give him that pleasure. I turn the page. In secret. Huddled under the covers. In the ashes. In the early-morning haze, from the window overlooking the East River, echoing with wailing sirens, I see some ships heading out to sea. It won't be long before I follow them. In my padlocked casket, "cabined, cribbed, confined." Peace at last. Moved only by the swell and pitching of the universe.

The bird is unable to reach the shore. Exhausted by his incredible journey, he has alighted on the furious waves. His storm-tossed body still floats on the surface with great thrusts of useless wings. The waves' pitch is steep. The black hole. Rain sweeps the sky. His feverish gaze is striped blood-red.

I gave the drawing to crazy Lola, but Andy the short-order cook jealously snatched it from her hands and tore it in half.

On one side, the sea. On the other, the drenched bird. Ridiculous now. With no sky or rain.

Clockwork came in to separate them. Screaming, squealing, making merry in the room full of rainbow-colored feathers. Flopped on gutted eiderdowns. Flaccid. Dead. They were carried, feet and arms dangling, into the next room. And I was able to get back the notebook. . . .

. . . a year later. A year later I still hadn't been able to give Milena a child. But rather than capitulate, recognize my own sterility, I threw myself even more fiercely into the whirlwind that was forcing us both to commit extremes. Both of us, because Milena, instead of reproaching me, offered her vitality freely. We both hoped she could free us from the destructive cycle we were in. Even now it's hard for me to say, but I was more unfaithful to Milena then than if I'd slept with every woman in Vienna. Yes, Milena was less and less in my thoughts. I would take her body, swearing I was entering her with my whole life, when I was restraining that life inside me, keeping it aside, as if the seed I sowed inside her had already slipped through the screen of my frailty and anxieties. Milena moved slowly under me, like a blanket being tugged away from you at the last moment, leaving your body bare, unprotected, and cold. And I would void a little dead substance.

Milena was marvelous. It is hard to describe the care she lavished on me, to help me over what she called my "temporary problems." I knew she loved me, that was a tragic certainty. I should have freed her. Instead of letting her take swift flight toward the savage space she had always loved, I had appropriated her for myself, under the pretext of my own self-indulgent Despair. And she—so aware, so lucid—loved me until she wasn't even aware of the chains that bound her, feet, hands, belly, chains I used to bind myself into false serenity.

One day after we'd made love, she said:

"I'm leaving Joseph. I'm coming to live with you."

"What about Marie?"

"She'll stay with her father for a while, till we find a bigger apartment. For her . . . and for our child."

Then came the great battle from which, as might have been predicted, I would emerge defeated. Would I, who made a living writing fantasies, have the necessary strength, the conviction and resistance, to live a "normal" life? Rather than lose myself in mazes inhabited by monsters, sirens, and apes with the gift of speech (in order to invent critical myths for mankind), would I be able finally to tell day from night, give acts and words their meaning and no more?

We were already too old. Fallen. In any case, I was.

Joseph reacted. And I wavered. Instead of helping Milena to resist him, to run away from him, not give in to his blackmail, I acted like an idiot and a coward. Nowadays, anyone can call me anything. Nothing matters, outside the gate of nothing. . . . They can stick insulting notices on the walls of the cell in which you're locked up forever, pin infamous stars to your lapel. To hell with posterity—I who couldn't generate a single scrap of posterity in my own image, my own flesh and blood. Who cares about the rest!

Joseph attacked:

"So this is the man who has made Milena break the deal we struck together, that we thought was indestructible. Never mind that for now," he said in an ironic tone that made me shudder. "What I cannot forgive, sir, is that you have also sabotaged Milena herself. You've destroyed her, unbalanced her—a woman who was harmony personified. Look at her. She has aged ten years in just a few months. She no longer takes care of herself as she always used to. She's let herself go. Because of you. For you. It hurts me to say so, but I believe she's done it to imitate you, to be like you in every respect, even your moral decay. . . ."

He had arrived at my place unannounced, at a time when he knew Milena wouldn't be there. We were sure he had been having us spied on, ever since the day Milena told him she was leaving him for me. Milena, truthful as she was, had told him everything. She had asked me to meet with Joseph to settle certain details he wanted to discuss. He hadn't tried to stop her. Not directly, but he did express certain reservations about Marie's education. For me, he was the light of revelation. If I loved Milena—and I did—then I would leave her. By doing so I would restore her freedom. What was hateful about it was that I, not Joseph, became responsible for Milena's downfall. And the worst was that Joseph was right. That was what I could never forgive him. For being an honest man, too perfect, too good, too proper. Flawless.

Since I loved Milena, I must leave her to him. I dare not believe or listen to the echo of the fatal poison that rises from deep in me as I write these lines, while night falls behind bars that frame a sky crossed by weeping gulls. If I let it out, to have its way, I think that the fragments of my endless madness will knot in my throat. Ah, how I wish they would choke me! So my life's irrevocable lie would finally end!

My true crime, the one I've always paid for, was abandoning Milena, leaving her too readily to our bankruptcy, our deluded hopes, without a real struggle, without believing in her enough to stop the night from burying us and killing memory altogether.

I packed and left at once. After announcing that my illness had returned. For good. Because I did believe that I was advancing deliberately toward my "first death."

I went to Marienbad and settled in. Carelessly, willingly. The journey was torture because it was taking me from Milena, but once I got there, far from the boardinghouse where we'd once been so happy, I shamelessly enjoyed the charms of a place I'd always loved. I began writing like a madman, and I *forgot* Milena. Not the right word, of course. How could I erase her from my body, from my memory? When body and memory were searing me, with bitter, unrelenting burns. No, on the contrary, I imprisoned her more completely than I'd ever done, but this time inside loops I traced with a noisy pen, on the yellowing pages of a notebook that had been a gift from Milena herself when we traveled to the mountains.

I went away without leaving an address, without telling anyone the reason for my journey. Did I know myself? I wanted to reflect, to take stock. Or perhaps to avoid having to face the fact that I'd never return to Vienna again. Weeks passed before Milena's first letter reached me. How had she known I was in Marienbad? No doubt she had looked for me everywhere she knew I might consider a refuge where I could hide from myself. Where better than in Marienbad could I wrap myself in the mantle of illness until I became invisible, hollow and nonexistent?

"My dear Anton (*why this restraint, this different tone, this shift in meaning—rift, distant abyss?*)

"I am too weak to describe how your sudden departure destroyed me, though I am foolish enough to hope you can imagine how it has ravaged me. Fortunately, Joseph was with me. (*God, already!*) In fact, I was ill. The doctors were afraid I might have caught your disease. (*No, no, not that!*) We are waiting for the results of the tests. I sleep a great deal, too much for my liking. I'm reading Proust, A *la Recherche du temps perdu*, but I'm making very slow progress. . . . This forced inactivity is hard to bear. I can't help thinking about the newspaper, everything that must be happening there, and in the outside world as well, everything that's escaping me— as you escaped me. As soon as I've recovered from this stupid false alarm I'll join you, my darling, and if we can't be properly married, we'll at least console each other during our convalescence! (*I recognized her style there, but the "darling" was too much, it was confused, affected, a false note.*) Work may help me even more. . . . (*There we go!*) I'll write you lovingly every day, between the lines of the articles I'll write while thinking of you. Tell me what you want. (*As if she didn't know!*). . . . Write and tell me when you're coming back. That's the greatest gift you could give me. It would take me from this foolish bed I'm stuck in. Are we condemned to love each other only with our doctors' blessing, in sad spas? It's not true, not possible! Ghastly cures! I hate them. Those places reek of death. Come back, I beg you.

"I love you.

"Milena."

She was not despondent. Not Milena! How her letter resembled her. And how it delighted me. But I didn't reply; every day I found a new reason to justify my silence. And the one that worked best—honestly—was the idea, the obsession that I was actually responsible for Milena's illness. If I myself was dying by slow torture, being eaten away, devoured by sparks from a hell of my own making, so be it. But not Milena; that was more than I could stand, confront directly, even in the mirror of the pages that I'd written. I told myself—rightly or wrongly, it doesn't matter—that the only way to save her was by staying away from her, so that she couldn't touch my sick body, my infected being. Let Milena be purified! Alive! And she survived, yes, she survived for Ravensbruck. Sometimes, in this silent hospital, I catch myself saying it would have been better if I'd taken her along the first time I went to the other side. But I came back—did I ever go away?—and now I'm raving like an old fool, here, half dead, looking back at a lost world, while the stars have gone out, lost in endless night. . . . Death would be better. Faster. More.

Milena wrote another letter. Sadder, more bitter. She was angry. She wrote about my illusions, my evasiveness, with an irony she'd never used with me before, reserving it for the idiots at the newspaper or elsewhere who smiled at her and criticized her the moment she turned away. That she grouped me with them brought me closer to the fall, confirmed my retreat. I wasn't upset, no, she was right in saying that the concept of failure which so fascinated me was alien to her. And in her third letter, which came the following month, I understood from her barely veiled allusions that she had taken a new lover. I reacted limply; her newfound freedom offered me a sort of freedom, too, broke the final links binding me to an image of Milena that was pure fabrication. She was herself again! At last! I was saved, redeemed. Poor me. Happy penitents!

This frenzied flight was easier for me to bear because another woman brought me the moral support I so needed. I had met Dora during a brief stay in the country, at Carlsbad, and was impressed from the outset by her seriousness and stability. During our first walks and thereafter, being with her gave me a feeling of security. I enjoyed being mothered by this woman who, from the day we first talked of betrothal, became my nurse. Until then I had never thought of marriage, aside from the proposal tossed in Milena's direction with obvious lack of success. This time, everything seemed to be working out just as Hermann might have wished. Dora was a practicing Orthodox Jew. She came from a very good family and went to Carlsbad with her parents every year. Her father was a senior functionary in Prague (just a few years later he was a victim of anti-Jewish purges). At that time not knowing all the sorrow to come, I had left forever the land where I was born and grew up. With Dora, everything happened according to the rules. Following the traditional ceremonies. Hermann would have rejoiced in the various stages, which progressed easily and monotonously. I didn't resist, just let myself be carried along. In six months we were engaged. And a few days before the Wall Street crash, I married Dora and settled with her in Prague. Since I hadn't been able to do so with Milena, I wanted to have a child with this woman. Though I didn't love her, I had agreed to be "united" with her in a final desperate attempt to establish my destiny.

I had paid no attention to the rise in interest rates and the brutal stop of price increases. Dora's father tried to warn me, recommending all kinds of transactions to safeguard my fortune (what am I saying—Hermann's fortune!). I was preoccupied with the return of my writer's block and—though it may seem too easy, too pat to Clockwork—my inability to do *anything at all*. I fell into a languor that held me, every day, at the edge of exhaustion. I had only a vague interest in what was supposed to be my new life. As for a child, that remained merely an intention. Dora aroused my friendship and compassion, but nothing else. Her body (as I should have anticipated) always left me cold. In any case, my disease didn't give me time for lengthy self-evaluation. Physical suffering returned in early November, and my condition quickly worsened. Fever trapped me in my room for a fortnight. Dora—I could see her only through a yellowish veil of fog—Dora never left my bedside but showered on me all the attention, all the consideration of her . . . love, because, when all's said and done, I think she did love me, in her way. Then suddenly I felt better, much better, and I was able to get up, to resume so-called activity—walks in the family garden, varied but listless reading in the library, vain attempts to write. My condition did, at least, enable me to escape the religious ceremonies that Dora and her family had briefly succeeded in imposing on me. To tell the truth, I'd put up little resistance. It was too easy to succumb to the tradition that had previously spawned my permanent defenses. In the end, Hermann was stronger.

Then, one afternoon I had a conversation with Dora: I told her it was impossible for me to live with her parents any longer; I wanted to go back to Vienna. In my excited speech I even promised that my affection would no longer be just that. It would take on all the means and accents of my passion for life, the passion I had left in that city. Whether to support my assertions or moved by a sudden burst of affection, I began to stroke her hair, her brow, and her lips. I even took her briefly in my arms and held her tightly against me. My mind was seething, scarlet, but my body was cold and dry.

We didn't even have time to carry out my plans. Scarcely had we arrived at the station in Vienna when I had to be put in hospital. Throughout the journey the symptoms had grown worse. A rapier through my chest. Sweating face. Fear in the belly. Bitter tears. A lump in my throat. Choking.

Overwhelmed on the white bed. Staring blankly away toward Milena, who on this Christmas Eve must be preparing the celebration for Marie. While outside they were breaking the windows of shops owned by Jews. While they were starting to burn books. Mine. All the books!

From my lungs, the vise had extended to clamp my entire body. I was an anvil hammered inside by death. I had sensed its peculiar way of testing every organ, every limb in turn, to determine which one would best ring out or which, finally, would sound the knell. Now I knew that the ultimate call would come from the larynx. I had always been fascinated by the organ, by its capacity to emit sounds, to link syllables through a complex and secret alchemy. And in the midst of my suffering I was strangely pleased to note, one morning when Dora was there on her daily visit, that my larynx was empty. Completely. The throat was blocked with a sort of nothingness that preceded any thought of being unable to speak. It had been wrenched away. . . . My true suffering was elsewhere, in the dense tingling that prickled the numb inside of my body unbearably. I was so weak I could scarcely move, but when I fell into a dizzy semicoma that shook me, I felt the white-smocked men and women tying me to the bed. When I came out of my somnambulist's sleep my hands and feet were bound to the metal bedposts. And my greatest relief, my greatest comfort came from my inability to cry out.

Inwardly I was screaming. As I'd always done. As I had perhaps never ceased to do. I wet myself. Soiled myself. Vomited inside myself. I wrote on myself. Donned my warpaint. A multicolored bird of death.

I hated it most of all when the doctor, by giving me morphine, plunged me into an ocean of somber bliss. I preferred suffering, the illusion of life, to oblivion, the illusion of death. I would rather they had left me alone, allowed me a faster, a *better* death. Their care, their temporary cures, their poisons: there was true murder. The one that gave birth to my second life. . . . From the day I realized I wasn't going to die, not for good, I resolved to escape from all of them—Dora, Maximilien, Milena, Hermann. . . . And the best way to do so was to make them believe that I'd died, convince them through illusion that my strange, abrupt disappearance could only be due to the subtle weavings of the Fates!

So it was that I took advantage of a period of remission and escaped from the Klosterneuburg sanatorium. On the night of

January 1, 1930. . . .

On the deserted beach, the waterlogged body, racked and rotten. He had been left behind, abandoned. Unable to fly, to make acrobatic circles in the sky, to drift along in rhythm on the course set by his people, he had been forsaken by all. Because he had unsuccessfully attempted the crossing, he no longer interested anyone. Even the children looked away, indifferent. The most daring, or the most unruly, had dared to nudge the corpse over with their toes "to see what it looked like" . . . but they very quickly found more amusing games.

One morning, however, the most mischievous child—or perhaps the most solitary—came prowling around the side of the beach where the decaying carcass lay, now dried by the sun. Seeing that predators were about to plant teeth, beaks, and claws in the black bird's ravaged flesh, he picked up a big stick and began to scream, brandishing his improvised weapon. As the birds of prey did not stir, he started running toward them, making a tremendous racket, showing his temerity. At last two heavy carrion crows flew away, clattering powerful wings, and rats threaded between the legs of the terrified young hero.

The black bird was in shreds. Neck slashed, oozing blood. Beak shut, Blank empty eyes. The wings, half torn from the body, lay on either side like a final hieroglyph drawn in the sand to attract unknown explorers who might ponder their strange meaning, men from another planet, perhaps, or simply future generations.

The child knelt. With his forefinger he traced the outline of the wing, and, as if deciphering a sign, he nodded. Then gingerly he took the bird in his hands, folded the wings, pressed the battered body against his warm chest, and headed once again into the forest. As he walked he stroked the bird's plum-

age, which soon looked almost normal again, as if the bird were alive, still warm, quivering, vibrant and cooing in the arms of his friend.

The bird was not very old. He must have succumbed in a fearful struggle with the elements. The child kissed the top of his head, tenderly, gently, murmuring words no one had taught him, words he would not have uttered elsewhere or to others. For him alone. . . .

When they came to the clearing, he knelt once more, set the bird delicately on the ground, and, picking up some of the dry leaves and twigs that lay all about him, began to build a small funeral pyre. When he was sure that the structure was solid, he laid the bird on it in such a way that the outspread wings fell on either side of the pile of wood, covering it almost completely. From a few paces away, the bird appeared to be sleeping, lying on its nest, or about to take flight.

Satisfied with his construction, the child rubbed two pieces of dry wood together, as his grandfather had taught him, as he would have been taught by the father he had never known, who had disappeared, gone up in smoke, without a trace. Not even a memory. Scarcely an idea. An abstraction. A dream, perhaps. . . .

And slowly the fire grew.

When the flames caught the bird's body the child stood up, then stepped back, a little frightened by what he had done. It seemed to him that the bird moved, and he gave a start. What he could not know was that the remains had greeted the fire like a final happiness that life had not granted. At last, cradled in the warmth, in the essence, in truth. . . . Crackling, shaking convulsively, he was opened from tail to neck, guts gaping, so he could be licked in the depths of his vitals by a thousand fiery tongues. And soon his eyes came to life. Glowing. Reddening coals. The pupils quickened with memories as if stirred by visions moving behind the curtain of flames.

Half-consumed, he stirred, feebly at first, then shook off his own ashes. The centuries began again to pulse in his blood, and time resumed its place in his heart. The feathers had lost

*their black color in the fire, turning first to brown, then red,
yellow, green, blue, until finally they seemed to become transparent, invisible.* The frightened child could no longer bear the sight, though
he himself had staged it. Like the artist terrified by his own
creation, he found the only way out: flight.

But if he had stayed, if he'd had the courage, the faith, or the
madness that alone can make the impossible happen, he would
have seen the white bird rise up in the sky. The fabulous bird,
who has no need of feet to stand proud, in its dwelling place:
the sun.

For the child retracing his steps, going back to meet himself
in these turn-of-the-century Viennese woods, the black bird
was already dead. Completely dead. Only dead.

19.
Clockwork's Notes (VI)

❧❧❧ As things stand now,
where I myself stand in this work *on* Blackie (*on*, not above,
not against, or toward . . .), I've concluded that the solution
might be to write a book *about* him. To approach him indirectly, to enclose him in a black pencil line, since I'm unable
to strip him bare on the page. I've put up with his presence for
too long. I even wonder how it is that after so many years he's
still here, in Bellevue Hospital, with no sign of a cure, and
that I'm here too, stepping up the effort, as if my career might
benefit from it, as if I had no other choice or prospects. As if
all the time was nothing. . . . And we're locked up here
together for the duration and the degeneration.

But to write that book, after my investigation in Paris and
even after the one in Vienna, which I will come back to, I
must begin at the beginning. In a more basic way. Start simply with words, with phrases. Because, after all, if Blackbird is
a writer, then he's a man of words. And a hell of an operator!
A maniac! He's been able to get this far with his neurosis
because of and thanks to words. And I let him have his way
. . . though I may never know if I was right or wrong. My
profession might have required me to shut him off, to sus-
pend his flow of fertile silt that constantly replenished our
fabricated wasteland. I have a feeling that, rather than become exhausted, he has enriched and improved himself,
grown fat on his own losses. He took me in. Unless, as I said,
instead of letting him use his fiction to inspire me, to float me
into an equally paranoid account, I had laid down a line of
behavior for myself: to dissect the words without sucking
them hollow of deceitful marrow. I should have broken them,

spread them across the dissecting table to get an inside look at the fabric of Anton Blackbird alias Antoine Choucas.

Blackie a sparrow? Easily tamed? Hell! Rather a blackbird, sly and shrewd! Or the elusive white crow, *rara avis*. . . . So I read or reread all the books, all the bird stories that resemble him even a little. Think about the fable about the blackbird and his mate in which the medieval peasant quarrels with his wife over the sex of thrushes and, repeating the same scene every year, marks the anniversary by flogging her buttocks. For seventeen years, until death ensues—the death of the peasant. . . . But it didn't matter. On the other hand, the fact that the dark-feathered bird doesn't exist in Africa could take my research in an interesting direction, but I must admit that, for the moment, I haven't figured out the connection. I lingered over its habits; the blackbird thrives in thickets and gardens, whereas the jackdaw, whom the French call *choucas*, lives in colonies, in belltowers and ruins. Both feed on insects and fruits, but the second is more harmful than the first. Dialectic between the true and the probable, counterpoint of day and night, twofold face of civilization and the apocalypse. . . . But as I'm about to faint into the dizzying vertigo of these ideas, I'm overtaken by chitchat, more seductive than ever. The blackbird chatters, whistles, flutes, babbles. He speaks in a muddle of tongues of his solitude, that of the North American solitary thrush or mockingbird. Caught in guano, by the gullet, the glottis, silenced by the pain that embraces him, the mockingbird knows just one thing: how to imitate other species, how to steal their songs, their cries, their flurries of excitement. A pirate of existence. A vulture of souls—or perhaps a conqueror of dreams, invader of continents, pioneer of new thoughts.

I went further, then, to the Antipodes, where "blackbird" refers to the kidnapping of Kanakas to be used as slaves on Australian plantations. The impertinence of hasty translations, of cannibal traditions! I would like to have been John James Audubon. A naturalist, not a psychiatrist. I would like to have crossed virgin lands in search of new species and

lovingly set them on paper, my skilled brush delicately brush-
ing in the colored plumage. To trace the outlines of the living
creature, capture the light in the eyes, instead of killing time
flattening, kneeling, grounding, sacking. . . . Audubon, son
of a French naval officer, was born in Santo Domingo. He
studied art in Louisiana and in France. But his father was up
to his ears in debt, so John James opened a bazaar in Louis-
ville, Kentucky. In fact, he would devote most of his time to
studying the birds of America. Until he too went bankrupt.
. . . I would like to have been Audubon. Perhaps then I'd
have had some understanding of Blackbird. Audubon died in
1851.

One day I showed Anton the magnificent plates repro-
duced in *The Birds of America*. The thrush, the woodcock,
the little owl, the shrike, the cuckoo, the whippoorwill, the
red crossbill, the dipper, the horned lark, the mockingbird
. . . He looked at them in silence, not moving a muscle,
showing no particular interest in any of the images that filed
past his eyes as I turned the pages. When it was over he got to
his feet, still without saying a word, left the room, and came
back a minute later carrying under his arm the portfolio in
which he kept his work. He tossed it on the floor, in a wide,
slow sweep that spread the paintings all over my office. The
colors burst out, clashing, violently thrown together. A blinding spectacle of aggression, carnage, malaise, death . . . scarlet feathers flying to the four corners of the room. Tremor of
cloistered air. I try to counterattack, to articulate some sort of
response. But nothing comes. The words stay knotted in my
throat. How could anyone, at a single glance, take in the
ravaged multitude of images and sounds? In spite of everything I look, blinking to avoid the bite. Serpents whistle in the
branches, stretch, embrace, crawl. Suffocation.

As if wanting to spare me, Blackie leaves the room, slamming the door. Brutal awakening.

Perhaps the documentation isn't that necessary. But it reas-
sures me. Gives me confirmation, hope, rules of behavior. A
way to set limits, ultimatums. Even so I feel as if I'm leaving

too much room for lies, as if the abundance of materials weren't enough (on the contrary!) for the ambiguity of the remarks.

I went to Vienna. I searched and found nothing. A futile, senseless journey. I had spent a year with the illusion that Vienna would provide the key to the mystery, that there, within walls laden with history too weighty for my feeble American shoulders to bear, the meaning of the mystery would burst open like a ripe fruit.

I'd been full of good intentions when I left. And when the airplane touched down at the Schwechat Airport, I caught myself saying: "To the two of us." *Which* two? I'd decided to pick up Antoine's trail where I'd left off—in Paris the year before. I had prepared my files. Gone over the facts. Put my ideas in order. Written down all the questions needing an answer. Everything seemed perfectly clear. Straight as an arrow, with no room for improvisation. And yet, on the first evening—probably because of jet lag, I told myself at the time—it all became confused in my mind. When I got to the Bohemia Hotel, I put my things away, took a bath, and lay down to smoke a final cigarette before going to sleep. At the same time, I reread my notes. Anton in Vienna until 1919, the Opera, Vera and her disappearance, the departure of Choucas himself, which overlapped, but with a gap, that of the Blackbird of the yellow notebooks. . . . Vienna had most certainly been a fulcrum, the break point where everything loosened, before coming undone and giving way to the fragments I was dealing with, like a disorganized geometric table with no lines of force, stripped of center and structure. A puzzle broken apart and turned upside down.

Once again, I planned to neglect the conference to which I'd been invited in order to devote myself to my investigation. The very next day I began wandering around the old city, not really knowing where to go, not really registering the signals that Graben, Kärntnerstrasse, or Judenplatz was undoubtedly sending me. For lack of anything better, I finally went to the university, to listen to the last paper of the day.

I spent the evening with colleagues. The head of our dele-
gation had invited some of our more eminent Austrian associ-
ates to dinner. I seized the opportunity to suggest the Rauchfangkehrer, which Blackie refers to in his book. The evening
was a success, but I looked around in vain for even a hint of
the shades of Anton and Vera (Milena?). I admit that my
attention was especially distracted by the presence of Dr.
Feldman at our table. Anna—for she had asked us all, at the
outset, to use her first name—Anna Feldman headed the
clinic at the Brothers of Mercy Hospital. I liked her at once.
Very much. She had a blend of charm and sensitivity, of
fragility and self-assurance, of aggressiveness and tender sensuality that I'd previously sought in vain. Captivated, I managed to sit next to her and to monopolize her conversation.
Happily, though Anna spoke poor English, her French was
nearly perfect. She'd learned it in Paris, while completing her
thesis at the Salpêtrière. We had something in common, and
I didn't hesitate to turn it to my advantage. I wanted to know
her better. I had a need to communicate that was hard to
explain at the time, though today I'm well aware of its repercussions. And of course the next day I forgot completely
about Blackbird, without regret, and attended all the psychiatric discussions with Anna. By noon we were both at a recep-
tion in our honor at the U.S. consulate. I didn't dare ask her
to dinner that evening, but she made matters easier by suggesting that the next morning, when we had a few hours'
break, we visit the Freud Museum. "After all, it's a must!" she
said with a characteristically charming smile.

Berggasse 19. A pilgrimage of sorts. Return to the source.
The emotion at the sight of the papers, paintings, statues,
knickknacks—and of course the couch. But I was most struck
by the *exterior*: the cold, gray, characterless facade; the elevator cage with its wrought-iron grilles and stone steps; the yellowish light; but stranger still, at the back of the courtyard, on
the ground floor, amid the shrubbery, a tiny Greek temple,
an anachronism stemming from some heedless fantasy—or

perhaps it acted as guardian of the ancient gods and myths. . . . And then, as Anna was lingering in the apartment of the man she referred to as "Master," I don't know why but I ventured upstairs. The goal of the visit, the tabernacle of our knowledge, the secret, perhaps, of our lives—all these I was supposed to find on the second floor, but ironically, paradoxically, almost incredibly (but it's absolutely true, it can be verified), it was on the third floor that I discovered *my own* truth, through the sort of coincidence that occurs so often in life that we dismiss it as *chance*, pushing us toward routes that are different (or perhaps always the same one, identical, unchanging, immutable, though we don't know the Law that governs it, we attribute to it some unknown force). As I was glancing about the third-floor corridor, then, I was surprised, even stunned at the brass plate that leaped to my eyes with its strange message: *Wilhelm Kafka—Private Detective*. At first I thought it was a joke or that I was hallucinating, as if I'd learned my lesson well downstairs and was projecting my desires onto a metal plate fastened to an oak door. But no. At close range I could see that I wasn't mistaken, I'd read it correctly: a private detective named Kafka. That was too much! I burst out laughing. So loudly it must have alerted Anna, for I heard her calling as she climbed the stairs. I came forward to meet her, as if I didn't want her to share the mystery. When she was halfway up the stairs, to disguise my lack of composure but also because I'd abstained for almost two hours, I lit a cigarette and offered one to Anna, who accepted.

"Why don't we have some lunch?" I suggested. "There must be a restaurant nearby."

"Not really," she replied as we descended to the ground floor, "but it's just a five-minute walk to the old city."

"Let's go."

She chose a Yugoslavian restaurant. "You'll see," she said, "you'll like it." We ordered shish kebabs of various meats. Then I excused myself, but instead of going to the toilet, I headed straight for the telephone. The number on the detective's brass plate at Berggasse 19 was engraved on my memory. Since we'd been at the Freud house I had only one idea: to put Kafka on Blackbird's trail. Sweet revenge!

In a few sentences I summed up the reason for my call. Kafka said he couldn't deal with such a matter over the phone, and we made an appointment for five o'clock that afternoon. When I went back to the table where Anna was waiting, I was overwhelmed with relief. Saved. Free of responsibility. Clutching my alibi. . . . Now I was free, free to act on my own, *outside* Blackie, free to take on whatever appearance I chose, to come right out and offer myself to a woman with no ulterior motive. Our meal was relaxed, warm, intimate. I already had Anna's friendship, but that day I attained a deeper part of her being, where two people come together who were previously strangers, but who quickly— perhaps too quickly—find themselves beyond complicity, beyond shared desires. I said nothing about Blackbird, of course, or about what had really brought me to Vienna. It was as though I were trying to convince myself that behind my decision to come to Austria was always the hope of meeting her, Anna. Similarly, she said nothing about her true nature, about who she *really* was. I only found out later that she was married, with a child. . . . But we decided to spend the afternoon together, to pretend we'd never part, congress or no congress. We skipped it, laughing like rebellious schoolchildren, as if that would make us brave. On the sidewalk outside the restaurant, Anna exclaimed:

"Let's go to the movies! *Morocco* is playing at the Burg Kino—the old von Sternberg film with Dietrich and Gary Cooper. Unless you'd rather see *The Maltese Falcon* with Bogart and Peter Lorre. . . ."

"I've already seen it. Let's go to *Morocco.*"

We thoroughly enjoyed ourselves. Children playing hooky. Concerned for nothing but the instant.

During the film, in the darkened room where I imagined

Anton bringing Milena (or so he said in his notebook . . .), I took Anna's hand. She didn't resist. We were no longer adolescents, but for the time being the rather innocent lacing of our fingers was enough.

After the film I went with Anna to some antique shops on the Dorotheum. We looked at everything but bought nothing. It didn't even occur to me to offer her a gift; we hadn't reached the point where we wanted souvenirs, substitutes for happiness. Still, I had to think about the passing time, which was bringing me closer to the appointment that, despite my desire to be with Anna, I couldn't avoid. I used a meeting with my American colleagues as a pretext for slipping away, after promising Anna to meet her at the university next morning. I had the impression she wanted to kiss me, but whether it was my impatient manner or my anxious expression that disturbed her, or her surprise at my own hesitation about taking her in my arms, she did nothing. I was somewhere else, unprepared.

I told the detective the story of Anton/Antoine as well as I could. He seemed disappointed at my relative inability to express things clearly. I was sorry I hadn't brought my notes, but how could I have known? I would bring them the next morning. How many days could I give him? Four at the most. Not much for something so complicated. It's easy! I wanted Anton in Vienna, and even more I wanted to find the person who could tell me what had really happened: Vera. I paid five hundred dollars in advance—all the cash I had on me—and promised the same amount if the results were satisfactory, though it would make a serious dent in the traveler's checks I'd been given to cover expenses. But to hell with that. Besides, I told Kafka, if you discover any new leads, if you find her after I've gone, write to me in New York (I gave him my card), and I guarantee you won't regret it. . . . As I was descending the stairs for the second time that day, I saw that ashtrays had been set out on every landing.

The rest of the evening I spent alone, in my hotel room. I

had sandwiches and a beer brought up. Once again I reread all my notes. But when I was finally in bed with the lights out, I had just one image in my mind: Anna.

Anna, with whom I would spend four days, the most intensely happy I'd ever had. Four days in which we loved one another in the hotel, in parks, museums, cafés, beer halls, at the Opera (Prokofiev's *Romeo and Juliet*, with choreography by John Cranko), everywhere! A mad race without a pause, without coming up for air or taking time to realize what was happening to us. Suddenly, without our realizing what it all meant, the eve of my departure was upon us. I began to make impossible plans. What if I were to stay in Vienna, throw everything over to start a new life, Anna—if I could only free myself of that miserable miserable Blackbird . . . Blackbird, she asked, who's that? As if I could tell her! But what difference does it make? Anna was the solution. Anna versus Blackbird.

"I'm staying."

"You can't."

"Why not?"

Then she talked about herself in a way I couldn't do. She told me about her life. (How could I have imagined that at thirty-five, her life was beginning with me!) About her husband, her son. In a sentence, with one stroke she sent me back to Blackbird and his fantasies. To the night that, for years, had wrapped my own life in a tissue of secrets laboriously wrenched from another's obscurity.

I backtracked, panic-stricken. Found every excuse, every justification I needed to remount the platform I'd been on, to face down this heartbreak. Not cynically, oh no, I couldn't do that. No, no, something far baser fueled me, a feeling more vulgar, more elemental, almost bestial. Like a subterranean instinct for self-preservation. A way to maintain my own integrity. Suddenly I had only one explanation for the terror that had taken hold of me: I had seen myself in Blackie's skin. I could tolerate anything but that. And I was far too frightened to mistake myself for Anton.

There was only one way out for me as well: flight. Forward,
or wherever, but escape! And I write that without shame,
because I'm starting the book I plan to write about Blackbird
at this point—though he concerns me only remotely—precisely because it is time to position the event in its purely
anecdotal nature. Reality almost took me too far, to the limits
of sanity. Let the novel I hope will emerge from these notes
settle things, put them in their proper place.

To get through the panic, I clung desperately to Kafka. The
detective, of course. On the phone he told me his research
was progressing well and I wouldn't be disappointed by the
results. Once again, he wouldn't give details but asked me to
come to his office. I went shortly after the farewell scene with
Anna. I wouldn't—now—be so bold and thoughtless as to
inflict the retelling on myself or on any possible readers. In
plain language, Kafka's "good results" were contained in
some concert programs from 1917 and '18, various contemporary newspaper clippings that, though they provided some
details about Antoine's repertoire, shed no new light on what
I already knew. The essential point, however—unfortunately
I should have suspected it—was that Vera had died in
Ravensbruck.

It's been months now—how many, I don't know—since
I've been back from Vienna. I've seen Blackbird again. The
same immutable. Like Bellevue itself. . . . Only a bit more
aged and tired from having written several chapters in the
notebooks that once again a little too readily he let me find, as
if he wanted to catch me in the web of his inventions, force
me to become interested in them again, so that I wouldn't
leave them, so that I'd never leave *him* . . . the monster! Will
I ever have the courage to admit to myself (to him!) that he's
ruined my life? Perhaps even my career: what must people
think about this strange case that's had me treading water for
years, unable to move on to something else? Of course I'm
responsible for other patients. I'd be lying if I denied that
Jerry, Snuffie, Linda, Lola, and the others fascinate me, but
even there, I have the feeling that Blackie knows and under-

stands all of them better than I do. Although I wouldn't make new medical history, I desperately want to write the book about Blackie, to make him cough it all up, flatten him, bring him to his knees, for good. . . . Now the only thing I'm sure of is that I can never give him free rein, allow him to be the only writer, to invent his life on paper. Otherwise I'll end up believing that he's right, that his version is the true one, that there's no reason for him to be locked up for life, no reason but my own madness, which makes me unable to distinguish day from night, right from wrong, up from down. My head is in the clouds, but I'm crestfallen, a tightrope walker on the ground. Disproving and destroying him would be the ultimate suicide, destined to annihilate all of us. . . .

. . . then, as all the doors are shut again, the corridors illumined in blinding succession, by lights that cut. The cameras are operating and I know that through the walls *he* is watching, observing me, eying my every move, listening to every murmur, spying on everything I do and write, so once again I must address only the essential, use new methodology to encircle him, starting with what we're taught by nature, that great cycle of living beings of which all of us (including *him*) are part.

Start from scratch. Reexamine our definitions. Grasp at theorems. Believe in axioms. For want of . . . No, settle into encyclopedic certitude, into . . . solitary reason.

Anton thinks he's a bird. Very well. From now on I'll treat him as pure instinct. Why should I believe him capable of intelligent reasoning? I'll show him! Yes, I'll make him work, like a bird, a circus animal. I'll train him. Why not, for a start, give him Kohler's test—you know, the one that uses two boxes. The cover of one has red dots on it like a card. That's the one he must open if he wants to show he has any kind of a brain. As much, at least, as a common trained jackdaw! If he makes it, we'll move on to the one that has food hidden in one of five boxes differentiated by irregular blotches of ink, that has the patient following arrows on a diagram. And for a start, no more piano. Enough piano. He hardly plays now anyway, just sits at the keyboard for hours at a time, daydreaming. With the money we'll save, we'll buy some new batteries of tests. The common blackbird has a life expectancy of less than nineteen months. And the North American thrush, scarcely seventeen. Patience: I'll soon be rid of him.

20.

Blackie's Notebooks (IX)

⩔⩔⩔ The time has come to reverse the process. My previous life was constructed to suit Clockwork. Now, half dead, it's up to me to take up the irons and put Clockwork behind bars, wean him from his usual meal and make him submit to an examination.

I've been spying on him for some time now. And observed clear signs of weakness, standing out clearer and clearer against the night that covers us both. He's noticed nothing, believing me more lost than ever on the peaks of unattainable dreams. But I've come down the other side of the mountain. I had sworn I'd stay up there, perched on the edge, waiting calmly until the abyss called so sweetly that I couldn't resist the fall. It took me years to get used to the idea of silence and vertigo. I had to go to sleep, give in to the attraction of heights, before I could accept the return to the plains, my need for flatness. Maybe ultimate courage is over on the other slope. Beyond exile.

I've found the place where Clockwork hides his notes about me. I went into his office one night. My patient spying took me quickly to the thick file hidden at the top of the sixth bookshelf, behind an 1846 edition of the complete works of Shakespeare bound in leather. As if he were ashamed . . . afraid of a bulky file, of the book he wanted to write.

I read and I understood. Understood at least that the game had gone on long enough. In the midst of gloom I'd conscientiously lived in all my life so I could cheat, forget, was still a glimmer of light I could hide from no longer. Clockwork's failure was in fact a success. He had circled the truth, ca-

186

ressed it so it sighed with ecstasy, tickling it so it fanned out under his clumsy fingers. So be it. But the main point was there. The proof: he loved me now. He loved me to the point of sharing my feelings, to the point of experiencing my own torments, of getting lost in the labyrinth of his own life. We were equals, interchangeable. I knew I must not stop Clockwork from being himself. Let him sink into madness, if he wants it. Then I too could be saved. . . .

Clockwork is right to say I don't have long to live. This time it will be permanent. It's no longer a matter of knowing if some disease will strike me down in the prime of life, if dark armies of chanting microbes will battle with my vital energy. No, it's simply time for day to give way to night. The pattern of the cycle. So, because I want to, I've started down the slopes of sleep. Even my ridiculous hunger strike makes no sense now: I don't know whether at this stage Clockwork will understand my message to him, but since yesterday he must have noticed, at least I hope he has, that I've started eating again. I was feeling thoroughly drained. I felt I was disappearing, as I was during my exile. I must still say a few words about that, since it was the blank intermission of my life, between two worlds, an equatorial divide where the writer gradually learns to be content with silence. Clockwork should have understood this long ago, instead of indulging in all his tricks and pranks. As soon as I started writing again, even this simple autobiography (though it's always beating against my brain like words imprisoned in a paper cage), I feel I am remaking myself in the image of everyday, ordinary, livable life that results in a *natural* death, not one brought about by a more or less grandiose *deus ex machina*.

It took me a long time to forget January 1, 1930. About eight years, while I wandered from one country to another, from intoxication to disillusion. . . . As things stand now I don't think anyone would be very interested in my expanding on those twilight years. Or maybe I lack the strength or the conviction to do so. Perhaps . . . but in reality, it seems to me—despite the horrible route I took to get there—my "second" life began on the day I set foot on the *Queen Mary*, where I felt beneath me the immensity of the ocean, of the opening I still had to do before I reached the other shore, the other side of my exile.

With the requisite blind self-sufficiency I'm about to risk enclosing in a few pages those hollow dark years from which I emerged only to find the apocalypse, as others find religion.

In the beginning, I hid. Thanks to Maximilien, good, kind Maximilien, who knew everything and asked for nothing. He let me stay with him for the first few days. After I'd made him promise to look after my affairs (not much was left, I was virtually ruined), I made him my authorized representative and full heir with special responsibilities regarding my papers and manuscripts. I told him to destroy them, then I disappeared. I know now that he did not follow my instructions. A few years later Maximilien would take everything with him to Palestine. And from there, contrary to my wishes at the time, he saw to my reputation, turning me into the great writer I'd always wanted to be but hadn't known how to become. I had hoped for oblivion, but Maximilien gave me glory, immortality. Initially, when I'd just entered Bellevue, I was angry with him for not keeping his word. Then the years passed, word of my fame reached me, ever louder, and I told myself that perhaps he was right. In fact my certainty began when I started filling these notebooks with the story of my life.

Maximilien had sent me to Goldstein in Berlin. I didn't have much to show, but he gave me a hefty advance toward my next book, though I hadn't yet written a word. So I was able to get by without too many problems—but this writing still pains me; I cry, thinking of the inconstant, wasteful moments—in Berlin (three weeks), Prague (incognito for ten days), Budapest (a month), Trieste (five weeks), and finally for almost a year in Venice. Venice, where I told myself without really believing it that I'd come to die! In that period between words, between acts, between wars, what could I do except,

ironically, come to Venice and die? Like the other I so feared
. . . my own ghosts I was prepared to forget, Vienna, Hermann, Milena, the growing perils accumulating behind my
closed door in a nauseating heap of garbage ready to rot—or
burn.

Because I'd run away from the fact that I couldn't trans-
form my suffering by writing, I forgot quickly, too quickly,
and my illness, unluckily for me, had, miraculously, almost
vanished. In its stead was a sort of syrupy, mediocre health. I
managed to convince myself that Venice was not conducive
to inspiration. What I needed was Paris, which had such a
dazzling intellectual aura at the time that no writer "worthy
of the name" could work outside it. And to be honest, I simply wanted to go back to Huguette, to the rue Haxo, the
Louvre—even perhaps to Cosette. So I outlined a novel I
wanted to write—in Paris and nowhere else. I wrote to Goldstein, to persuade him I needed more help. That wise and
splendid man responded that since he'd been waiting in vain
for some results from his prior generosity, although he understood the creative problems a writer of my caliber must en-
counter, as he lacked any detailed information about my writing plans, he could not, under the circumstances, offer me an
additional advance. However, for encouragement and as a
sign of his grateful friendship, he would send me enough
money to get me to Paris.

Paris, of course, was no help at all. I'd intended to move
into the pension on rue Haxo, but I was unpleasantly surprised to find in its place the "Institution Sainte-Marie" for
young girls. And Huguette had disappeared without a trace
. . . The people in the neighborhood could tell me only one
thing: Huguette had been forced to close up shop and move
to the south of France because of her daughter's health. But
they didn't know any details.

So I took a small furnished room in an inexpensive hotel on
rue Gît-le-Coeur, in the heart of the Latin Quarter. I sent
Maximilien a long letter bringing him up to date, asking him
to be sure to destroy the letter after he'd read it. And I did get

down to writing . . . the story of Cosette. That was what I had in mind. I'd sworn not to try to see her. On the contrary. The fewer real traces of her I could find, the more alive my memories would be. A *Married Woman*. That was the title I wrote in the middle of an impeccable blank page. And I wrote, yes I wrote ten, fifteen pages. Then nothing. A quick sketch in the French manner, the sort of thing I didn't think I could do. Pure, crisp, chiseled, ground to a find point, with all the bitterness of a poisoned pen. In fact, that was sufficient, that in itself was sufficient. The novel remained open and so became a short story. Superstitiously, though, I wrote the word "novel" above the title and, on the first page of the manuscript, "Chapter One." I made a copy, which I sent to Goldstein, with no comment. His response was enthusiastic and took the form of a considerable sum deposited to my account. Goldstein hoped to read the rest shortly. Need I add that there was never a "Chapter Two"?

The months passed. Nothing happened.

One day, Maximilien sent me a very large sum of money— the result of liquidating my belongings. It let me reestablish my customary confinement, which even seemed to have acquired an acrid taste, like beneficent dust. For months now I'd been spending my days in the Bibliothèque Nationale, where, with a single-mindedness that contrasted with the fragmented state of my senses, I read ancient books, many of which I hadn't known before. I became fascinated with subjects and authors I'd considered saccharine or useless in the past. It was as if I'd decided to inhale, devour, assimilate, digest everything, to get to the end of the chain of words that had imprisoned me—and perhaps find the very source of writing. Fascinated by the tons of paper, I came to think of literature in terms of weights, of stacks, of kilometers of shelf space, of inventory, of storage space. Larder, storeroom, cold room, antique store. . . .

With Goldstein's advance and the money from Maximilien, I was able to buy a small business. I opened an antiquarian bookshop just a few steps from my hotel, on rue Saint-

André-des-Arts. My specialty was the Romantics. I survived that way for a little over three years, pressed between pages stained with fragments of forgotten verse and self-indulgent literary brews. Worse, I found myself in a businessman's skin—one I'd struggled to shed—Hermann's. Though I took ceremonious precautions before burying myself in the dust, under the jumble of priceless, untouchable documents, I too was a butcher, one who disemboweled books, carved up pages, boned bindings, feasted on spoiled meat! Playing the role of the great curator, eking out matter to be absorbed, was too easy an alibi. How can I ever tell what it meant to me! If I really had to describe it honestly, those three years alone would warrant that I tear up everything I've written in this notebook and start again. . . . I'm strongly tempted. But I have too little time left to pretend I could take such a risk. If I were strong, I'd have tempted the devil, played the game, for in doing so I would undoubtedly have briefly raised my youthful genius once again. Instead, I've scattered myself, emptied like the overflowing wineskin that I am.

But those years were not as empty as I pretend—this is enough to justify them, to give them some interest—I happened on a *Historia Eclesiástica* by Rivas, published in Madrid in 1877. One chapter in particular caught my eye, the one on Pope Benedict XIII, artisan of the Great Schism. Afterward I learned everything I could about him, beginning with Don Pedro Martínez de Luna y Pérez de Gotor, born in 1328 in Illueca, a province of Saragossa.

This cardinal of Aragon and future pope was a small, puny man with bright eyes and a straight nose. A keen observer combining humility and inflexibility, he showed himself both austere and tenacious in his actions and his ideas. He was immensely cultured.

As a sign of the political and religious unrest of the time, on March 25, 1409, the Council of Pisa canceled his election as Benedict XIII in Avignon, in 1394. Cardinal de Luna was accused of demoniacal sorcery. He was exiled first to Barcelona, then to Tarragon and Saragossa. Finally, on July 21, was sent to Peñiscola, within the walls of the Templars' fortress, where he was imprisoned for more than twelve years, unbroken until his death. . . . *"I am pope, pope of the sea. Tell those who send you: You have made me king, yet now you send me to the desert!"* Captivity, solitude, martyrdom. . . . *"I cannot and I shall not abdicate!"* Fiercely attached to his ideals. Fortified by books and study. Relieved with writing, ceaseless and unshakable. Surrounded by those walls facing the sea. Oblivious to any tricks, any bargaining, any abuse of authority. Until that day in July 1418, when the false pope was brought some poisoned sweetmeats. For nine days and nights he hovered between life and death, but incredible though it may seem, he was able to fight off the poison. It was then said that a witch imprisoned in a Florentine jail had predicted both the attempt on his life and his recovery.

In 1430, on April 9 to be precise, when the body of Pedro de Luna was exhumed, to be transferred to the palace at Illueca, his native city, people marveled at the sight of the remains, intact and perfectly mummified. Today, the skull rests in a crystal urn in the chapel of the counts of Aragon, at Sabiñan in the province of Saragossa.

What fascinated me about this individual had something to do with the irrational ascendancy of faith. As you know, I was not and never had been a man of faith. But somehow . . . this person who, in the face of every opposition, had defied both monarch and laws, both temporal and spiritual powers, to shut himself away in certain, prideful solitude, immeasurable . . . he filled my mind completely. I wanted to write a book with him as hero. My next novel would be devoted to the pope of the sea. Strengthened by this notion, I decided to sell the store and set out for Spain, on the trail of Señor de Luna. I forgot everything else, absolutely everything: Hitler, who had come to power in Germany and was yelling louder and louder into loudspeakers that deafened, the riots in Paris, everything happening in the world . . . engulfed, escaping, dispossessed . . . I thought this new story that obsessed me could draw me from the comfortable mental cell in which my mind was so molded. I could no longer write as I used to. The rock of Peñiscola had given me the illusion that new horizons were opening. Useless placebo. But despite everything that happened, I was unable to control History, which was catching up with me in front of the sumptuous waves of the Mediterranean—blood-red. History: the true, the present, too present and intolerable contemporary History!

I left, then, to shut myself away in a little fisherman's house beside the medieval fortress. For months, I made notes and comments, picking over and digesting from the local archives anything remotely concerned with my man. But that was all. The writing in progress stopped there. Without ever being injected with life. I was living on exotic things, on salt and pimiento, and I'd started confusing experience with truth. I elaborated, I constructed, I worked, but nothing was happening. I was just playing at changing identities.

The civil war broke out. I was so caught up in my network of papal bulls, annals, and chronicles I didn't realize what was happening. I was the Pope of the Sea. And His Holiness didn't hear, or pretended not to hear, the sound of cannons, until the din became so terrible, he finally had to stick his nose outside and see the black birds set ablaze in the sky. Then, awakened at last, he exposed his body to the storm, greeting the rain of fire with open arms.

Such were the circumstances of my meeting with Antoine Choucas. I recognized him at once. Despite the lined face and the warrior's uniform he wore as elegantly as a tailcoat, he hadn't changed greatly. We had met in Vienna, in Paris as well, and I'd attended many of his concerts.

He was commanding a coastal battery in the International Brigade. One day I left the fortified part of the village for a walk on the beach toward Vinaroz, where I came upon a group of soldiers. One had strolled toward the sea and was standing in the water. He seemed to be staring at some unknown point through his binoculars. When he turned around, obviously very excited, he couldn't avoid seeing me there, quite close by, ten feet from him, staring in amazement.

He walked over and joined me and said without further ado, as if we'd seen each other just the day before:

"Can you imagine? Two French warships cruising peacefully in the open sea. While we . . . I'll tell them what they can do with their nonintervention!"

And he started running toward his men, barking orders I couldn't really understand. While I, I don't know why, began following a few yards behind the group that was now heading north.

That was how I came to be with Choucas until he died, in April 1939, in the camp at Gurs, on the other side of the Pyrenees.

That day on the beach he resisted temptation. Perhaps because of my passive, silent presence. . . . I had no right. But the fact is, he didn't do it, he didn't point his guns at the French ships—an action that could, as he briefly seemed to hope, have drawn his country into a conflict it had refused. "I'd have arranged it to look like the work of the Fascists," he confided with a smile. I remember too, on the night of his death, just before I escaped from the camp many of our companions would leave only for the Nazi death camps, one of his last whispered remarks: "I'm sorry . . . I'm sorry I didn't give the order to shoot. . . ."

At the moment of our meeting on the beach I became the chronicler of Antoine Choucas's life. I followed him everywhere, with a disregard for danger, an indifference to death that surprised even me. On the front line facing the Moorish infantry. On the Ebro, in the flotilla that was our last hope. In the trenches at Aragon. On the tragic roads of exile. Toward the frontier.

And I started to become Blackbird. It was the *nom de guerre* with which I signed the articles Choucas sent to Barcelona. So people would know. All over the world, across the ocean, to the shores of America . . . where Blackbird was to alight for the first time.

Then Anton Blackbird managed to have false papers issued by some absentminded or ignorant French gendarmes, and to escape once more a fate that was too carefully drawn, too well established to be borne, to escape—definitively, he hoped, from his past. . . . To save his skin, if you like!

No, I never wrote the story of the pope of the sea, but I learned how to forge an identity for myself, how to copy a signature, to counterfeit a life.

In Spain, I never met our great writer Toller, whom I should have, could have, tried to see. Even better, though, I slipped into the skin of another man. Choucas, with his superb despair, offered me a treasure that would become the sanctuary of my existence: Blackbird.

Gurs. Valley of Oloron. It is cold, a fine rain is falling that adds to our barbed-wire confinement. The horizon is gone. You cannot see the Pyrenees; they have disappeared behind a dense curtain of fog.

The sentinel paces past his sentry box. He must be cold too. We have been put in the first block with Choucas, the one that stands next to the surveillance post and is surrounded by a double row of barbed wire. We are "Reds," stateless, unknown . . . more undesirable and dangerous than the Spaniards themselves.

Choucas is sick. During the retreat I watched him fade away, refusing food and prone to coughing fits that left him weak and drained. Today the fever has cast him into a state of exhaustion from which, I'm sad to say, I doubt he can recover. He has been put in what is pompously called the "infirmary," in reality a drafty shed. There is no bed, and no drugs, no doctor . . . no doors. No door, not even in the barracks. Only barbed wire and wind.

The food is execrable: water faintly tinted with coffee, more water and a few chick peas by way of soup, a crust of bread . . . bread that we share with no argument. The habits of war, of solidarity. Of men who have fought for freedom.

We could have cut each other's throats. Instead, in the few days that I was interned in the camp at Gurs, I had proof—perhaps the one time in my life—that man is not a beast. It was without any doubt a necessary circumstance for my survival, but it was not enough, not nearly enough. . . . One ray is not light. One star is not a galaxy. The universe had long since been extinguished.

I looked away, my eyes searched the night. Soundlessly, I crawled to the trench. Dirt on my hands, under my nails, in my mouth, on my eyelids. And when I straightened up, a clay statue drenched by searchlights, I leaped into the void, into the dark, without turning around.

The window on Hester Street. The twelfth floor. The ocean.

Do you understand, Clockwork? Do you finally understand? So what, I don't give a damn. It's all so ridiculous. Hideous. Why should I expose myself to some grotesque uproar? Why don't I display myself in a shop window too, offer my charms to the avid eyes of passersby, give myself entirely, open my mouth and ass wide so they can see right through me? As if that's what it was all about! What happened in the end: a fifty-year-old Jew got off the boat at New York when his coreligionists were starting to be massacred on the other side of the ocean. They had to make such a fuss about it! Mr. so-called Alias, or whoever, even denied his guilt for having escaped the Holocaust. Yeah, sure, in spite of everything. What was he complaining about? He still has his skin, it was still attached to his flesh, and it wasn't worth the trouble to keep harping on the fact that he'd bled. The parade of offended genius, that was something else! By what right, what immortality abruptly turned institutional, could old Blackie lay claim to the uniqueness, the interest even, of his particular fate?

There was nothing to say. There was nothing left for him to say.

21.
Final Bestiary of the Yellow Notebook

⩒⩒⩒ Myrddin has taken refuge in the forest. He wanders helpless through the appalling maze of shadows. Close murmurs whisper that Myrddin is mad and soon must die. The prophet screams his death. He senses it, he knows it is there, close at hand, hidden at the rim of the woods where a pack of dogs is baying. He sees it clearly, he who must pay for the visions in which he announced the queen's adultery and the death of knights in battle. He had been forgiven for being born an orphan—for being born without a father, mysteriously: it had delighted the imagination of lords and serfs. But after a period when he held the post of eccentric public entertainer, his power to denounce the false and evil actions of secret chambers and antechambers had finally been exhausted. Came the day when, prey to a fearful trembling, he cast his thunderbolts at the life of the kingdom itself, predicting its ruin and destruction. No jest, no magic trick could help him escape punishment then. Myrddin was condemned to roam the woods.

Until now, he had managed to escape his persecutors. When hunters' arrows whistled toward him he could utter the ritual words and his wings would push him above the treetops, toward celestial heights beyond the reach of man. And if he hadn't enough time, he would blend into the dense foliage of oak and larch, become bark, branch, acorn, needle—invisible. When his seekers disappeared, a sad Myrddin would take up his lyre and sing his despair. It was said that he was mad; but he was simply immortal.

197

Utterly unconcerned whether Christ had descended to hell, the drunken Antichrist had torn the young virgin's skirts and his burning penis had pushed apart her thighs. Blood had flowed, mingling in a sinister gurgling with the seed of the demon, who was furious that the virgin resisted. He thrust loins and belly forward in vain, for he encountered a wall of flesh that was too alive to be easily pierced. He reprimanded his acolytes, insulting them copiously to make them force the girl to drink from the bottle. From time to time, as if to restore his own courage, the Antichrist snatched the flask from them and drank without touching his lips to the glass. At the end, for want of anything better, he began to vomit on his victim. At the sight of the rats, frogs, and snakes that started running over her naked body, the poor creature let out a long scream, and at once, briefly, he released her thighs. The scalding liquid surged into the rift.

And so it was, thought Merlin the Enchanter—for it was he—that I was, in a manner of speaking, begotten.

They have started beating the bushes once again. The dogs are not far. I have only a little time left. Scarcely a few hours. I know how it all will end, for I've told it before, many times, before the assembled court. They listened to my account, laughed, and did not believe me. And Vivien, my love, my one and only passion, it was I who taught her, for her pleasure, how to make me her slave. Escape is no longer possible. I am condemned to flee and to pretend to die, though I disappear only into the trees or clouds. Eternally.

As there is no way out, I have let myself be shut up in the magic circle. Ultimate locus, locus of distress. And the worst is that behind this invisible boundary where I am buried, the power has been given me to speak the truth. My prison is the very instrument of prophecy. I no longer know how to fly; my wings have been clipped. I am no longer a bird, yet I cheep, squawk, chatter, cry, jabber, and scream more than ever.

22.

Clockwork's Notes (VII)

↯↯↯ I've lost interest in Black-
bird. I accept him. And his story. All of it. Even if I know,
medically speaking, that neither one is true. No, Blackie no
longer interests me. Doddering silly old fool—let him die.
And leave me in peace so I can live for myself a little. By
myself.

I've lost the thread, I've lost the trail. Because of him. All
the others—Linda, Snuffie, Jack, Andy, Pat, Jerry, Hans,
Lola, and Garry—I've forgotten them along the way. Even
though they, too, were sending me desperate signs I didn't
even try to interpret.

Anton will drive me crazy. If I let him, if I let *myself*.

I do have *one* thing left to do. Me too. To write my story.
My own. Starting now.

He's ruined my life. Made me lose all the Annas on this
earth. And I've let myself be taken over by words scrawled on
paper, paper accumulated over months and years . . . for
him, just for him. In vain. If I still had the strength I'd smash
his face, demolish the portrait of that wreck who drags himself from his room to the dining hall, from the library to the
art room, down all the corridors without even seeing that
there are other human beings there beside him, loudly pro-
claiming their own suffering, the misery of their bodies and
their lives. I'm not brave enough, never have been. I could
have gotten rid of Blackbird long ago. What weakness, what
innocence made me let this zombie go wandering through
the hospital, counter to all the rules of therapy and public
health? He could have infected them, all of them. But instead

of that, a subtle poison, he's taken on the strongest. Me. And he's gotten to me.

So today, in full self-awareness, since I've been unable to exterminate that vermin, I've decided not to write another line about what is, after all, a typical case. Now it's my turn. I'm leaving here. My letter of resignation is ready. Tonight I'll take it to the hospital director. I don't think he'll turn me down. For a long time now my professional performance hasn't been brilliant. Besides, I'll soon be fifty-nine years old. It's time to make way for younger people. Isn't it? It seems they have new methods that are more appropriate for the extreme situations of our time. In the end, my mistake will have been due essentially to my amateurishness, my aestheticism, and my overactive imagination.

I'll leave tomorrow, yes, and retire to the house where I was born, near Brewster, Massachusetts. I'll shut the door, open just one window, the one that faces the sea and the unleashed elements of winter, and there I'll begin to write. . . .

. . . I was born on December 25, 1918, the youngest in a family of five. My father, a pastor, read this as a sign from heaven that the fate of his youngest child would be different from that of the others. He dedicated me to the ministry, while my brothers and sister, according to his enlightened views (which were inviolate), were intended for careers in industry and business. Amidst these fallen yet highly useful angels, I found myself in the position of archangel bearing a message of never-failing family redemption, guaranteed pure-blooded, colorfast, resistant to washing and bad weather. A prefabricated gadget. Despite her willing piety, my mother soon realized I didn't exactly correspond to the heavenly model the pastor had imagined. My favorite reading material, once I could decipher the black letters I found so intriguing, was not the Bible, but books by Mark Twain and James Fenimore Cooper. And my heroes were called not Abraham and Isaiah, but such barbaric names as Huckleberry Finn and Chingachgook.

Even though my tastes weren't shared, my passion for

books was accepted. In time they would try to guide me toward more serious subjects and authors. My father contentedly ruminated, telling whoever would listen that I would be an intellectual, well-read, erudite. A theologian, perhaps. He was all the more convinced because I never balked at any of the constraints of the church. They recognized my musical gifts: As a matter of course I was assigned to the choir. I didn't rebel; singing brought me pleasures unrelated to spiritual richness, at least according to the pastor's definition. What my mother called my "vocation," a term that always aroused a vigorous retort from Father, gave me the privilege of private piano lessons in the next town. Every week she drove my older brother Tom and me to Brewster in the horse and buggy, and while they shopped for our weekly provisions, I had my lesson with Mrs. Stone, my first teacher. Later, when I started college, I got permission to study at the local music school. Around that time, my father began to have doubts about my infallible destiny. My mother, on the other hand, enthusiastically pushed me along the path I seemed to have chosen. Until the day of the great argument, the great quarrel. . . .

I put everything into it—let it all out at once: I'd lost my faith, probably never had it, and I'd never become a pastor. Not like Father. I'd rather die. And if they wouldn't let me be a musician, very well—Father could pretend to have a fit if he wanted, but I'd decided to become a writer.

I think I'm still scarred from the thrashing Father gave me with his belt that night. But I persisted. To put on a good front, I made a provisional compromise. To allay their suspicions, I told them I'd enter medical school next fall, in Boston. But that wouldn't stop me. . . .

Need I add that I was never able to carry through? I was very soon swept up in the whirlwind of the university, and by a real passion for medicine. I didn't realize what was happening. Except that one day I thought to myself, Very well, if I cannot save souls I'll take care of bodies . . . and later perhaps I'll be able to heal souls as well. . . .

I'll begin like this. Why not? Then the rest of the story will follow by itself. Without interruption. To the very end. And if I get there I don't think my undertaking will have been useless. Maybe, a psychiatrist's memoirs could end up a bestseller.

As long as I come out of it alive. . . .

23.
Blackie's Notebooks (END)

🌿🌿🌿 Really, there's something not quite right about C. I feel sorry for him now. Is there a sadder punishment? There have been times when I've hated him. But why bother now? Pathetic sentiment. . . . Once I could have prevented him from taking the wrong path, the one that would lead nowhere. But it was soon too late. Play became necessity. Two years ago I threw him a line, as he said at the time, inviting me to get beyond the false dialogue that had begun between us. I talked to him about Maximilien, Tel Aviv, Israel. . . . Once again he made the trip, he invented a pretext. And on his return he came to see me, grief-stricken, to tell me my friend had died long ago. Maximilien, he told me, had been killed during the Six-Day War. Nothing is left now. Not a trace. No family. No writing, no document. "You made it all up."

That day, I knew he wanted me to die. Seriously. He was trembling, dared not look me in the eye. And the papers in the file he held in stiff fingers fell and scattered on the floor. I helped him pick them up, reassemble and sort them. I saw the unbelievable notes, nonsensical documents, untranslatable misunderstandings. C. looked at me for the last time. He was no longer pleading, no longer giving orders. A blank stare. Only, behind the crystalline lens, a vague glimmer of terror or weariness. . . .

That night, I wept in my bed.

I wept for Maximilien, who had thought he could, by some miracle, keep alive the memory of one who had willingly eluded history, *his own* history. I had imagined him married,

with children—that seemed likely. And that Daniel and Na-
than were now working on the Golan Heights . . . at the
wrong time, backs against the sunlight, against the grain perhaps. In any case, away from me, part of a story that wasn't
mine, that *refused* the one their father and I, each in his own
way, each in turn, had lived.

I wept for C. and for his mortal remains.

I wept for Linda, Snuffie, Garry, Pat, and all the others
he'd forgotten because of me, who were still in search of
themselves, unaware that they'd long since been defined by
the walls.

I realized as well that I had no right to obliterate the earlier
life, the dreamed-of life of people who deserved a place in the
story as much as I or C. From that moment I began (but
wasn't I too old, too tired to begin anything?) *truly* to live with
them. Now I must assume the madness that has encased
me since the spring of 1945 when the letter came from
Vienna. . . .

I had taught piano and Hebrew to Jewish children from the
Bronx and Upper West Side, the two neighborhoods I'd lived
in since 1939. And now when I must restore everything to its
proper place, I tell myself that throughout these notebooks I
never revealed that Hermann had once bent his rules con-
cerning educational principles. Yielding to his own suppressed passion for music, he'd started me on lessons when I
was a young child. Until I turned twelve or thirteen, I'd seen
this as just another mark of his authority, as one of the
signs—perhaps the most subtle—of the constraints he im-
posed on me. I went to all the family concerts, to the re-
hearsals of the good souls who sat around the paternal table.
Sonatas and waltzes, Mozart and Chopin, Jewish folksongs.
. . . I can't pin down the exact moment when tedium gave
way to passion. Starting at the conservatory, the bar mitzvah;
playing four hands with my mother; meeting my blind old
teacher . . . the temptation of a double career, starting university and giving concerts at the same time. Cosette in the
front row. . . . And then, Semmering and the musical eve-

nings when I performed for my fellow patients in the sanatorium, in mourning, in disability, in weakness . . . the better to fall asleep, to lament, throw suffering off the track. While writing was rising from the depths, tumultuous, throbbing, giddy, and gasping. Then Milena . . . and the fresh outbreak of wild arpeggios, of solitary variations, of difficult harmonies. I composed pieces then that no one has ever heard. Sometimes they wash up in my ears, like weary waves clean of foam. I remember the dissonances, abrupt syncopations, but the melodic lines generally escape me. What is left of these fragments snatched from a silent time now gone forever, of a work that has been suppressed? Dazzling, ephemeral images: Choucas at the organ of the Tarragon cathedral in 1937, while bullets whistled by in the neighboring streets . . . myself in Marienbad, before an audience of the dying, all of whom resembled me . . . and little Sarah Friedman, my first pupil in New York, who today—it's C. who told me—is one of the leading pianists of her generation.

I'd made up my mind to close the door to temptations. Aware of the paradox—I saw the inherent contradiction of an extreme departure—I had made the trip, the crossing, the leap. Across the sea, the cage was closing by itself and I wouldn't even have to push the door. At least that was what I believed and desired. There were plenty of immigrants on the boat. Jews, of course, many Jews, fleeing though they didn't know why. And others too. A multitude of stray souls who lived for the notion that life was finer elsewhere, simply dreaming. I didn't share that illusion. The Atlantic did not console me: my ocean of tears had long since dried up. I was no conqueror. Glory was behind me, not out there in the open, in the wind and fog. . . . I took no treasure with me, and no gold mine awaited me on the other side. I was drained. Hollow. And the waves tossed me like a nutshell. The epic ended with excruciating, purely physical seasickness. Endless days shut away in the second-class cabin. Alone, shaking, vomiting, beyond any rational thought.

I can, however, describe how I was shocked by New York,

fascinated by Manhattan, how I felt I was coming to a land where everything was possible. . . . But in reality I refused to see, to look, to raise my head. The Friedmans, who came from France and whom I'd met on the boat when we set sail and then on the last day of the crossing, had taken me under their wing. We talked about Paris, but I said nothing when they brought up their background and the family who had stayed behind in Austria. I simply introduced myself as Blackbird. They were insistent.

"But perhaps you have some relatives in America?"

"Not one."

"An uncle, a cousin, friends—with such a name!"

"I have no one."

Mr. Friedman, a decent man around forty, was a tailor, and he told me he was opening a shop in the Bronx.

"What about you?" he added. "What are you going to do?"

I was silent.

Then his wife, a plain, scrawny little woman, smiled at me.

"And where are you going to live, Mr. . . . Blackbird?"

"I don't know."

"I'm sure David wouldn't mind if you came with us. . . . There's a little cubbyhole behind the shop and we could always slip in a bed, couldn't we, David?"

"Of course, Rachel darling . . . we must help each other in difficult times, and anyway, we'll have the apartment upstairs."

I stammered a few words which, since they weren't a refusal, almost passed muster as thanks. I was torn between my desire to flee and my immediate happiness at encountering these pleasant people who asked for nothing in exchange for their friendship.

"And what do you do, Mr. Blackbird?"

That question surprised me even more. A terrible, unexpected knee in the groin. But I didn't take offense. I swallowed, and the only reply that came to me, without really knowing why, seemed to surprise no one, not even me.

"I give piano lessons."

On the contrary, their daughter Sarah, who must have been six or seven, took my hand and said, looking directly at me with her gleaming black eyes:

"Oh please, sir, say you'll teach me the piano."

Her words and her expression were undoubtedly what attached me to life most firmly during my first months in New York, a place that completely eluded my thoughts, ideas, nightmares. For in reality I was still back there. On the Graben . . . on streets drenched in the sound of stomping boots . . . under the rain of bullets . . . chocked by incendiary bombs and barbed wire . . . with Milena!

But I'd been adopted.

I'd dreamed only of some sort of survival, but here I was with the family I'd never known. And so, in desperation, I clung to this image of a possible harmony, one that was all the more necessary as we guessed, though no one breathed a word of it, what was happening in Europe.

One year . . . a semblance of that kind of happiness when you believe that you are still hanging on lasted almost a year. The Friedmans helped me rent my first piano, urged me to entertain and be entertained by the Jewish community that surrounded us, and David kept rounding up new pupils. They often invited me to eat with them, whenever—as little Rachel put it—friend Blackbird really looked too sad. And Sarah's progress was stunning. Every day she came down from the apartment to practice, even if it wasn't time for her lesson. I would pretend to be engrossed in a newspaper or a book (one of the volumes lent me by the Friedmans, which I never read), and I listened. And I saw again. It all came back. At those times I came close to experiencing ecstasy once more, when I thought I had forever banished both desire for it and its existence.

Sarah had the skill and talent I had tried to forget. I no longer believed in creativity, but here was a little creature who told me the opposite every day. Anton Huka had wanted to disappear, Antoine Choucas had wanted to die, but Sarah Freidman was bringing them a troubling denial. There were days when I couldn't resist the pleasure, the consolation, the grace. My emptiness was inhabited by the dead, and yet a blast of life was forcing its way into the breach, the only breach that still remained in me. Everything was beginning again. Was everything to be done again?

No. For although there were the Friedmans, and above all Sarah and the piano, there were also the Roths and the Bernsteins, all parents of pupils who lived on our street and resembled like brothers, like apparitions of blood-sucking ghosts, the Roths and the Bernsteins I had wanted to leave behind, to deny, to kill. I was gradually caught up all over again in the litany of ready-made phrases, of supposedly sacred remarks, and the cult of origins. Though the Roths and the Bernsteins were honorable people, honest immigrant workers and part of the great democratic beehive of the United States, they were still a myth to me, the myth of going back in time. As if I had stayed behind and nothing had happened in the meantime. There was no doubt of that. And the guilt of the Roths and Bernsteins was nothing compared with the vertical anguish that rubbed me against the grain, stripping me bare as I faced my unreal survival. Before, I based my life, my passions, and my art on the idea that I was a monster, but now I must bow to the facts, I did not belong to that species. Monsters, the real ones, had been born. Under our eyes. And we'd let them have their way. *I* had left them. Now they could swallow us whole. I was on the victim's side. Out on bail. All the more threatened because, outrageously, I was temporarily safe from their fangs and claws.

The Freidmans, though, knew better. One day they told me they were going back to Europe, despite everything, to see, to speak out, to fight, to refuse. They could no longer bear to be willing victims. Little Sarah? She would go to some cousins in Indianapolis. Everything would work out. Not to worry. Kind Mr. Blackbird.

And they left to die.

I moved to Hester Street. As I didn't find any pupils immediately, I gave Hebrew lessons to the Rossman boy, my landlord's offspring. I'd gone back to it with the Friedmans, though I avoided the ceremonies in which they always took part. I'd returned to the sacred texts, as if goaded by some ultimate need for proof. I was well aware there was a possibility of dangerous regression, but realizing the suspect nature of my undertaking, I issued myself a final rule of behavior. Because I knew, I was aware of what was going on, I ardently desired to revert to the same old story. Another way to drown, to deny my existence. . . .

Until the day Gold the furrier pulled up in his Packard convertible, with his money, his ambition, and his patronage. He was one of the richest men in the neighborhood, a second-generation immigrant of Polish stock. Born in New York, he was free of the tenacious humility that still clung to those Jews who had recently arrived in the United States. Gold was American.

"Rossman told me you taught piano in the Bronx," he announced in the self-assured tone of the businessman who gives his listener no choice. "I want you to come to the house for my sons. Little idiots, don't know how lucky they are; greenhorns, they think America was built in a day and they're the only people in the world. But so it goes. I'll pay, pay whatever I have to, to avoid their growing up savage. Nobody's going to say that Gold can't face up to facts. Here's a hundred dollars in advance. You start tomorrow."

He held out his card. And the next day I went to the Madison Avenue address printed on it. I had no reason not to. From the outset, of course, Gold had struck me as a disgusting person, the personification of everything I disliked. In a way, as well, he reminded me of my father, Hermann; and perhaps it was that conflict, that fascination, which compelled me there.

Goldman absorbed my time and energy, he digested me and in the end annihilated me, all the more easily because his chosen approach corresponded closely to the one I'd deliberately chosen for myself. I let myself float unthinking on the oppressive ebb and flow of the dialectic between master and slave. I lent myself, I gave myself. I was a private tutor with nothing, or not much, to reject. I was there to teach two apathetic boys every subject—languages and literature, mathematics and music—without interruption, eight hours a day, five days a week. Finally, for the second time in my life, I had a job. I was like other human beings. I was becoming almost normal again.

On Saturdays there was the walk in Central Park or on the docks in Battery Park. Sunday, I'd go to the beach on Coney Island or sometimes, following the crowd of New Yorkers in their Sunday best, as far as Long Island. By bus at first, then in a little car I'd bought on credit.

By the time the thundercloud burst over Pearl Harbor I'd become an average American, and, like all average Americans, I began following events—with stupefaction, with anguish, but also without really believing it or, at most, assuming that the American dream could never become a nightmare.

So I had constructed a new shell for myself. Apparently my wild venture had been successful. Without changing my life, I had been content to change lives. And I'd done well. Life was comfortable, reasonable, safe. The temptation to write had been repressed, thousands of kilometers away, buried under bomb craters, inside damp, dark blockhouses, relegated to the bunker of the soul. . . . But that didn't take into account the explosive charge which existed under the building! The scarlet rain of memories that sometimes came and beat against my windows . . . ideas that—especially at night—would start crawling through the mud among the cadavers . . . the forced marches . . . ambushes. And then I was filled with the strongest feeling of all, the feeling that I was in hell, in the pay of a devil named Gold. How many times did I tell myself I would run away to escape him, tell myself I must rid myself of him, one way or another? And yet I waited, just waited, without really knowing why.

It wouldn't take much for me to lose my way in this labyrinth again, to go out again in search of the truth that always seems to disappear. The smallest thing, a gleam of hope, a moment of reprieve—another few days—and today I would almost start this nameless story again, though I know it is of lesser importance. But one must choose. I know full well the time has come when life must be confirmed, when memories must be buried. I no longer have the time, I no longer have the right to seek any road but the straight one—and to follow it to the end.

One stop along that road was fatal. For me, Milena's death was all deaths. I was cast outside myself, outside the purgatory of the living dead. . . .

I don't know how the bastard—but why use an epithet that now seems so insignificant?—how Joseph Weiss tracked me down. I thought I was safe from the Blackbird mystery. Wrongly, it seems, for Weiss discovered how to reach me, sent me the letter in which he recounted the end of Milena's life. Had Maximilien betrayed me? Perhaps he had been unable to withstand the urgent questions of Milena (who, I was still convinced, had continued to love me in spite of everything, just as my body had not ceased to burn, my soul to be rent, at the mere memory of her). She would have known what was happening all along, followed my itinerary, tried to get information . . . who knows . . . from town to town, from exile to exile, she would have spied on me, though without daring or wanting to intervene more directly, for fear of compromising a fragile equilibrium, a building already crumbling beneath the fatal weight of memory. Out of love. Quite simply.

That thought leaves a taste of wild honey in my mouth. Rough, tart, yet sugary. And I spit out my disgust, my shame, my accumulated bile. There was only one reason for my first death, one I experienced through and for Milena. I can't keep silent anymore: I was no longer a man, no longer capable of an erection (as on that day with Oscar, in the luminous forest!). Since then—have I said it often enough?—it has been a question of death in life. The final stakes today, I hasten to add, result once more from a simple desire: not to grow senile. Unless the delicacy whose bittersweet juices I was savoring concealed a more tender, more facile poison. The exotic form of suicide that keeps finding new reasons for putting off till tomorrow the validation and justification of the act . . . that's probably what happened with the Pope of the Sea. You remember that, don't you, Doctor?

The dull, shameless words of the letter were engraved on me forever. "It's true that Milena suffered. But you of all people know her strength of character. To the very end she was the dignified woman both of us loved." Weiss was still consistent with his own image of a peaceful father steeped in moral precepts and humanistic values. For a moment I railed against this man who, I don't know how, had slipped through the Nazi net. Without realizing that I too . . . and perhaps Weiss was now too a citizen of the United States of America, happy and proud of her "liberty" and her "democracy"! The thought that we had followed the same route no doubt helped push me out the window, only to land quite gently on soft and soothing mattresses, in the hospital of lesser evil. "At least," Weiss added, "Milena suffered only the torments of her illness. Tuberculosis allowed her to escape the gas chambers."

Tonight—I have no idea of the date—will be the madmen's ball. At last. I've been thinking about it for a long time. Not the charitable afternoons, not the entertainments organized around an occasion, not the Christmas dinners, but our own party—the real thing. I simply hadn't known how to go about it. Hadn't known how to talk to them, how to suggest a convincing plan. Satisfied with suspicions, with scraps, I'd never managed to get Pat, Hans, Linda, Lola, Garry, Snuffie, and the whole gang beyond the little scuffle in the canteen or corridors that always ended with some of them cooling off in the disciplinary cell, while I, looking impassive and virtuous, got at worst an unofficial reprimand from Clockwork or one of his henchmen, who never dreamed I could have instigated these fleeting disturbances. Only those who were punished seemed to hate me, for a few days expressing themselves with low blows I'd take without a word. Or they'd scream in my face, but since their screams were inarticulate, they never reached their target, but disappeared in sullen echoes. I didn't hold it against them. On the contrary, I wished I spoke their language so that I, like them, could express my mental distress, and—for lack of anything better—scream my guts out. They were pure and inviolate. I was soiled and locked in the present, too solid to be true.

This time, we've seen to everything. Together. Andy will bring the saucepans from the kitchen. Pat, Linda, and Lola the costumes and makeup. Jack and Garry have baked cakes on the sly. Jerry the ape-man has performed some balancing act to get at the head guard's liquor supply. We'll bang on the saucepans and in the midst of the cacophony we'll baptize Hans the Nazi with bourbon. And when his clothes are well soaked, we'll set fire to him with the matches Snuffie pinched from the orderly's pocket. And we'll lacerate our costumes with light, till nothing is left of them, till the marks of our claws appear on our bare, bleeding flesh.

And then we'll sit on the ground in a circle, holding hands. And each will tell his story. The night will be filled with stories. . . .

Garry nods as napalm burns the Vietnamese rice paddies. Garry drifts along the Mekong, while Andy shakes all over at the thought that bombs have just fallen on Pearl Harbor, wiping out his hopes of a fortune and giving the starting signal to the Pacific Forces commandos. Jerry plays at being a monkey in the Korean underbrush. The jungle catches fire. Panic-stricken, the wild beasts roar. A shell bursts and the ape looks at his amputated leg lying a few meters away. He hoists himself up, climbs to the top of a tree, where he will be found half dead, numb with cold and forever lost to reason. I sketch a few pictures recognizable only to myself: I am talking, without being precise, about Guernica, about the fire that rained

down on Vienna in 1945, but Pat cuts me off and launches
into a speech on the massacre of the Palestinians. The others
laugh. Heartily. Hysterically. Until the chain that we form,
welded by our protean stories, starts trembling hideously, terrible spasms that shake it in every direction. And yet the
chain holds fast. The hands do not let go. The cries are
united, one neutralizing the other, and calm is soon restored.
A keen silence. Then, in her lovely adolescent voice, Lola
starts to sing. A melody that is dear to me, one I taught her
months ago when I came close to telling her about my past. A
song I'd composed for Milena. In counterpoint, the recitative
of Garry and Snuffie, who combine and exchange a mercenary's Africa for an exile's Cambodia. Their voices are strong
and sonorous. They rise up to assault the gloom that sur-
rounds us. The fire has consumed them and only a few red-
dish ashes now remain, casting invertebrate glimmers on our
faces flushed with warriors' disguise. Song alone brings order
to the night.

We can drop our hands now, the circle exists. And Linda
can start to dance. The fat woman's dance, the dance of life,
stout, cooing, gelled and trembling. Her arms envelop us in
flesh, in warmth, in a womb that contains us all. Belly first,
Linda draws close to each of us and takes us in turn in her lap,
then delivers us a little further with much panting and heaving of back muscles. The gestation is painful but the result is
fine. Linda the stripper shows, perhaps for the final time, how
a woman can bestow life.

Jack leaps up then and surprises us all in the midst of our
rapture. As if he had guessed how I feel, as if he wanted to
forestall my own desire, he starts to scream. Shouting lies,
morals, deceit, blackmail! And the oddest, the most surprising thing is that little Lola joins in. Now the party takes an
unexpected turn, turns to disaster. Would I have presumed
on their strength, on their will to deliverance, their power to
survive? Lola says she doesn't give a shit about our stories, she
isn't interested, she's sixteen years old and has no reason to

believe any of it ever happened and she doesn't give a damn if it did, because she wants to live, that's all, to live. Get it?

Silence, weighty now, has descended on the room.

It must not end like that. No, I don't want it. It can't be. Too harsh, too derisory. Unlivable! I hadn't expected that. Find a way to get the party going again. One final artifice.

Then a thought occurs to me. (Yes, I'm sure it will come, this idea or another. . . .) What if I were to take all these friends of mine (for they are friends now, flesh-and-blood creatures like all those who have crossed my life, and together we form a community of lives and interests, in a word, a veritable social *class!*), what if I were to take them all to the theater. There, before rows of empty seats, upon an empty stage (what does it matter if C. has taken away the piano!), we'll put on a play of our own making. We'll begin the aborted stories again, but this time certain that the recent ritual will be replaced by an even more effective ceremony. Instead of believing we possess an exhaustive liturgy, a barbaric way of speaking that nurtures nothing, very well, we'll perform for ourselves the comedy of our intimate little low masses. We'll ruminate, we'll sniff, we'll murmur. We shall coat ourselves giddily and complacently with borborygmi and onomatopoeias, plunge into a litany of farting and gurgling, belch and spit in one another's face. And when it's all been said, when it's all been poured out and stripped bare on the stage of despair, we shall soil one another with our excrement and use our own vomit as libations.

Doctor, never mind your patients. I'm taking them on. For after all, who says that you and I are the geniuses? In fact we're the offspring of Pat and Linda crossed with the ape-man and the Nazi short-order cook. They're the ones who invented us. And if we hadn't existed, we'd have had to invent them.

I always thought I would die young. In the end, this weakness explains my entire life. I've submitted to myths, dreaming of just one thing: becoming a myth, my own myth. The

ambition of a fallen god! And now I am stagnating, old, doddering, besotted by life and by words, in the antechamber of a
beyond that does not exist!

The truce is ending. Tomorrow, it will all be over for me.
Let them have their way with me, if at least I'm still—un-
justly—alive. I've found one final truth; I hope this time it will
be a lesser evil, less disturbed, less irrational. Tonight, or
rather at dawn, when the party's over . . . I shall go and kill
Dr. Clockwork.